Also by Lorie O'Clare

THE BOUNTY HUNTERS

Play Dirty

Get Lucky

Stay Hungry

THE FBI SERIES

Tall, Dark and Deadly

Long, Lean and Lethal

Strong, Sleek and Sinful

ANTHOLOGIES

The Bodyguard

Men of Danger

Run
Wild

Lorie O'Clare

St. Martin's Paperbacks

This is a work of fiction. All of the characters, organizations, and events portrayed in this novel are either products of the author's imagination or are used fictitiously.

RUN WILD

Copyright © 2012 by Lorie O'Clare.
Excerpt from *Slow Heat* copyright © 2012 by Lorie O'Clare.

For information address St. Martin's Press, 175 Fifth Avenue, New York, NY 10010.

ISBN: 978-0-312-53456-1

Printed in the United States of America

St. Martin's Paperbacks edition / April 2012

St. Martin's Paperbacks are published by St. Martin's Press, 175 Fifth Avenue, New York, NY 10010.

10 9 8 7 6 5 4 3 2 1

Chapter One

"Natasha?" Greg King glanced up from the file in his hand. "Natasha, the phone?"

"Got it." Natasha grabbed the phone from her desk, ignoring Uncle Greg's disapproving frown.

Patricia Barton, Patty, hurried into the office. "Here's the file you were looking for," she announced, handing the file to Greg before giving Natasha a winning smile.

KFA, King Fugitive Apprehension, had recently hired on two new bounty hunters. Two weeks ago Uncle Greg also had hired a new office assistant. Natasha appreciated the help in the office, but Patty was intent on showing Natasha up, making their daily jobs more of a competition than a team effort. It sucked. Natasha was competitive, and if the prissy little girl wanted to be shown who was the better woman, Natasha would take her down. She had created this job Patty was determined to show her, and everyone else, she could do better.

There was no way Natasha would give Patty the satisfaction of knowing how much she affected her. She returned an indifferent nod and looked away, staring outside through the large windows as she answered the phone.

"KFA," she said quietly, calmly. "How may I help you?"

"I need to speak with Natasha King," a deep, male voice demanded.

Natasha blinked. She'd been answering KFA's phones for seven years, since her uncle opened up shop, and couldn't remember when anyone last called this number for her. She had her own cell, and if anyone wanted to reach her, they called her number, not KFA's. Yet this was the second time today someone had called and asked to speak to her. The first call had distracted her. Now her nerves were on edge.

"This is Natasha." She turned her back on Uncle Greg and Patty and walked around her desk. "May I help you?"

"This is Natasha Nadine King?"

Natasha's heart stopped and she froze. Then her teeth clamped shut when she plopped into her office chair behind her desk, which faced the rest of the office. Natasha didn't use her middle name. Sure, it was on her birth certificate, but Nadine was her mother's name, the woman who'd left Natasha and her father when she'd been four years old. "Nadine" wasn't even on her driver's license. Not even the middle initial.

"Who wants to know?" she demanded, keeping her voice low as she shot a furtive glance toward her uncle. For once she was glad Patty was kissing up to him. It was keeping him busy. Otherwise he'd be towering over Natasha wanting to know who was harassing her.

"This is a personal matter between Natasha King and her family."

Her family? Her family, for the most part, was standing five feet from her. There were her two cousins, Marc and Jake, but both of them had moved out and weren't working for KFA anymore. And Aunt Haley, of course, who didn't like Patty any more than Natasha did, was probably either in the kitchen or somewhere else in the King house, which was attached to the KFA office. The office had once been a screened-in front porch, but Uncle Greg had converted it over shortly after he'd opened his doors for business.

"This is Natasha," she said hurriedly. "What can I do for you?"

"Natasha." There was no emotion in the man's tone. "Where's your father?"

"My—" Natasha bit off the word "father." Who the hell would be asking her about her father? Obviously no one who knew her. She was the last person to ask if anyone wanted to find George King.

"Yes, your father, Natasha," the man said crisply. "Tell me where he is." He was rather demanding.

"I have no idea," she drawled, her heart beating once again as she leaned back in her chair and examined her fingernails. It was the second time today. The first caller had been more polite, more conversational, but the question had been the same. Why did they want to know where her father was? What had he done?

She waited out the silence, curiosity besting her. At the same time she straightened her hand and stared at her short nails and the recent manicure she'd given herself. After her last breakup and Bill Sanders' informing her he couldn't be in a relationship when he wasn't sure who wore the pants between them, Natasha had decided to confiscate some of Aunt Haley's nail polish and paint her nails and her toes. They even matched. There was a first.

"Miss King."

Natasha wasn't in the mood to offer the caller a more informal title.

"I need you to come to Weaverville."

"Weaverville?"

"Yes, Weaverville, California."

She ran her fingers through her long black hair, immediately tangling them when she neared the ends, then yanked her hand free and stared at the tousled ends with casual indifference. Somewhere in her desk drawer was a hair stick she could wrap her hair around and pin to the back of her head.

Natasha opened the drawer and spotted it immediately. At the same time she glanced up, which was a mistake. Uncle Greg was watching her, raising an eyebrow. He was listening. Patty had returned to her smaller desk along the adjacent wall and was tapping away at her keyboard, probably blogging.

The stupid twit seemed to forget anyone could read it. Natasha would check Patty's blog later and read all the hateful things she wrote about her.

"Where is Weaverville, California?"

"We're in the Trinity Alps."

"I'm in L.A. That's eight or nine hours from here."

This time her caller waited out the silence.

"You can come here, fax, or mail any information." Natasha wasn't in the mood for nutcases. What was her father up to now?

"Your father is in serious trouble. You're needed in Weaverville if you have any intention of helping him."

She blew out a breath. Answering the phone for KFA all these years didn't make dealing with people like this any easier. Everyone thought their world was coming to an end and KFA needed to drop everything and run to their assistance immediately. All she could do was slow the caller down and gather information. "Sir, I'm sorry. I didn't get your name."

"Trent, Trent Oakley. Does Monday work for you, around two P.M.?"

"Why are you asking where my father is and demanding to see me?" she asked. "I've already told you I don't know where he is and no, Monday at two P.M. doesn't work for me at all."

She pictured Trent Oakley to be some bulging-gut mountain man, wearing a cowboy hat and plaid shirt and spitting chew after every other sentence. If he called her "little woman" she would hang up on him.

"This needs to be discussed in person." Trent allowed another pause.

Maybe he didn't realize what Natasha did for a living. He'd have to do a hell of a lot more than that to persuade her into doing what he wanted.

"Natasha," Trent said, lowering his voice. Apparently, he felt they'd spoken long enough to address her by her first name. "I'm extending you a courtesy. I'm giving you the opportunity to meet with me before any charges are officially made."

Natasha sighed. "Give me your number and I'll call you back," she said, resigned. "We're a busy office. Don't count on me being there."

He merely grunted, gave her his number, and hung up without saying good-bye. She pulled her phone away from her ear slowly, trying to digest everything he'd just said or, better yet, what he hadn't said.

This was two calls now. The first caller hadn't identified himself but had simply asked if she were related to George King. They'd asked where he was. She'd said she didn't know and they'd hung up. Now this caller, this Trent Oakley, had taken the conversation a bit further. It was all too bizarre. It had been years since she'd last seen her father.

Even if she did take off from work, which wasn't an option, drive clear up to Northern California, which she couldn't do, it made absolutely no sense at all why anyone would want to talk to her before pressing charges against her father. She had no say in her father's life and never had.

"What was that all about?"

Natasha jumped and stared at her uncle, who loomed over her desk, watching her carefully. "Is something wrong with George?"

Patty hopped around her desk and sidled in next to Greg, her bright brown eyes wide with curiosity. "Is there something I can help with?" Which was her way of snooping into a conversation.

"No," Natasha and Greg said at the same time.

"Oh." Others might be offended by the snub, but Patty rocked up on her heels, spinning around with the files she held in her hands, and disappeared from Natasha's line of vision. Uncle Greg was a large man and initially Patty's not cowering around him had impressed Natasha.

Most people took one look at her uncle, who was six feet, four inches tall and built like one of those professional wrestlers on the WWE shows, and forgot what they were going to say. He could be intimidating as hell, and he did have a temper. But he was also the man who practically raised her and was more of a father than her real father had ever been.

Natasha saw the concern in his eyes, and although she hated talking about either of her parents with anyone, she and her uncle were also talking about his brother. She'd overheard more than once what her uncle thought of Natasha's father, not only for willingly dropping Natasha off at Uncle Greg and Aunt Haley's house several times a week throughout her childhood, but for eventually leaving her with them permanently. They didn't care for George's self-focused lifestyle and indifference for anyone but himself.

Her father was a gambler, a con artist, and a lady's man. Natasha had overheard him telling Uncle Greg that his world was no place for an adorable little girl. At the time, Natasha had hung on to the words "adorable little girl." She'd adored her dad, and truth be told, she didn't hate him now. George King wasn't a bad man, just a bad father, which made the conversation she'd just had with Trent Oakley even more mysterious, if not just plain weird.

"I don't know if he's in trouble, or not," she said, and gathered her hair behind her head, twisted it into a knot, then slid her hair stick through it to hold.

"What was that phone call about?"

Uncle Greg had been a cop for twenty years before becoming a bounty hunter and had taught Natasha to focus on details and on how to read people. The look on his face suggested he believed his brother had done something wrong. Greg's large stature suddenly appeared harder than stone and he crossed his thick arms against his chest as he stared down at her. He'd already drawn his conclusions and wasn't happy.

Natasha felt a wave of defensiveness as she looked up at him.

"I need a drink." Natasha pushed her way out from behind her desk. "Patty, can you handle the phones for a few minutes?"

"I can handle them all day." Patty waved over her shoulder, suddenly no longer acting interested in Natasha's conversation. She jumped on the opportunity to show Greg she was quite capable of handling the office without Natasha's help.

Greg followed Natasha out of the KFA office and into his home. Once Natasha had loved it here but with her cousins off doing their own thing, and new bounty hunters and an annoying office assistant on staff, there were days when she dreaded coming to work. It never used to be like that.

Natasha walked through the spacious living room, down the hall, and into the kitchen. It still smelled of bacon and maple syrup from breakfast. In spite of the house being an empty nest, more or less, Haley King still didn't know how to make a small breakfast. Natasha wouldn't be the one to point it out to Haley. There were days when bacon, toast, and juice grabbed from the kitchen was all she ate all day. She really should be more grateful for her new assistant, in spite of Patty's prying methods and competitive nature. It was nice not wearing a Bluetooth all the time and being able to have a conversation without continual interruption. Or at least it should feel nice.

Natasha entered the empty kitchen, wondering what was wrong with her. She loved her job. She'd always loved this job. Or was it being needed that made her truly happy? She sighed heavily. That was just plain stupid. She was needed around here as much as she'd always been. It was just these strange phone calls about her father that had her upset.

"What's going on?" Greg didn't waste time the moment they were in the kitchen. He stood in the doorway and crossed his arms, resuming the stance he'd held at her desk, and watched her walk around the island to the refrigerator.

Natasha helped herself to a cold bottle of water. "This morning someone called about Dad." She might as well start at the beginning. That phone call had bothered her, but she'd done her best to put it out of her head and not worry about it. Her father was a grown man, and he'd never sought her out for help. It didn't appear he would this time, either. If he was in a jam, there wasn't anyone on the planet better at getting themselves out of trouble than her dad.

"Oh? Why didn't you tell me?" Greg cared about his brother, which was why he treated Natasha as a daughter. Greg was all about family. Her father didn't get any of those qualities.

She'd always been grateful to her aunt and uncle. Natasha was always included in their family vacations. They had made sure she got to school every morning, and even during college her aunt and uncle were always there to help out financially and sing her praises when she did well.

Unscrewing the bottle, she put the lid on the counter and stared at the perspiration dripping onto her hand. "You were still out in the field working the Murry case." It wasn't a good answer, or even accurate. There had been times she could have mentioned it. Talking about her father made her feel awkward for some reason. "A man called asking questions about him."

"What questions?"

"He asked if we were related and if I knew where he was." She glanced up. "That was it."

"Where was he from?"

She frowned. That should have been something she remembered foremost about the first phone call. Natasha might not be a private investigator, cop, or bounty hunter. But she'd been surrounded by law enforcement all her life. There were a few things she'd picked up along the way.

"His number was blocked." She shook her head. "Uncle Greg, I guess it upset me a little."

"You've been distracted all day."

"And I'm sorry." She wasn't worried about her job being on the line. There was an unwritten clause in her job description: She would never be fired. As long as she kept up her work performance. She could do this job in her sleep, and had a few times. "The first phone call struck me as odd, although I couldn't put my finger on why," she admitted. "But this second caller was a bit more blunt. Dad's in some kind of trouble, Uncle Greg."

Her uncle didn't bat an eye. "Tell me about the second call."

"He was annoying." She began pacing the length of the island. Downing more of the water before she put the bottle on the counter, she then pulled out the stick she'd just wrapped her hair around and began combing through her hair with her fingers. "Obviously, whoever these people are who are looking for Dad, they don't know a lot about him. If they did, they sure as hell wouldn't be calling me asking about him. Or demanding I drive up to Weaverville," she explained, throwing her hands in the air.

"Weaverville?" Greg frowned. "Isn't that up in the Trinity Alps?"

"Yup. Whoever called this morning wasn't the same man who called me just now. The caller just now had a deeper, gravelly voice." She gathered her hair at her nape and scowled ahead of her, staring at a bowl of fruit on the counter. "The first guy who called was gruff, almost mean sounding. He wanted to know if I was related to George King. I said I was. He wanted to know where Dad was. I said I didn't know. He hung up. That was it."

Natasha grabbed one of the apricots, took a bite, and looked at her uncle. He was watching her, waiting to hear the rest.

"The second guy, the call just now, was more conversational, I guess." He had annoyed the hell out of her. She took another big bite of the fruit and began pacing. "I didn't like the way he demanded I drop everything and come talk to him in person. Like he thought I would be able to give him more information about Dad if I saw him than over the phone."

"Which you couldn't do."

"Which I couldn't do," she repeated. "I told him I didn't know where Dad was, and although he seemed a bit surprised by that, he accepted my answer."

Her uncle tapped his lips with his finger, studying her. Natasha knew the look. He wasn't so much focusing on her as he was processing what she'd just said. Her uncle had always looked out for his younger brother, even when he hadn't deserved it. Maybe George King was Natasha's father, but she wasn't under some childhood illusion that he was a good man.

Her father loved her and was always happy to talk to her, when he was around, but he treated her like a distant friend, not a daughter. The man she stared at now was the closest she'd ever had to a dad.

"Did he tell you anything else?" Greg finally prompted.

Natasha finished off the apricot, tossed the pit in the trash can next to the refrigerator, then wiped the juice from her hands on the dishcloth hanging from the refrigerator handle. "He told me his name was Trent Oakley. He's in Weaverville, California, and wants me there Monday at two P.M. to discuss my father."

"Are you going?"

Natasha hadn't given any thought to actually following through with the demand. Her uncle studied her, appearing serious about wanting to know. She admitted curiosity over these sudden phone calls. If her father was in some kind of serious trouble, she should help him, shouldn't she?

She glanced through the other kitchen door that led into the adjoining dining room and in the direction of the office. "Honestly, I hadn't thought about it. I guess Patty is trained," she began, musing out loud. "She'd probably love the office to herself," she muttered.

"It wouldn't be more than an overnight trip." Her uncle sounded as if she'd already made up her mind. "You can take one of the Avalanches. Number three is running well."

Natasha needed to switch gears quickly to keep up with her uncle. He never let her use any of the Avalanches. Ever since he had bought two more black trucks that matched the first one he owned, the three trucks were used out in the field and by her uncle and aunt but no one else. Natasha had never considered asking to use any of them. City transportation had worked nicely for her over the past few years. The bus picked her up outside her apartment and dropped her off a block from KFA.

The back door opened and Aunt Haley entered, her hair windblown and her cheeks red. "I can't believe I feel cold," she said, grinning broadly at both of them. "It's in the seventies and I'm ready to dig out a jacket."

"Natasha might be heading up north Monday," Uncle Greg announced, his voice a low grumble, although unless Patty had snuck into the living room she wouldn't overhear them.

"What? Why?" Haley pulled a coffee cup out of the cabinet and reached for the coffeepot. "Where up north?"

"Someone wants me to go to Weaverville, California, to talk to me about Dad," Natasha explained, giving the incredibly abridged answer.

"About George?" Aunt Haley's interest was piqued. Although she just got her private investigator's license a couple years ago, she had bounty hunter's blood in her, too. Aunt Haley loved a good hunt and a good mystery.

"Natasha has received two phone calls today asking about George," Greg explained, pushing away from the doorway and moving to the counter to pull down his cup.

Haley immediately took it from him and filled it with coffee. "You have?" she asked Natasha. "Are you okay, sweetheart? Did they upset you?"

"No," Natasha answered slowly. "The first call didn't bother me as much as it struck me as weird that they would call me. And I just hung up the phone from the second call," she added, waving her hand in the direction of the office. "Uncle Greg overheard the call and thinks I should go up there."

"What did they say to you?" Aunt Haley nursed her full cup as she sat at the kitchen table.

Natasha grabbed her water bottle, understanding they would now hash through and dissect every word of her phone conversations. It was what her family did, and overall, this usually meant she left the table with a clearer head. Although at the moment she was still pretty upset with Trent Oakley being so demanding.

Both her aunt and uncle sat facing her, listening attentively as she went over both phone conversations again. "The second call made me mad because the guy was such an ass," she added. "He made it sound as if I didn't have a choice about seeing him on Monday."

"Sounds like George is in some serious trouble," Haley said, glancing at her husband.

The two exchanged looks and Natasha watched them, knowing they were speaking volumes with the glances they exchanged with each other.

"I'm not sure if I have a current phone number for him, or not," Greg muttered, digging in his pocket and pulling out his cell phone.

"Try giving him a call." Haley looked ready to grab her husband's phone and make the call herself.

Greg scrolled through his phone and shook his head. "I don't have his number. I'll do some checking, though," he said.

"I'll go up there," Natasha decided. "I admit I'm curious about Dad."

"Something isn't right." Aunt Haley blew on her coffee as she held it between her hands and rested her elbows on the table.

"I'd have to agree." Uncle Greg leaned back, stretching his legs under the table. "Is there anything else you can think of about either call, Natasha? Even if it's trivial, we need all information on the table."

"Trent Oakley might be some kind of cop, or something. He said it was urgent he talked to me before deciding if any formal charges were pressed, or not."

Her uncle was a good man, but a bit too protective at times. When he shifted his attention in her direction she felt it coming on.

"Maybe it would be better if I drove up there with you."

"You don't have to do that." She didn't hesitate. "I'm going alone, Uncle Greg. But I'll call you the second I know anything."

He stood without commenting and she watched, wary and knowing looking to her aunt wouldn't offer her support. Aunt Haley would side with Uncle Greg.

"What was that man's name again? Trent Oakley?" he asked, walking out of the kitchen.

Natasha didn't go into her uncle's downstairs office very often. It was his private sanctuary and where he often brooded when a hunt turned bad. She followed him now, though, with her aunt on her heels, and stood next to his desk, watching as he ran the check on the name. There were advantages to so much law enforcement surrounding her. Her uncle had some kick-ass programs at his fingertips.

"Trent Oakley," Greg announced. "Or make that Sheriff Oakley."

"Sheriff?" Aunt Haley said, leaning in from where she was on the other side of her husband.

Natasha didn't say anything but instead stared at the picture of the man who'd demanded she appear on Monday.

"Thirty-five years old, black hair, green eyes, two hundred pounds, and six foot, one inch, according to his driver's license." Greg read the computer screen. "He was born and raised in Weaverville, California, and has been sheriff of Trinity County for six years now. Kind of young for a sheriff," he muttered, running his cursor over the screen as he debated where to click next.

Even after Greg changed pages, searching for more information on Oakley, the picture of him stuck in Natasha's head. Trent Oakley wasn't at all how she'd imagined him looking. When she placed the gruff voice she'd heard on the phone with the picture of him online, which came from a driver's license, it created a more thorough mental image.

Trent had thick black hair that waved around his face in soft curls. His green eyes were dark in the picture and stared hard at whoever took the shot. He wasn't smiling, nor was he frowning. Instead it looked as if he would take the camera from the photographer if he believed them incompetent in any way. He was a lot taller than her but not as tall as her uncle or cousins. At two hundred pounds she imagined him well built, a regular mountain man. The picture had shown glimpses of a plaid shirt. She'd gotten one attribute about him right.

There was a tilt to his head. She'd learned to read people's body language from the best in the business. That slight tilt often indicated strong confidence or, at least, a high self-esteem. Natasha imagined him competent in his job, thorough, and well aware of his bad-boy good looks. He'd spoken to her on the phone as if he wasn't used to anyone telling him no. She wondered how many ladies in his county told him yes. The report on him didn't say he was married.

"He's not bad looking," her aunt murmured, glancing past her husband at Natasha.

"We don't care how he looks," her uncle grumbled.

Natasha worried her thoughts must have shown on her face when her aunt gave her a small smile.

"I'll call Sheriff Oakley back and let him know I'll meet him on Monday." Natasha left her aunt and uncle and headed through the house to the KFA office, her stomach twisted in knots over her unexpected road trip and concern for her father.

Patty sat at Natasha's desk, typing in reports Natasha usually handled.

"Thanks for holding down the fort," Natasha said, moving around her desk.

Patty didn't turn to acknowledge her but continued entering the report. "No problem at all. The filing is done. Would you run a couple messages to Greg?" she asked, as if it were her job to find something for Natasha to do.

It was on the tip of Natasha's tongue to snap at Patty and demand she get out of her chair. Natasha allowed a second to pass, but Patty never stopped typing.

"The report can wait a minute, Patty. I need to talk to you."

That got Patty's attention and she looked over her shoulder, giving Natasha a quick once-over before raising her lashes and lifting one eyebrow. "Yes?"

"Get up." Natasha didn't snap. She remained calm, staring at Patty until the woman sighed, reluctantly scooted the office chair back, and stood. "Have a seat," Natasha said, waving a hand to one of the chairs on the other side of her desk.

Patty might be attractive if she weren't such a bitch. The woman stuck out her chin, walking with indignation around the desk, then plopped down hard enough in the chair that her ass slapped against the smooth surface. She made a show of clearing any expression from her face as she clasped her hands rigidly in her lap and stared Natasha down.

"What is it?" she asked.

"I'm going to be gone Monday and Tuesday of next week. I think you're up to speed on how we do things around here, but if you aren't, now is the time to let me know so we can familiarize you and make sure you're comfortable."

Patty's entire expression transformed. "Really? You're leaving? For two days?"

Natasha bit her lip so she wouldn't make a sly remark about Patty's enthusiasm. The woman couldn't make it any clearer that she wanted Natasha's job.

"Yes, I am. I'm going to make a few phone calls, but then I'm going to head out for a couple hours. It will be a good opportunity to see how you do running the office on your own. I'll be back before five, and of course you can reach me on my cell. If you have questions, we'll go over them when I return. Sound good?"

"Yes, it does." Patty licked her lips, her excitement making her beam.

Natasha didn't care what Patty thought. Her being here made leaving possible, and for that much Natasha needed to be grateful. She reached for her phone and held the pose for a moment, staring at Patty until the woman came back down to earth, more than likely stuffing her dreams of victory to the back of her head.

"Oh," she said, giggling and making a show of running her hands down her pristine gray high-cut dress. "I'll run these messages to Greg."

"A piece of advice." Natasha had to speak quickly when Patty ignored her and headed to the door leading into the house. "Greg prefers business not be brought to him when he's inside his home. He'll come get his messages. Unless it's a life-or-death emergency, don't chase him down with phone calls. He won't like that."

"Okay," Patty said slowly, staring longingly at the door leading into the living room. Then returning the messages to the message spindle, she stabbed the papers on it and turned to her small, simple desk and organized the few pieces of paper on it.

Natasha ignored Patty, turning her attention to the phone call she needed to make. Her message pad had been pushed to the side when Patty had made herself at home at Natasha's desk. After a moment of reorganizing her things, Natasha placed the pad next to her phone and dialed the number.

She mentally prepared herself for what she'd say and a few questions she wanted answered before leaving. Trent picked up the phone after the first ring.

"Trent Oakley," he answered, his deep voice crisp and authoritative.

Natasha breathed in, ignoring the quick flutter in her stomach as she straightened. "Sheriff Oakley, this is Natasha King with KFA," she began.

"Yes, ma'am."

"I'm calling to confirm our two o'clock meeting on Monday."

"Good. I've taken the liberty of making reservations for you at Pearl's. It's a bed-and-breakfast. If you have something to write with, I'll give you the address and phone number now."

She had hit it on the mark when she'd guessed him so confident he wouldn't imagine anyone telling him no. Grabbing her pen, she wrote down the address to Pearl's Bed-and-Breakfast along with the phone number. "You were mighty sure of yourself that I'd agree to come up," she couldn't help saying.

"We're talking about your daddy here. Most people care about their parents." There wasn't any indication he was making fun of her or joking in any way. He sounded serious.

"I would like to know what this meeting is about."

"We'll talk in person."

"Sheriff Oakley, quote me a law that says you can't tell me over the phone, or tell me now why you want to see me in person."

There was silence before he muttered something Natasha didn't catch. "Ms. King, I'm doing you a favor and giving you the opportunity to defend your father."

Natasha's breath caught in her throat. "Is my dad up there?" she asked, her voice catching.

"How long has it been since you last saw your father?"

She hated people asking her that question. Everyone jumped to conclusions when she answered. Over the years, she'd never found a perfect answer to prevent more questions or looks of pity. She and her dad didn't have a typical father-daughter relationship, but she still loved him and knew he loved her.

"It's been a while."

"You care to narrow that down for me?"

He was a pushy bastard. Something told her by Monday evening, after meeting this Trent Oakley, she'd no longer think him handsome. He was going to be one of those people whose abrasive personality stole all good looks away from them.

She wouldn't give him the satisfaction of sounding defensive. "I'd have to say around three or four years."

"Three or four years, huh. Are you telling me you don't remember when you last saw your father?"

She remembered. It had been right before Christmas. When he'd shown up unannounced, Natasha had hurried out and bought presents for him, thrilled he would be with them over the holidays. Her father left on Christmas Eve, forgot to say good-bye, and called that night, laughing good-heartedly at his absentmindedness, and told her some friends had invited him out for Christmas. It had never crossed George King's mind that his daughter might want him there for the holiday.

"It was almost four years ago," she said, hearing the chill in her tone.

Trent Oakley let out a low whistle. "You sure about that?" he asked.

"Yes, I'm sure. Are you suggesting I'm lying?"

"Are you?"

"No. I am not lying," she snapped, gripping the phone harder as she pressed it against her ear. She began pushing the end of her pen, opening and closing it repeatedly as she frowned. "You haven't told me yet what this is about."

"We'll discuss all the details Monday. I'd suggest driving up Sunday. I reserved your room for Sunday night. Once you've checked in give me a call. You'll get your details then." Trent hung up the phone.

"Of all the—" Natasha slammed her phone on the receiver.

"What's wrong?" Patty's eyes flashed as she spun her chair to face Natasha.

"Nothing." Natasha stormed out of the office. So much for having fun shopping for a new outfit or two before heading up to the mountains. She had half a mind to cancel the trip and tell the pompous sheriff to go to hell.

Sheriff Oakley didn't know George King very well. Her father had never needed her help before and probably didn't need, or want, her help now.

Chapter Two

Weaverville, California, turned out to be a very small town, obviously not very wealthy but somehow holding on to a content, peaceful atmosphere Natasha noticed immediately when she slowed to the posted speed limit and relied on the GPS system built into the dash of the Avalanche to show her how to get to the bed-and-breakfast. In spite of heavy clouds looming overhead that looked like bad weather, people on the sidewalks moved slower than they did in L.A. No one was darting around her or honking for her to get out of their way, and there wasn't a taxi in sight.

She'd just entered a different dimension; she was sure of it.

"Turn right at the next corner."

Natasha followed the automated woman's voice and turned. A dark, midnight blue Suburban passed Natasha on the road just as she turned and she caught the logo on the driver's side door. It was the sheriff. Would there be more than one sheriff in this tiny, timeless community?

"Drive two blocks," the female voice said soothingly. Even its programming sounded less stressed and seemed to speak with a slower drawl.

"I'm losing it," Natasha said, rolling her eyes.

"Pearl's Bed-and-Breakfast is on the left. You have reached your destination."

Natasha eyed the large front porch and potted plants hanging on hooks over the railing. They had to be fake at this time of the year. It was a hell of a lot colder up here than it had been in L.A. Not that Natasha didn't already know it would be, but she wasn't used to seeing her own breath, let alone turning on the heater in the truck. A large wooden sign in the front yard said simply: PEARL'S. Natasha turned off the road onto a gravel drive that ran alongside the large, old house to a square gravel parking lot where a backyard might once have been.

"Wow," she whispered, after parking and getting out of her truck, then standing and stretching. "Who would have known places like this really existed?"

Even the back of the old, glorious home made her think at any moment a horse and buggy would drive by and women would scurry past her in long dresses with children at their feet. Natasha shook her head, reminding herself why she was here. This wasn't time for silly fantasies, and she wasn't the type of woman to stare at the world through rose-colored glasses. Maybe she wasn't walking into a life-or-death situation, which she'd certainly done more than once in the past, but she was here on business.

Was her dad somewhere in this tiny town?

The place didn't seem quite up to his speed.

Natasha opened the passenger door to the black truck and pulled out her suitcase and laptop, then, nudging the door closed with her elbow, pushed the button on the keys to lock it and headed to a covered back porch with a WELCOME sign nailed to the screen door.

The back porch led to a small room, and she thought of KFA back home and how this house had also been converted over to a business. The small room was an office, with a high counter and a bell in the middle of it. A handwritten three-by-five card next to it told her she should ring for service.

Natasha did just that and put her suitcase and laptop on the floor next to her.

"Hi there." A middle-aged woman with an apron tied around her thick middle and her gray hair falling out of a tight bun behind her head hustled in from the other room. She dried her hands on a dish towel and dropped it unceremoniously on the counter next to her.

"I'm Natasha King," Natasha offered, watching the woman grab a three-by-five-card box and open it. "I have reservations."

"Yes, Miss King." The woman pulled out a card, read it, then met Natasha with gray eyes as she gave her a curious once-over. "I hope you had a pleasant trip."

"As pleasant as can be driving up the state of California."

"Well, now that you've reached the beauty of it all, we sure hope you enjoy your stay here." The woman pulled out an adding machine and began punching numbers. Then quoting Natasha the rate, she added, "We accept cash or most major credit cards, but no personal checks."

Natasha pulled her credit card from her purse. "That seems a bit high. Your rates on your Web Site—"

"Ninety-five dollars per night for one week," the woman stated, reading her three-by-five card. "That includes your meals, maid service each morning, and there is information in the living room on tours and the local dude ranches. I'm sure you'll be visiting Trinity Ranch," she said, narrowing her brow and again giving Natasha a shrewd look.

Natasha had no idea what Trinity Ranch was and at the moment didn't care. "One week? I'm not paying for one week. I have an appointment here tomorrow afternoon and will head home after that. All I'm doing is staying the night."

"I see." The woman frowned and redid her math, ran Natasha's credit card, and handed it back to her along with a receipt for her to sign. "I'm Matilda Patterson. Here is the key to your room," she continued, handing Natasha an actual key on a small, nondescript key chain. "If you'll follow me I'll show you the way."

"Coldhearted city girl," Matilda muttered as she bustled down the stairs and returned to the kitchen. "Oh, Trent, there you are. Well, she's here. Can't say much about her, but she's checked in."

Trent Oakley helped himself to Matilda's coffee, then

blew on the hot brew. "You can't say much about her?" He knew Matilda well enough to know the woman would have a lot to say about anyone, even if they'd just met.

Matilda pursed her lips, wiping her hands on her apron as her chin puckered into tiny dimples. "As cool as she could be. She prances in here, looking as pretty as a picture, but turns into a heartless big-city tramp within less than a minute. You know what the first thing is she says to me?"

"What's that?" Trent leaned against the wooden countertop on the large island in the middle of Matilda's large kitchen, getting comfortable. Matilda was just getting started.

"She informs me she isn't here for a week. She tells me as smooth as can be she's got an appointment tomorrow and will be leaving right after that. Heartless woman," Matilda muttered, turning her back on Trent as she began clattering pots in her large lower kitchen drawer until she found one large enough to boil a bag of potatoes. Hefting it to her kitchen sink, she turned on the water. "I showed her to the Emerald Room, the nicest room we have, everyone knows that, and she doesn't say a word. I even mentioned Trinity Ranch. She didn't say a word, stared at me as if she'd never heard of the place." Matilda huffed, her pudgy arms not even bulging when she lifted the heavy pot of water to her stove. "Don't get me started on how bad blood breeds bad blood. You know I'm right about this."

He wouldn't get her started. Matilda would offer good insight on Natasha King once the woman was settled. All Matilda would need was time spent with her, possibly over dinner, and Trent would have all the details on her that he couldn't find online. Matilda was a pro at getting people to talk, then forming strong opinions about them. With Matilda it was love or hate, no middle ground.

Trent didn't know enough about Natasha, yet. He'd done a background check on her. Natasha King lived in Los Angeles, had attended a two-year community college, lived in an apartment that was priced way too high, and had worked for her uncle, the renowned bounty hunter Greg King, for seven years now. Trent guessed Natasha's father was Greg's brother, which would undoubtedly make things a bit trickier. It wouldn't take Trent long, once he sat and visited with Natasha, to learn how well she, and possibly the rest of her family, upheld the law.

Trent knew a good-looking woman when he saw one, and Natasha blew any notions he had on beauty out of the water. From just her driver's license picture it was obvious she was hot as hell. He'd found it interesting her eye color was listed as "tan." He wasn't sure such an eye color existed. There weren't any other photographs of her online anywhere. Trent knew she was twenty-six years old, five feet, seven inches tall, and 150 pounds, although no one stated their true weight for their license. She had a sultry smile and smooth-looking tan skin that definitely wasn't the same shade as her eyes. The woman was absolutely gorgeous, and that was from a chest-up snapshot.

Of course, Matilda wouldn't see her with the same eyes Trent would, which was why he valued the older woman's opinion and knew it would take little to get it out of her. Trent sipped his coffee, then took a bigger gulp and enjoyed its rich, smooth texture. It was already too cold in the mornings and not warming up much by afternoon, a sign of an early and hard winter around the corner. He put his cup on her counter as he watched Matilda move methodically in her kitchen.

"Good coffee," he muttered.

"Thank you." She started running a very sharp knife through potatoes.

Trent hadn't been able to stop the gossip from flowing once the newspaper reported the murder at Trinity Ranch. He knew most everyone in Weaverville, having been born on his family's ranch north of town, but reporters flew in, camped out, and didn't give a rat's ass about his investigation, other than to question why he hadn't caught the murderer yet. Trent had his methods. This wasn't his first case, and it wasn't the first time he'd dealt with snooping reporters.

When his father had passed, no one had questioned Trent filling his shoes. Trent was elected as sheriff almost unanimously and learned, as his father had, to use gossip to his advantage instead of trying to keep a lid on it. There wasn't any reason to add to speculation, though, when he'd told Matilda to reserve a room for Natasha King. Matilda made her own assumptions when she believed Natasha would know any details about what had transpired over the past month.

There was a crunch of gravel alongside the house, and Matilda left her task of peeling and slicing potatoes as she scuttled through the doorway leading into the dining room. Long, narrow windows lined the far wall and allowed her to see whoever might be driving to her back parking lot.

"Jerry Packard," she mumbled, immediately fussing with her hair. "You fill your thermos with hot coffee before you leave, Sheriff," she said, waving her hand over her shoulder as she hurried into her outer office.

Trent didn't bother saying anything. Matilda and Jerry, the mailman, would stand out there at the counter and gossip a good thirty minutes. Natasha King couldn't have timed her arrival better.

Trent topped off his coffee and walked through the large, old house. Matilda did a wonderful job of keeping the place authentic looking. The long, narrow windows in the dining and living room had thin, veneer curtains hanging, which allowed natural light to flood over shiny hardwood floors and antique furniture in both rooms.

An older couple, probably in their sixties, glanced up from the love seat where they sat glancing over brochures. Trent nodded, wondering how many guests Matilda had here at the moment. He made a note to find out as he turned into the formal entryway and headed for the stairs.

Pearl's was a three-story house built in the late 1800s and on the National Register of Historic places, as were many houses in Weaverville. The community was proud of their history and did a good job of preserving it. They also relied heavily on revenue from tourists who came here to escape fast-paced city life and stressful jobs.

More than once Trent had considered kicking the dust from the place off his boots and heading out for some of that big-city life. He wasn't sure what kept him here. He'd been sheriff for six years and as far as anyone in town was concerned would be until he retired, just like his father had been. Maybe it was Trent's mother's blood. She had always yearned for big-city lights and fast-moving cars. Trent's father, Bill Oakley, did his best to oblige Sharon Oakley. When Trent was ten Sharon asked for a divorce. Bill never denied her anything, and he didn't fight the divorce. The only thing Sharon didn't get as she left town without turning back was custody of Trent.

He'd been out of high school and working part-time at the grocery store bagging groceries, as well as helping out on the ranch next door, when his mother sailed back into town. Suddenly she wanted to be a mother and a wife. Trent hadn't been able to see her as anything but a big-city woman, who talked too fast and dressed flashy enough to be spotted a block away. His father saw a completely different woman.

There were times when Trent wondered how different his life would have been if he'd taken off when his father retired, after his third heart attack. Trent could have gone to college, seen the country, hit the road, and enjoyed his youth. But the town pressured him to fill the role of the new sheriff. Trent might have been able to ignore their persuasion, but it was hard as hell telling his father no when he pressured Trent as well. Three months after he was sworn in, his mother died of cancer. It had hit so hard and fast there was no saving her. His father passed away less than a year later.

After burying him on their property next to Trent's mother, he thought he'd remain sheriff a year or so, then take off for those big-city lights his mother had always talked about. Six years later he was still here, the longing to see the world not quite as strong. It was the same thing that happened to his father. The land and mountains were part of Trent. It was more than just a job protecting them. When something like this went down, a murder on a ranch and a drifter disappearing at the same time, Trent had to set things back to right.

He climbed to the third floor where the Emerald Room was, breathing in the thick smell of flowers from bowls of dried petals Matilda had on practically every table in the house. Taking a drink of his coffee, he stared down the dust-free hallway. It was time to meet Miss Natasha King, niece and employee to Greg King. A lady in her position, with captivating good looks and experience with hunts and mystery solving, would probably be better trained to lie then most. He reminded himself of this as he moved down the hallway, passing the two other bedrooms on that floor and stopping in front of the large, thick, highly polished heavy wooden door with a small wooden plaque nailed to it that said: EMERALD ROOM. He also reminded himself that even law-enforcement people could turn bad, or be bad blood, as Matilda put it.

Did Natasha King agree to meet him because curiosity bested her? Was she concerned about her father? Or was it that she did know his whereabouts and felt a need to drive up here and do damage control?

She might be from L.A. and work for a prestigious bounty hunter, but she wasn't any better than Trent was. He knew how to play the simple, small-town lawman, though. He didn't have a problem with keeping it low-key until he knew this woman's nature.

Trent knocked firmly on the door and waited, relaxing and holding his cup in one hand as he stared down the hallway. He listened for sounds on the other side of the door, and heard none. Not until the lock clicked. This house was sturdy enough to stand another hundred years. It shouldn't surprise him he wasn't able to hear anything behind the closed door. He glanced at the doorknob, watching it turn, then lifted his gaze as the door opened.

"Natasha King," he said, and stared into eyes captivating with their unique color. He wasn't sure who had decided to call them tan. But they were definitely wrong. Natasha's eyes were possibly the way natural, raw gems might appear, straight from the ground. Not the shiny, flashy color of gold worn in jewelry but a more primitive, basic shade. They flashed at him, the compelling intensity of her stare as captivating as her eye color.

Her dark skin suggested a mixed background, although he wouldn't begin to speculate on what nationalities. George King was Caucasian, so whatever mixed heritage was in her came from her mother. Long black hair tumbled over Natasha's shoulders and matched the color of her thick lashes, which lowered as she hooded her gaze and took him in as well.

"I'm Sheriff Trent Oakley," he offered. He noticed how she held on to the door knob. He wasn't sure whether he'd compare her to a trapped animal, ready to run, or something more dangerous on the verge of attacking. "Call me Trent. Welcome to Weaverville."

"Thank you." She didn't have a problem taking in every inch of him, as if putting him to memory from his boots to the top of his head.

One thing was very clear: Natasha was more than distractingly beautiful. He noticed she wasn't wearing makeup, which in itself was refreshing to see. She didn't have on any jewelry he could see. She wore blue jeans that hugged her incredible figure and a sweater that ended at her waist. She might be trying, but Natasha King would never be able to pull off nondescript.

"Do you have a minute to talk?"

"I thought our meeting was tomorrow." Her voice was smooth, soft, and alluring. There was a strong sense of confidence about her that not enough women had. And although she didn't open the door far enough for him to see beyond her into her room, there was no fear or wariness in her eyes.

"Just trying to be neighborly." Trent offered her a grin he'd been told more than once added to his bad-boy good looks. Not that he'd bought into much of what ladies he'd gone to high school with suggested when he knew they either wanted to get laid or had ideas of becoming a sheriff's wife. "You're a stranger in our town and we do our best to make anyone welcome," he added; that was until they did someone, or something, wrong.

The smile didn't change Natasha's expression. "I think you're here to check me out."

"You're blunt." He liked that.

"I'm honest." Her expression didn't change.

He'd be the judge of that, and the only way to learn a person's nature was to spend time with them. "I take it you do have a minute to talk."

"There's a couple more things I need to get out of the truck," she said after considering him a moment. "I'll meet you outside in a minute."

"Good enough." Trent backed up and turned but glanced over his shoulder when the door slowly closed and the lock clicked into place. Typical big-city girl to lock up everything as if she had something to fear. Although maybe she did.

Folks in the area were incredibly spooked after what had happened over at Trinity Ranch. He needed to wrap up this murder investigation soon. Once snow started falling on a regular basis, it would be harder finding the clues needed to put the terrible crime behind all of them. Not that he hadn't found his guy before during blizzards. But nothing like this had ever happened in Trent's territory. However, it had happened. His people needed closure and so did he.

Trent headed downstairs and wasn't surprised when he pushed through the swinging door from the dining room to the back office and Matilda and Jerry were sipping coffee and leaning on the counter facing each other.

"I wondered where you went off to," Matilda said, giving Trent a side-glance before smiling at her mailman. "Jerry and I were just speculating about our murder. The two of us might solve it for you." Matilda had a deep, throaty laugh and her large breasts jiggled as she grinned.

Jerry sipped coffee, eyeing Trent when he came around the counter. "Any new leads?" Jerry asked, adjusting his bag of mail on his shoulder. "We were just talking about that woman who just got here, King's daughter."

"He's keeping that drifter's daughter upstairs," Matilda told Jerry, dropping her voice to a low whisper as she thumbed in the direction of the house. "Trent knows I'll keep a close eye on her here in my house."

"I thought we agreed to keep that between ourselves." Trent knew Matilda wouldn't keep the knowledge of Natasha King coming to town a secret but didn't have a problem reminding her. Possibly she'd only hand out the news to a few people instead of half the town that way.

"Oh for heaven's sake, Trent, it's just Jerry. We both know he won't tell anyone." Matilda blushed in spite of herself, then huffed and ran her hand over the counter.

Jerry Packard was known for delivering the latest gossip as efficiently as he delivered mail.

"Just keep it quiet for now," Trent said, opening the back door. "It will make my job a lot easier."

"No problem," both of them announced eagerly, and he left them to continue speculating on why he had brought Miss King to town.

Natasha returned outside the same way she'd been led upstairs. When she came to the door leading to the closed-in back porch where the high counter was and where Matilda had checked her in, she hesitated when she heard voices.

"It's got to be the only reason he brought her here, Mat," a man said.

"Well, you know it wasn't just for her good looks. The sheriff could have his pick of the county."

Matilda and the man laughed at her comment. Natasha froze, her hand on the door, wondering if they would say more. They had to be talking about her. Trent was the sheriff, and how many other people had he brought here? She scowled, looking down, listening for something more revealing to be said.

"Do you think she knows about the murder?" the man asked.

"Of course she does. The sheriff said she didn't hesitate in coming here. He'll use her to flush out George King. You mark my words."

"Are you a private dick now?"

Matilda found that question very funny and broke out into a deep, gut-clenching laugh.

Natasha was suddenly numb. Murder? Was her father somehow messed up in a murder investigation? She fought to swallow. It was the last thing she had expected to hear. Maybe he would have conned someone. There might have been people in this peaceful town incredibly outraged and believing George King had swindled them out of a lot of money. But murder?

There was no way her father would ever kill someone. These people had led a slow, uneventful life for too long if they were even considering her dad might have anything to do with a murder. It just wasn't in his nature.

Natasha pushed the door open, knowing if she stood there a moment longer she'd hear something that would really piss her off. Besides, the sheriff was waiting for her outside. If she took too long, he'd come looking for her. She didn't doubt he was a man on a mission and for some reason believed she could help him achieve his goal. But if his goal was connecting her father to a murder, she'd set him straight real fast.

Matilda and a mailman held coffee cups and looked as if they could be posing for a postcard when she pushed through the door. They stopped talking, and the mailman held his cup in front of him, as if he were bringing it to his lips and seeing Natasha made him forget what he was about to do.

"Hello," she said, nodding, then headed past them out the back door. She heard her name whispered before the door closed behind her.

Natasha needed answers now. One man would have all the facts, or at least more than anyone else in Weaverville, and his gaze locked with hers when she stepped outside.

The crisp air was dropping in temperature quickly as the sun began setting. Natasha pushed the button on her key chain to unlock the Avalanche but focused on Trent Oakley. He leaned against the back of a black Suburban but pushed away and approached when she neared her uncle's truck.

Trent wore a button-down plaid shirt with the sleeves

rolled up to his elbows. Natasha had noticed upstairs how muscular he was. She now saw how his skin was sprinkled with coarse-looking black hair. Trent wore a T-shirt under the flannel shirt, which stretched over broad shoulders. He appeared not to have an ounce of fat on him. The mountain man sheriff kept in shape. If she had to guess, she'd put him in his thirties somewhere, which begged the next question: why was he single?

Not that she cared. At the moment, he was her adversary. So far he'd been very ambiguous about why he wanted her here. Now she understood it was because he had a murder of some sort on his hands. The sooner she cleared up any thoughts of her father having any involvement with it, the better. This backward town was starting to give her the creeps.

Trent moved silently across the parking lot, which was impressive given his black boots and the gravel. Her own shoes crunched over the fine white pebbles, but she didn't care. Any more than she cared how Sheriff Oakley reminded her of a deadly predator, approaching with skills so fine-tuned and a body so virile she imagined every inch of him was hard packed under his rugged exterior. His faded jeans looked comfortable and hugged long, muscular legs. He was tall and his black wavy hair was as dark as a starless sky. He definitely didn't fit the image of how a sheriff of such a small community like this would be.

He had a lazy stroll, moving as everyone else here seemed to do. She doubted there was anything lazy about Trent Oakley, though. The way he watched her gave her the impression he didn't miss a thing that went on around him.

She was also acutely aware of how he seemed to be studying her, as if trying to understand something about her that he didn't want to ask. Natasha was beginning to worry that the sheriff, and his town, had drawn a conclusion about some horrific crime and had named her father their primary suspect. It made her want to scream. She would bet they had no proof.

Just ask what you want to know and I'll tell you, if it's any of your business, she wanted to say. His scrutinizing stare was about business, but Natasha didn't miss the sizzling sexual undertones surrounding him as well.

Something in his eyes made her wary. They were a simple green, although the way they pierced through her made them seem anything other than ordinary. His thick black hair helped set off his sharp facial features, his straight nose, broad cheekbones, and mouth, which was currently pressed into a thin line. The man was beyond gorgeous, and as he moved closer he seemed to set the air around them into a charged state of anticipation. This was a guy who made things happen, took the bull by the horns, possibly literally, and controlled even the air she breathed when he paused next to her. Her skin prickled from all the sexual energy charged around her and she told herself it came completely from him.

"Need help carrying anything to your room?" he asked, his slow drawl sounding as dangerous as the rest of him appeared.

"No, but thanks." She'd decided on impulse, as a way to avoid allowing the sheriff into her room, that she'd come downstairs and pull out of the dash the GPS system her uncle had installed in each truck. She was able to do the same with the CD player. Better safe than sorry and she didn't want it stolen. "The room is nice by the way. Thanks for recommending this place."

"Matilda will be thrilled to hear that." Trent followed her around to her driver's side and paused, resting his hand on the roof of the Avalanche. "This your truck?"

Natasha looked at him, but he was focused on the truck's interior. "Why do I think you already know the answer to that question?" she asked. If it had been her, she would have already run the tags.

He didn't answer her question, nor did his expression change when she slid into the driver's seat and snapped the GPS out of the dash. She did the same with the CD player.

Trent glanced at both items in her hands when she slid out of the truck, and the corner of his mouth curved. "Is that what you came down here to get?"

"There's no reason to invite someone to break into my truck," she informed him, watching when those alert eyes of his lifted to her face.

"Nope. I agree." He still looked amused.

"What?" she demanded. It was so incredibly tempting to flirt with him, or spar a bit. She was only here for a day, and he was one hell of a sexy man. A bit of exchange would help him show off his true nature.

"Nothing." He dropped his attention to the GPS system and CD player, or maybe it was her breasts.

"Do you find it amusing when people lock everything and remove valuables from their cars?" she demanded. "Let me guess: no one around here locks anything."

"Not until recently," he said, his voice lowering a notch and his facial features turning harder than they were a moment before.

"And why is that?" she asked, lowering her voice as well and turning to face him. She hugged the two items against her as she squared off with the sheriff.

"Because up until recently, crime wasn't something folks around here talked about."

"What's changed that?"

The sheriff didn't answer right away. He searched her face, possibly looking for signs of deception. Natasha wasn't sure why he believed she would know anything about what was going on in this small town when she lived in L.A. She had her own crimes and criminals to keep her busy. She didn't break eye contact but wasn't going to remain under his compelling gaze for long.

Natasha let another moment pass, then shrugged. "Tomorrow at two P.M.," she said, shut the truck door, and started around the front of the truck, once again pushing the button on her key chain and making the truck beep as it locked.

Trent grabbed her arm.

Natasha froze, glancing down at where strong, long fingers wrapped around her biceps.

"If you're hiding anything, Miss King, I will find out." He

barely whispered and his fingers tightened around her arm. "Don't judge someone's abilities because they come from a small town."

"And I'm sure you aren't judging someone's abilities based on their gender," she shot back at him. "Let go of my arm now, Sheriff," she said, matching his low, dangerous tone.

Trent studied her, really studied her, holding her firmly and taking his time as his gaze traveled from her head to her feet and back up again. Natasha hated the fire that ignited inside her the longer he kept her pinned in front of him.

"Why did you agree to come up here?" he asked when he looked at her face once again.

There wasn't any reason to lie. "If there is something wrong with my dad, I'm going to help him," she said flatly.

"I see."

"Wouldn't you do the same?"

"Yup."

"You're still holding my arm."

Trent lazily studied his fingers, moving them over the sleeve of her sweater, but not letting go. Natasha breathed in a cleansing breath, fighting to keep her cool when she ached to show this chauvinistic brute exactly what she thought of being manhandled.

"Let go of me, Sheriff. Unless you'd rather I make you let go of me."

Trent's gaze shot to hers. A fire ignited in his eyes that hadn't been there a second ago.

"Is that a threat?"

"It's a promise," she informed him.

"You could force me to let go of you?" He seriously sounded amused now.

But when the corner of his mouth twitched she knew he was fighting a grin. Nothing pissed her off more than a man who believed a woman wasn't as competent or as good in every area as he was. Natasha's blood boiled. He thought he could belittle her because she was a woman. Well, he asked for it.

She smiled. "Would you mind placing these on the hood

of my truck, please?" she asked, handing him the GPS and CD player. "Gently. Don't hurt my paint."

Trent didn't let go of her but took both with his free hand and placed them on the hood. The moment he gave her his attention, Natasha jumped into action, using a simple karate move that allowed her to lift more than her own body weight using her legs. With Trent holding firmly onto her arm, he gave her the leverage to carry the move through smoothly. Having a black belt in karate came in handy from time to time.

Trent went flying over her head to the ground, howling loudly and hitting the ground hard enough it shook under her feet as his body landed with a thud. He freed her arm and Natasha started to straighten, grabbing her hair and shoving it behind her shoulders. He had asked for it.

She barely had time to acknowledge the back door to the bed-and-breakfast swinging open when two large hands grabbed her with more force than he'd held her arm with a moment before. Trent yanked her down on top of him, flipped over, and in her next breath she lay flat on the hard parking lot ground with every inch of him pressing down on top of her.

"Impressive, Miss King," he rumbled, sounding like a dangerous cat who enjoyed playing with its prey before devouring it.

Natasha stared up at him wide-eyed. Not only could she not catch her breath, but she also was acutely aware of everywhere their bodies touched. Roped muscle bulged against his shirt and down his arms. His black hair fell around his face as he stared down at her, his expression gloating victoriously.

She didn't move, didn't dare suck in a breath and risk pressing their chests closer to each other. Her nipples were painfully hard and her breasts swollen with the weight of so much raw masculinity bearing down on top of her. Their legs were intertwined and his were longer than hers and hard and trapping her so she couldn't move.

The ground underneath her was cold, hard, and uneven, with small gravel pinching through her sweater and threatening to scrape her skin if she tried moving. Natasha wasn't sure she would feel the pain, though. Her nerve endings were suddenly hyper-sensitive, and when he exhaled, apparently near the end of his moment of savoring his victory, his breath tickled her flesh.

He remained on top of her, more than likely only a second or two, although it seemed as if time stopped. They lay there, pressed against each other and becoming incredibly familiar with each other's bodies. She looked up as something else became apparent. Trent's cock was incredibly hard, long, and thick.

Natasha shot him a warning look when it jerked between them.

"Know any other moves you'd like to share?" Trent whispered.

"Oh my goodness! Oh my!" Matilda ran toward them, which might have been a humorous sight if Natasha could see anything beyond Trent's face and his thick black hair twisting in soft waves. "What happened? Is anyone hurt? What did she try to do? Trent, I told you—"

"Everyone is fine," Trent announced, cutting off Matilda. He pushed himself off Natasha and reached for her hand, pulling her to her feet before giving her a chance to stand on her own. "Miss King is a black belt in karate and offered to show me one of her moves. I haven't won awards, but I held my own, don't you think, Miss King?"

"For crying out loud, Trent Oakley." Matilda suddenly sounded as if she were a mother scolding her ornery son. "And I don't suppose you let on that you were a black belt, too?"

Trent released Natasha's hand and made a show of wiping gravel and dust off his clothes. "I don't think I mentioned that." He didn't sound apologetic.

Natasha made quick inventory, determined nothing was hurt, or bruised, other than her ego. The score might be one to nothing in favor of Sheriff Oakley, but there would be another round. She walked around him and grabbed her things off the hood of the truck.

"Thanks for the lesson," she muttered when she passed him. "I'll be sure to remember that move next time."

"And there will be a next time," he said under his breath.

Natasha didn't bother looking to see if Matilda heard Trent or if she would put in another comment. She hurried past the mailman, who'd remained back toward the house watching in dazed confusion, and headed inside to her overly frilly room. There she would lick her wounds. As she climbed the stairs she decided she was right in thanking the sheriff for the lesson. He'd just shown her how he didn't play fair. It was a lesson she'd do well to remember.

"Tomorrow all of this will be over," she muttered under her breath, and reached the third floor, her adrenaline spiked so high she could have easily climbed three more flights. Tomorrow couldn't get here soon enough.

Trent usually headed home around five or so, depending on the day he was having. There were steaks individually wrapped in his icebox and a variety of vegetables packaged and frozen. It wouldn't take thirty minutes before he could put a nice meal on the table. Tonight he decided to remain in town a bit longer, opting to eat at the Nugget Diner. It just happened to be across the street from Pearl's where he could keep an eye and see if Natasha went anywhere.

Nodding at Helen, the only waitress on duty at the moment, he took a booth that allowed him a good view of the driveway in and out of Pearl's. Even as the sun went down, he would notice the Avalanche's headlights.

"Haven't seen you around here lately," Helen said, sauntering up to him with a gentle swish of her hips and steaming coffee in her hand. She bent over, her pink uniform dress unbuttoned just enough to show off some decent cleavage if she was so inclined. Apparently he rated receiving the full package deal. "We've got trout on special tonight. I know you like that," she suggested, filling his cup and straightening, then winking as she smiled. "There's also the meat loaf. What's your poison, darling?"

Helen had gone to school with Trent and was a decent woman. She'd run with the wrong crowd right after high school and ended up with a son and no husband. Today she raised a sharp young boy and worked her ass off to make sure he was brought up right.

"Meat loaf sounds good." Trent sipped coffee and leaned back in his booth, glancing around the diner and noting everyone in there. There wasn't anyone eating he didn't know.

Helen brought him his meal and hurried off as the diner started filling up. Trent took his time eating, enjoying the hot meal. He tried relaxing although he was barely able to take his attention from the drive across the street, even after it grew dark and became impossible to see through the large windows facing the road. He still knew where it was and willed headlights to appear and head to the road.

Trent couldn't explain why he was so eager to see Natasha again. Very likely, she was a primary part of his murder investigation. So far, she'd given the impression she didn't have a clue where her father was and that they weren't close. She'd made a bit too much of a show trying to prove to Trent she didn't know anything about what was going on in town. When she acted as if she hadn't heard about a murder happening, his radar went up a notch. Natasha had access to all the best search engines and programs in her line of work, especially considering who she worked for. He'd done his homework and Natasha wasn't a licensed PI, which was a requirement in the state of California for all bounty hunters. But she'd been with KFA for just over seven years and was the office manager. He'd found a few newspaper articles that put her on location when KFA captured the criminals they'd been hunting. Trent didn't doubt she knew at least as much as he did about how to hunt and investigate. If she had something to hide, she quite possibly would be better at doing it than most.

Trent ate his supper, barely tasting it, as he remembered how she'd felt pinned underneath him. The look on her face when he'd grabbed her off guard had been priceless. He had to admit he'd been surprised and, after the immediate shock, more than a bit impressed that she'd taken on such a tough move and pulled it off perfectly. He hadn't planned on taking her down or revealing pertinent information about himself, such as being a black belt. Natasha would notice his move was more that of mixed martial arts than karate, though.

Maybe he simply wasn't able to let a woman take him down without proving he could be the man and put her where she belonged, or at least where he wanted her.

Damn. He'd enjoyed the hell out of having every inch of her sexy body pressed against him. It wasn't often a woman got him that hard. Usually he had better control over his actions, and his dick.

There were blessings in disguise, though. For once, Matilda's interruption was needed. He'd told Miss King even more about himself. She now knew how much she turned him on. Not that he wasn't fully aware the feeling was mutual. Nonetheless, he would have to tread carefully if he was going to learn what she knew.

Trent glanced down at his plate, realized he'd scraped it clean, and pushed it toward the center of the table. Helen was immediately by his side, taking the plate and refilling his coffee. A retired ranch hand and his wife sat at a nearby table and grabbed Helen's attention. She gave Trent a wink and hurried off to take care of the couple. The three of them started in on local gossip and catching one another up on everything going on in town.

It wouldn't hurt to clear his head of Natasha, and the case, for at least the evening. Relaxing a bit, listening in as folks around him gossiped and caught up on one another's lives, might help him keep a better perspective on everything. Getting worked up over a dark-haired seductress wasn't a smart move.

He shifted his attention each time the door opened and someone entered the diner. Trent noted almost all tables were taken. When the door opened again, he watched Natasha enter and hesitate. Helen was across the room, greeting her with a menu and a smile, then escorting her to one of the round, small tables at the other side of the diner. It was a small miracle when Helen sat Natasha with her back to Trent.

"Pie for dessert?" Helen asked when she returned to his table.

"Coffee is fine."

"Take your time then," she said with a grin.

Trent stared at Natasha's long black hair streaming down her slender back. He never cared for women who were overly muscular. Natasha was a hell of a lot stronger than she looked. There were few capable of lifting him off the ground, not to mention throwing him off balance and taking him down. She hadn't suspected he was the type of man who actually did believe in treating both sexes fairly. What was good for him was good for her. If Natasha could throw him to the ground, he could do the same. Granted, he had held her arm after pulling her on top of him and made sure not all his weight pressed into her when he rolled her to her back.

Her stunned reaction had been worth giving her a taste of her own medicine. But Trent hadn't been ready for how perfect she felt pressed underneath his body. They had molded together, every inch of her touching him; her soft curves, large breasts, and temptuous body caressed every inch of his until he'd turned harder than stone. It had taken more than just a bit of concentration to make himself presentable before standing and listening to Matilda rattle on. That had sobered him even more. Although it would take more than listening to idle gossip tonight to make him forget what Natasha's alluring body was like pressed against his.

Helen waited on Natasha, bringing her an iced tea and a salad. If Natasha was one of those women who refused to eat meat, it wouldn't surprise him a bit. She was thin, although not anorexic looking, as some women tried to be these days. Trent preferred a healthy woman, one with curves a man could hold on to, and not sickly from a diet of rabbit food. Natasha had sure as hell felt healthy.

He watched, patient, taking in her backside and every now and then glancing around the diner as he nursed his coffee and allowed his meal to settle. When Helen returned to Natasha, the two women engaged in a rather lengthy conversation. Most everyone in the diner was eating now, and Helen probably had a moment to catch her breath. Instead of sitting, waiting until she needed to dish out bills or bring dessert, Helen seemed content to chat away with the new lady in town.

Natasha didn't appear concerned about keeping a low profile. Not that she could with a body like that. A sexy body wouldn't taint Trent's judgment. If she was hiding her father or knew information that would help solve this murder and was keeping it from Trent, he'd treat her the same as any other criminal.

Natasha finally pulled out a few bills, handed them to Helen, and waved off change. Then grabbing a coat that was much too light for this time of year, she headed out of the diner. Trent straightened, relieved when Natasha didn't notice him as she left. He still planned on following her, allowing just enough time before he walked out so she wouldn't notice him especially if she didn't return to Pearl's. When he stood, Helen hurried to his side.

"What were you talking to Miss King about?" he asked without formality.

"She's quite the looker, isn't she?" Helen wagged her eyebrows at him. When she got the hint he wanted an answer, she cleared her throat. "Nothing much. We talked about Weaverville. I told her some of our local history. When I started telling her about Trinity Ranch and the murder we had out there, she suddenly had to go. She did ask where it was located when she paid me."

"She asked where Trinity Ranch was located?"

Helen nodded before turning when a couple ranch hands waved her over. He'd waited long enough. Heading outside, he spotted Natasha hurrying alongside the bed-and-breakfast. Her long hair swaying down her back and the cute way her ass swayed noticeably, even in the dark, distracted him only a moment. She hadn't spotted him, or if she had, she was better at concealing her thoughts than he'd give her credit. Not once had she looked his way.

Trent slipped into his heavy coat he'd kept in his Suburban all day, knowing he'd need it now that it was dark. It appeared he wouldn't be heading home as soon as he thought. He'd parked around the side of the restaurant where his vehicle wouldn't have been obvious and given away that he was inside. It was an old trick he'd learned from his father. As a kid, Trent used to complain how far they had to walk to get inside a business when there were parking spaces close to the door. Now he understood his father's intentions. People behaved differently when they didn't know the law was within earshot. Trent watched the Avalanche pull out of Pearl's and turn north, in the direction of Trinity Ranch.

He waited until she had gone through the intersection, then jumped into his Suburban and fired it up. When he hit the road, he still had a view of Natasha King's taillights ahead of him.

Chapter Three

Natasha had typed in the address Helen had given her for the exact location of Trinity Ranch. Her head still buzzed with everything the friendly waitress had told her. Helen had been as eager to share what had happened out at Trinity Ranch as she had been to tell Natasha all she knew about their sexy sheriff.

Natasha would find out soon enough how much of a gossip Helen was. She'd asked Helen not to mention to Trent any of their conversation or the questions Natasha had asked. When Helen had cocked an eyebrow over that request, Natasha offered a version of the truth as an explanation.

"He doesn't think a female bounty hunter can solve this case as well as he can," she'd offered.

Helen's reaction had surprised her. "Really? That doesn't sound like Trent."

"Turn right in half a mile." Natasha's GPS navigator interrupted her thoughts. Already she was outside of town, and she flipped on her brights as she slowed the truck.

Something caught her attention in the road and she slowed more, leaning forward against her seat belt and squinting to better see what lie in the road.

"Shit!" she cried out, screeching the truck to a stop and swerving on the road as she tried to avoid hitting some kind of giant animal lying lifeless right before her turn. "What the fuck!" she yelled, white-knuckling the steering wheel as her heart hammered so hard in her chest she couldn't catch her breath.

She stopped the Avalanche within yards of what looked like a very big dead deer, at least by the large set of antlers sticking out from his head. She'd never seen one so close before, and staring at the motionless creature didn't help get her bearings. It took a moment for her to realize the truck was almost sideways in the road, its rear end sticking into the next lane. For a two-lane highway so close outside of town, it was dark as hell outside.

Natasha took a moment to find her purse, which had slid to the floor on the passenger side, grab a flashlight out of the glove box, and fish out her cell phone as she worked to put her wallet and lipstick as well as hand lotion that had fallen out of her purse back into it.

"Okay, it's obviously dead or it would have moved by now." The last thing she needed was to try to move the truck and have the thing realize sleeping in the road was a bad idea and try to stampede her with all those antlers. If that was what deer did. She didn't know a thing about deer, other than they were obviously a lot larger than she'd imagined.

Slipping the truck into gear, she checked her mirrors before moving the truck back into her lane. Immediately she heard a flapping sound and felt the hard pull in the steering wheel.

"Oh my God, you're kidding me," she complained loudly, slapping the steering wheel when she'd only succeeded in pulling closer to the dead animal as she maneuvered the truck into her lane, then parked alongside the road. Now she had to deal with a flat tire.

Her cell phone didn't have a signal. She held it up before her, to her side, even out her window. Nothing. She couldn't use her phone to call for help. Why hadn't she pushed her aunt and uncle into activating the roadside assistance program that had come with the truck? She was completely on her own with this ordeal.

Too bad the sexy sheriff hadn't decided to follow her from the diner, instead of trying to pretend he didn't know she was there. What an unpredictable man! He'd been all over her earlier, but when both of them were in a public diner he'd never sought her out. Natasha hadn't complained when the waitress sat her with her back facing Trent. She'd used her compact to confirm he'd remained sitting facing her backside the entire time she'd been there. And the tingles up and down her spine throughout her meal were proof enough he'd seldom taken his eyes off her.

"Wouldn't he just love playing the knight in shining armor come to rescue the damsel in distress?" Natasha grabbed her flashlight as she slid out of the truck and closed the door, which turned off the interior light and engulfed her in darkness. "And I don't suppose there is roadside assistance out here," she grumbled under her breath.

She flipped on the flashlight, giving the dead beast in the road a speculative look. "You'd be smart to stay dead. Do you hear me?" she asked the deer, waving her flashlight at him. Then glancing around at the incredibly dark night, she hopped back into the truck and fished out the small pistol in the glove box.

She'd fired a gun a few times over the years, although mostly during target practice Uncle Greg had taken her and her cousins to when he had time while they were growing up. Uncle Greg believed they needed to understand and respect weapons. It had been an education Natasha had taken to heart. And it gave her a bit of reassurance when she slipped out into the chilly night once again.

Natasha tucked the cold metal inside the back of her jeans, feeling the hard, chilled outline of it pressed against her rear end. It seemed to drop her body temperature a bit and she shivered. It looked a lot cooler when she watched cops and bad guys stuff their guns into their pants in movies. In real life the thing bugged her, didn't feel really secure, and made it hard to squat down next to the deflated tire when she reached the back of the truck.

Now to remember the lesson on changing tires. She

glanced up and down the road, not seeing a soul or any indication of headlights. Natasha shifted in her squatting pose and searched the other highway she would have turned onto if she hadn't run into the dead deer, or almost run into him. There wasn't any sign of life down that road, either. An eerie sensation that she was completely alone in this inky black night unnerved her and she shuddered, insisting her imagination choose another time to go overactive on her.

Glancing the way she'd come one more time, Natasha aimed the flashlight beam down the road, honestly surprised the sheriff hadn't followed her. Either he had something better to do with his time that night, the waitress hadn't shared her question-and-answer session with Natasha with him, or he wasn't concerned with her desire to check out Trinity Ranch.

What the hell had she thought to accomplish by driving by the ranch anyway? It was dark as hell and getting colder by the moment.

"Damn it," she grumbled, not seeing anyone on the road.

The tire wouldn't change itself and she wasn't going to leave her uncle's new truck parked here and walk back into town. Damn it! She could do this. She needed to prove to herself, and the sheriff for that matter, who one way or another would probably hear about her outing this evening, that she was quite capable of handling herself regardless of what might happen. It really sucked at the moment, though, growing up with two male cousins so close in age to her. She'd only had one blowout in her life; it was when she was a teenager and not too far from the high school she, Marc, and Jake had attended. She'd pulled over at the gas station where all the kids stopped before and after school, and word had traveled fast that she'd gotten a flat. Marc and Jake had come to her rescue before she'd figured out how to assemble the jack.

"Well, they aren't coming to help you out tonight," she pointed out to herself, speaking out loud, although interrupting the chilled silence around her didn't help soothe her nerves any.

Standing, she moved to the back of the truck, then found

the jack and the pole that would help lower the spare. Tingles shot up and down her spine and she spun around, dropping part of the jack, and searched the dark road behind her. She got an eerie sensation someone was watching her.

The last thing she needed to do was scare the crap out of herself while changing a tire alone on a dark night. Nonetheless, she aimed the flashlight at the road behind her and took her time searching both sides of the road.

That's when she spotted him. "Son of a bitch," she hissed, clenching her teeth together when a cold wind whipped around her.

She was almost positive the sheriff's Suburban was parked in the dark, maybe a quarter of a mile behind her, headlights off and looking as black and isolated as the night.

Why would he just be sitting there and not coming to help her?

The moment that thought popped into her head, another followed suit quickly. He was waiting for her to admit defeat, acknowledge she shouldn't be out here by herself late at night and would not be able to make it without his help.

"Like hell," she muttered, and her teeth started chattering when she returned her attention to the task at hand.

Natasha put the jack together, lowered the spare tire, then managed to prop the jack under the truck so she could raise the flat tire off the ground. Her fingers were numb from the cold, and she was shaking uncontrollably. It was hard as hell trying to get the tire off the truck and hold the flashlight so she could see what she was doing. Finally, resolved to change the tire in the dark, she put the flashlight on the ground. It immediately rolled off behind her into the narrow ditch alongside the road.

Natasha stared down at the flashlight, which was at least still on, so she could see where it was, as its beam glared off along the ground, highlighting every blade of grass and each weed in its path of light. The headlights on the Suburban parked just a ways back on the road popped on, startling her and hyping up the nervous trepidation already rushing through her system. She reached for the gun in the back of her pants and slid into the ditch to retrieve the flashlight. When the truck accelerated, driving toward her in the ditch, it crossed her mind to shoot out one of its tires if it didn't stop soon. Although that would leave her and whoever was in that Suburban both stranded out here, at least until one of them managed to change their tire.

The Suburban slowed, then parked behind her, its headlights making it impossible for her to see who was driving it. She hadn't taken Trent's Suburban to memory, other than the sheriff's logo on the doors. In the dark, she couldn't see whether there were logos on the doors or not.

The driver's side door opened and Natasha pulled her gun. She didn't aim in the direction where she would guess someone would be getting out but held it aimed at the ground, her arms straight and both hands clutching the cold metal. Suddenly that small weapon was her lifeline and clutching it as she did offered a tremendous amount of reassurance. She wasn't helpless and she'd be damned if anyone in this town saw her that way.

The bright lights kicked on, blinding her and temporarily leaving her teetering as she experienced the sensation that she was losing her balance. Natasha had read how manipulation with lights often helped during interrogation. They were just lights, though, and if they were turned on, the person who did so was standing right by the driver's side door. She raised her gun and aimed.

"For Christ's sake, put that thing down!" Trent barked.

"Turn off your headlights."

"You prefer changing the tire in the dark?" There was that amused tone again.

She couldn't see a damned thing and listened carefully for any sound of him walking toward her.

"I prefer to see who I'm talking to," she informed him, tilting her head when she thought she heard boots crunch on the road. "Turn them off now," she ordered.

Once again she was engulfed in darkness. Or almost darkness. Trent flipped off the headlights but left his running lights on. He was standing with his car door serving as a shield, and his gun was drawn, too.

Natasha blinked. Helen, the waitress, had told her Sheriff Oakley knew who killed the ranch hand at Trinity Ranch. Everyone knew. Apparently the news had gotten ahold of her father's name. George King was wanted for murder. Helen hadn't been able to tell her what proof the sheriff had. She'd planned on driving by Trinity Ranch, then returning to her room and finding the articles that supposedly had been published recently about her father. There was also at least one newscast, which she'd intended finding as well. Experience told her reporters often glamorized an unsolved crime, not only making it tougher for investigators to learn the truth but tipping off criminals as well, which sent them on the run. Even if the person was innocent, as she tended to believe her father was, being charged with murder was one hell of a good reason to go into hiding.

"Why did you ask me to come up here?" she asked, reluctantly lowering her gun. It had given her an overwhelming rush of power when she'd held it in both hands and pointed it.

"I need to find your father."

"Whom you've charged with murder," she accused.

Trent walked around the front of his Suburban, his boots crunching on the gravel along the side of the road. "Yup," he agreed without hesitating.

She wanted to point the gun at him again and demand he admit he knew her father didn't kill anyone. Instead she stuffed it down the back of her pants and pulled her sweater over the barrel. "Obviously, you don't know my father very well."

"You said you hadn't seen him in a few years. Sounds like you might not know him that well, either."

"Then it seems rather pointless that I'm here," she countered, putting her hands on her hips when he stopped in front of her.

His green eyes pinned her where she stood, incredibly

focused and way too sexy for his own good. "It's easier to tell if a person is telling the truth when you talk to them in person."

"I'm here. In person," she added, feeling her anger grow. She didn't break eye contact, but Trent did.

He walked around her, squatted in front of her flat tire, and began unscrewing the lug nuts. The glow of his running lights reflected off his black hair. Muscles bulged in his arms as he fought each one loose. After a moment, Natasha left him, marched around his Suburban, and opened his truck door. His hands clamped down on her when she reached inside.

"Back out slowly," he ordered, and at the same time removed her gun from under her sweater.

Natasha spun around, or tried to. Trent grabbed her arm, pulled it up her back, and pushed her against the side of his truck.

"You're hurting me!" she wailed, twisting against him, but this time couldn't free herself from his grasp. He had her pinned against the cold metal of the Suburban as if she were a dangerous criminal. "What the hell are you doing?"

"Enough, Natasha." The sheriff's voice was unnervingly calm. He pushed against her, his hot, rugged body burning against her backside while the brutally cold metal of his truck froze her front side. "Calm down," he ordered. "Then you can tell me exactly what you think you were doing."

"I think I was turning on the headlights," she said, speaking slowly through her teeth as she kept them pressed together so they wouldn't chatter, between the cold Suburban, a vicious breeze picking up around them, and his incredibly warm body scorching more than her flesh as he used his body to imprison her. "Then I think I was going to tell you I could change my own tire," she added.

"Oh really."

"Yes. Really. Let go of my arm!" If he pulled her wrist much higher up her back he'd break her arm.

Trent released her arm and backed away. But not far enough for her to get around him. Natasha edged away from the cold car and found herself trapped between the driver's side door, Trent's muscular body, and the heat rushing toward her from inside his Suburban. He took her arm, although gently this time, leaned into her, and turned on the headlights. Then, keeping his hold on her, he pulled her away from the warmth she was suddenly embracing.

"Look here, Sheriff," she said, unable to keep her teeth from chattering this time. "I've never liked being manhandled and I care for bullies even less."

"And this is supposed to hurt my feelings?" He sounded pissed.

Natasha glanced up at his face. "For some reason, you've concocted this belief in your head that I'm going to be some great help in solving your murder case. You don't want me as an enemy."

"I've had worse enemies." He pushed her toward the flat tire.

Natasha maintained her balance, but her fingers burned when she grabbed the cold tools. She was shaking from the cold and nerves. Getting pissed might help warm her up, but it wouldn't get the tire changed any faster. So she bent down and put muscle into it, using her adrenaline to keep from freezing to death.

Trent remained standing over her, although he did move to allow the passenger headlight to offer its maximum light. Her hand slipped a few times as she struggled to get the tire off, but she managed and finally slipped it off. Trent stepped out of her way so she could roll it to the rear of the truck. He didn't help her when she rolled the spare tire from the back of the Avalanche and stood silently as she used all her strength to lift it into place, then began putting the lug nuts back on.

Her hands were freezing and burning. She'd broken two fingernails, and her knees hurt from kneeling on the road. There weren't any records broken, but she finally had the spare on and tools put away. Trent stayed within a foot or two of her the entire time. He didn't trust her.

"Are you going to give my gun back to me?" she asked.

He still held it in his hand and looked down at it as if considering the idea.

"It's registered. I'm not breaking any law by having it and, if you don't mind, I'd rather not be unarmed. After all, there is a murderer loose somewhere in your town."

Her last comment rubbed a raw nerve. She saw it in his eyes when he shot her a scathing look.

"I know how to use it."

"That's what has me worried." He was reluctant when he handed it to her.

She snorted and walked away from him, opening her driver's side door and sliding inside the truck, immediately turning on the heat before returning the gun to the glove box.

"What about the deer?"

Trent frowned.

"That's why I had the blowout. I slammed on the brakes to avoid it and slid the truck sideways. If it weren't for my GPS warning me I needed to turn and so slowing down, I would have run over it."

Trent left her for the first time as he walked toward the dead animal. Her headlights were still on and she remained in the truck, wishing the heat would warm her up faster as she watched him stop next to the dead animal and stare down at him. Trent then bent over, gave the creature a closer look before pulling his phone from his belt and placing a call.

"Someone will be out here shortly to get him off the road," he said when he returned to her. Then taking his time searching her face, before letting his gaze travel down her slowly, he gripped her door and met her gaze. "Did you do it?"

"Do what?"

She watched a twitch play at the corner of his mouth. "Murder Carl Williams."

"Was that his name?"

"He was twenty-two years old," Trent offered, looking away from her and staring at the top of the Avalanche. "I met him once or twice. He was a kid, in love with life, psyched that he had a job, and spending most of his paycheck on booze. He chased any lady who would let him. He came from Washington State, and notifying his parents was one of the worst things I've ever had to do."

"It does suck," she whispered, knowing the pain from having experienced it a couple times herself. "My uncle believes a woman's touch makes it easier for the next of kin."

"He passed the buck to you."

Trent was right, but Natasha still felt defensive. "You don't know Greg King."

"No," he said slowly. "And you didn't answer my question."

She frowned. "Oh no. I didn't kill Carl Williams."

Trent didn't wait a heartbeat before asking his next question, as if it wasn't the answer so much as her answering his questions that mattered to him. "Did Helen tell you how he was killed?"

Natasha had asked Helen not to repeat their conversation and so decided it was only fair she give the waitress the same respect. "She and I agreed we wouldn't discuss our conversation with anyone."

Trent nodded. "She's the one who told me you'd asked about Trinity Ranch."

Natasha hoped her smile was sincere looking. "That isn't exactly sharing the details of our conversation."

His green eyes flared with emotion again, although she wasn't sure what emotion she saw. It crossed her mind to ask why he suspected her father, but she wasn't sure the sheriff would be open with her. In a few hours she barely considered herself close enough to him in order to read him accurately. He'd said it was easier to tell if someone was lying in person. But the truth was, it wasn't possible to know whether someone was lying or not until enough time passed to learn certain characteristics about an individual. Natasha barely knew the sheriff. And all she was sure about at the moment was that Sheriff Oakley was dangerously hot and distracting to a fault.

"Why were you heading out to Trinity Ranch?" He changed the subject and pulled her out of her thoughts, which once again were heading in the wrong direction.

She shrugged, then extended her hand toward the heat that now blew out of the vent and warmed her up. "It's the scene of the crime."

"And you were going to search for clues in the dark?"

"No. I'm not a trespasser, either." She stared into those compelling green eyes and didn't notice his facial expression change. Just to be safe, Natasha didn't dwell on how many times she'd trespassed while on the clock over the years. "I thought I'd do a drive-by, learn how far out the ranch was, then return to my room and do a search online and learn what I could about the murder that way," she told him honestly.

"I'll have all links I know of ready for you to check out tomorrow when we meet." He looked past her, glancing behind them at the road.

Natasha caught headlights in her rearview mirror. A large vehicle rumbled to a stop behind Trent's Suburban.

"Don't leave yet. I'm going to help Ronnie get that buck off the road." Trent started around her car door but then paused. "Once we have it off the road you can follow me out to Trinity Ranch so you can see where it is. Then you can follow me back to your room."

Chapter Four

Trent sat in his office the next day, going over notes and documents he had so far on the Carl Williams case. Something told him Natasha would be punctual for their appointment, if not early. Matilda had agreed to let him know if Natasha left the bed-and-breakfast. He hadn't heard from her all day.

"Sheriff's office," he said, glancing at the clock and guessing it was Matilda telling him Natasha had just left, which would get her here about fifteen minutes early. It wouldn't surprise him. His sexy newcomer to town would try keeping him on his toes, and showing up early was a great tactic to capture someone off guard and, as well, witness them in their own environment and not necessarily prepared for their appointment.

He'd been ready to see her since he woke up this morning. For business reasons, he told himself. Natasha might be hotter than any other lady he'd ever laid eyes on and willful enough to push every button of his she could find, but he was a professional investigator and knew how to keep his mind on work.

"Sheriff, it's Lana Bishop," Weaverville's local veterinarian said when he answered. "Didn't you tell me that buck was roadkill?"

He shoved a snapshot of Natasha he'd been staring at the last few minutes, which didn't help his argument to himself that he wasn't affected by that sexy body of hers, back into the file. He'd found it online this morning, printed it, and included it in his file on her. It was on a Web site he hadn't run across before this morning and part of an article about a case in Arizona from a couple years ago. She looked as good then as she did now.

"I never said he was roadkill."

"Okay. Well, good. I must have misunderstood." Lana Bishop worked a full-time job as their only vet and ran a household with a doting husband and three very active boys. There were times when she probably didn't remember what day of the week it was. Although a bit absentminded, she was a good veterinarian and a good wife and mother. "I wanted to call you because whoever shot this animal shouldn't have left him in the road."

"Shot him?" Trent hadn't taken time to look and see how the animal had died the night before. Once he had helped Ronnie Powell get the deer in the back of his pickup truck, Trent had hurried back to Natasha. "The animal was shot?"

"Hunting rifle," Lana concurred. "Maybe someone didn't realize they'd shot themselves a buck and the poor animal wandered into the road to die. But the bullet didn't kill him right away. This poor guy bled to death slowly."

"Damn," Trent muttered, and stared at his phone when his other line started beeping. "Hold on a second, Lana."

This time it was Matilda, speaking in hushed tones when she informed Trent the L.A. woman had left the building. It would have been comical if Matilda had laughed at her own joke, but she wasn't joking, taking her task as the sheriff's spy very seriously. He thanked her, cutting her off when she started asking questions about the murder and promising to update her when he could but that he had another call now.

"Thanks for holding, Lana," he said, and began straightening up the Carl Williams file. Trent would pull everything back out again as needed once he started talking with Natasha.

"No problem, Sheriff. I'm sure this murder has you busier than normal. Terrible thing that happened to that young ranch hand."

"Yes, ma'am." It was beyond terrible, and he would find the killer no matter who he had to get tough with and interrogate. "Tell me what kind of bullets were used to shoot it. I doubt it will help, but if I can find out who our careless hunter was I'll give him a good lecture."

"Good, and thank you. I knew you would see it that way. I'm surprised he wasn't run over out there on the highway. He was found right before the turnoff to Trinity Ranch?"

"Yup. Right before it." He hadn't mentioned who had stopped just short of hitting the buck. It wouldn't surprise Trent if Lana already knew. She had the public in and out of her office all day long, and if he knew anything about his town it was that his people loved to gossip.

"If Jim or Ethel Burrows had been heading home to their ranch after dark, they could have wiped out one of their cars," Lana pointed out.

Trent had picked up his pen and began clicking it as he stared at the closed manila folder on his desk. "You're right. It could have been a lot worse."

"Oh yeah, those bullets." There was a shuffling of paperwork on the other end of the line.

Trent glanced up toward the large windows on either side of the door leading into the sheriff's office. He had a private office off the main lobby but often sat at the dispatcher's desk to do his work and make phone calls. He liked being able to see out on the street and spotting anyone as they walked up to the entrance to the station. His budget didn't allow for a full-time dispatcher, which meant he often answered his own 911 calls. His father had done the same, had the station phone transferred to his phone at night, and before 911 was around, their home phone and sheriff's phone were the same number.

"I can't think of anyone out that way who can't shoot a buck," she said after a moment. "I guess maybe a kid. But the bullet went through this buck's lung and came out on the other side. By the looks I'd say it was a twenty-four caliber from the size of the bullet hole. But that doesn't help you know who shot it. Whoever it was, they would have known they didn't kill it."

Trent jotted down a few notes, but Lana was probably right. Every rancher in the area, not to mention most of their ranch hands, had rifles. Many of them were similar brands. He wouldn't find out who had killed that buck and left him on the road unless someone saw them do it, which Trent doubted, or he would have received a phone call. All he could do about it at this point was keep his ears to the ground, see if anyone slipped up during conversation and offered evidence they'd been out that way at the right time in the evening to have shot the buck or seen anyone driving by or up to anything out of the ordinary.

Trent's town usually talked to him about any detail, or event, they found odd. His people helped keep crime in the area to a minimum. Everyone looked out for everyone, as it should be. But this damned murder had the entire town and all ranches in the area squeamish. People weren't thinking, or behaving, as they usually did.

"Thanks, Lana. My appointment is here, but I appreciate the phone call."

"Glad to help." She said her good-byes and hung up before Trent could do the same.

He placed the phone on the receiver and stood as Natasha walked in the door.

"Right on time."

"I am?" She glanced at the large, round clock on the wall behind him. "Looks like I'm fifteen minutes early."

"Like I said," he muttered, starting around the desk.

Her expression changed slightly, although he couldn't guess at what emotion, or reaction, he'd just pulled out of her. More than likely, working among a family of bounty hunters, Natasha had to be quick and alert to pull anything past them. Either she'd just learned this sheriff of a rural county might measure up to her standards more than she'd originally thought or he'd actually just busted her trying to catch him off guard. He doubted he'd get the truth out of her.

His phone rang again and he stopped, grabbing it and holding a finger up for her to give him a moment. "Sheriff's office," he said, then glanced at the caller ID.

"It's me, Matilda, again," Matilda whispered. "I forgot to tell you. Natasha King told me yesterday she wouldn't be staying a week but just overnight. Well, I told you that part already. But I forgot to tell you this part."

Trent stared down at his desk, not showing exasperation or any reaction at all to his long-winded and easily excited bed-and-breakfast owner. Anything he said would just keep them on the phone longer.

"Our suspect requested her room for one more night. She isn't going home yet."

"I appreciate your letting me know."

"She's there right now, isn't she?" Matilda was still whispering but doing it very loudly and with a shrill edge from excitement in her tone.

"Yes, ma'am."

"I'll let you go."

"I appreciate it. Good-bye." This time he hung up on Matilda while she was saying good-bye. The older lady meant well, though, and believed herself a good and loyal citizen. He'd have to make a point of stopping by later and thanking her personally.

Natasha was tilting her head, watching him when he held the Carl Williams file and gestured for her to follow him. They weren't going to have this discussion in the main office where anyone might walk in.

"How many people do you have watching me, Sheriff?" she asked as she stepped inside his office.

Trent sighed, seeing how Matilda might have taken his simple request to an extreme. Although technically, he hadn't asked anyone to watch Natasha.

He moved around his desk and sat. "Paranoid, Miss King?"

"Hardly." She slumped into one of the two wooden chairs facing his desk.

They were incredibly uncomfortable chairs, a tactic his father had firmly believed in, since quite often the only people who sat in them were people the sheriff needed to question. Trent had never bothered to replace them.

She didn't act as if she noticed, rested the file she'd brought with her on her lap, and stared at him with her unusual shade of eyes. "I wouldn't complain except it's not common for maid service, even at a bed-and-breakfast, to enter your room while you're showering and claim to be cleaning."

"'Claim to be cleaning'?" He leaned back in his chair, watching her almost golden eyes glow, although she kept a straight face otherwise. "What exactly do you think Matilda was doing?"

"I *know* she was going through my things." Her voice was soft, easy to listen to, and her expression didn't change in spite of her accusations. "I wasn't yet in the shower when she entered my room. She announced that Housekeeping was there so softly I wouldn't have heard her if I'd already started the water. She didn't hear me open the door a crack and spot her bent over my suitcase, rifling through it."

"Was anything missing?" Trent had always considered Matilda fairly levelheaded. She was a good businesswoman, although a nasty gossip. But she could keep her mouth shut when asked, which was why when he'd contemplated trying to leave a bug on Natasha's Avalanche, or make that her uncle's Avalanche since the tags were registered to him, and Matilda had come outside and offered to put the bug among Natasha's personal things, Trent had taken her up on her offer.

In retrospect, maybe it wasn't his best professional move, but Trent had liked the idea of knowing where Natasha was when she wasn't with her truck and had seriously doubted he'd be able to get that close to her belongings, at least not yet. He had every intention of spending quite a bit of time with Miss Natasha King while she was a guest in his town, but it was what she did on her own time from the moment she arrived here that might be relevant. Except so far, the modern, fancy little bug hadn't offered him a thing he hadn't been able to find out simply by paying attention.

"No, nothing was missing. Which is why I know she's watching me," Natasha told him. "And, my guess is, taking your request to do so a bit too seriously. Please ask her to tone it down a bit."

He waited a heartbeat and, when she appeared to be done but wasn't demanding he tell her whether her accusation was accurate, he decided to let the subject die and move forward.

"Did you bring something to show me?" he asked, nodding and looking at her lap.

She fingered the file. "Maybe. Let's hear what you have to tell me, first. I'd like to start with the details of this murder and, more specifically, all proof you have against my father."

Natasha was all business. Trent sensed her defensive edge, though, which made him even more curious what she might have brought with her.

"What I plan on doing is giving you the details about the murder, of which I'm sure you have a lot now if you listened to the newscast videos online."

"You know as well as I do reporters aren't always accurate."

"If they were I wouldn't be doing my job right."

"Exactly." Her full lips curved into the softest of smiles at his comment, and she leaned back against the upright wooden back of her chair.

Both chairs were set far back enough from his desk to make it difficult for anyone to use any part of it for their own things. It wasn't that he didn't like sharing his desktop, but with the chair back this far Trent could lean back in his comfortable office chair and see all of Natasha to her knees.

With anyone else, it allowed him to be assured no one would pull out a weapon without him seeing. At the moment, he enjoyed how flat her stomach was when she leaned back. She wore blue jeans that looked comfortable, not too tight. Yet they showed off how round her hips were and how long and slender her legs were. She was dressed in warmer clothes than she had been yesterday. More than likely her thin blood from living in L.A. her entire life wasn't handling their cooler weather very well. The short-sleeved knit sweater she wore clung to decent-sized breasts and hugged her thin figure. Natasha gripped her file and crossed one leg over the other. He kept his eyes on her face and didn't lower his gaze, not needing to since he'd already taken her incredibly hot, distracting good looks to memory.

"What details about the murder have you found out?" he asked.

"It was a very disgusting, gruesome murder. You've got a sick son of a bitch running around up here." She opened her mouth as if she'd say more, and he leaned forward, eager to hear what it might be. But she licked her lips instead of saying anything else and stared at him with her stunning eyes.

"You were going to say," he prompted.

"I was going to say I don't blame my dad a bit for getting the hell out of Dodge."

He frowned. She smiled again, this time looking triumphant.

"I would have, too," she added, licked her lips again, and waited.

He lowered his attention to his file, opening it, then began pulling out pictures. Maybe she needed to see exactly how sick their murderer was.

Trent began laying eight-by-ten crime scene photos out in front of him, creating a row of them and tapping each one with his finger as he placed it next to the one before it. Natasha knew his tricks. They were the oldest investigative ploys in the world. She'd witnessed her uncle pulling the same stunts on more than one occasion.

The sheriff would now lay out the details of the crime, intentionally leaving out a detail or two or even stating the order of events wrong on purpose to see if he could trip her up. If she had any first-hand knowledge about this murder, getting wrapped up in the gory details, laid out in pictures, might make her slip and reveal she knew a detail he hadn't mentioned. Since her uncle had reminded her that the sheriff might use that type of interrogation to satisfy his curiosity about whether she was involved or not, Natasha had printed off the Web site pages she'd browsed through prior to talking to Uncle Greg. She might know something Sheriff Oakley wouldn't mention, but it would be because she had read every article she could find about the terrible murder before talking to him.

She had half a mind to tell him she was on to his game. Instead, she decided to use another tactic. Standing and pressing her hands against the edge of Trent's desk, she leaned over him and the pictures.

"Oh God," she gasped, her jaw dropping at the sight of the horrific pictures.

Trent looked up at her and his gaze dropped. The short-sleeved sweater she had on was a V-neck, and with her arms straight and hands bracing the edge of his desk she knew she offered a damn nice view of cleavage. They'd already determined Trent was a healthy red-blooded man in his prime. She was using her body to distract him, only because he was using his line of questioning to trip her up. A mixture of pleasure and satisfaction that she could so easily sway his attention turned to an equal amount of frustration, then anger. This was about her father.

Natasha stared at pictures of the most horrific murder she'd ever seen in her life. Trent truly believed her father could have something to do with how this poor young ranch hand had died. To think anyone could believe her father—and she didn't care how long it had been since she'd last seen him—had anything to do with this was beyond preposterous. George King didn't have it in him to be a killer. The more she thought about it the more it made her mad. And the angrier she got, instead of yelling at the sheriff, she wanted to scream at her dad. How could he have gotten himself messed up in something like this?

Trent stood as well. "Ethel Burrows found Carl Williams." He tapped a snapshot of a man stretched out between two poles, his arms and legs bound to each pole so his body resembled the letter *X*. "Now Ethel was a ranch hand's wife before she married Jim. She's grown up around livestock and wouldn't be as weak in the knees as some women." He picked up the eight-by-ten and held it up to Natasha's face. "Not everyone witnesses a decapitated body during their lifetime, though."

"My God," she whispered. That bit of news hadn't been printed anywhere or mentioned in any of the news pods she'd watched that morning. Her hand went to her mouth as her stomach churned. Her eyes remained glued to the gruesome photograph as Trent continued talking.

"Ethel was crossing the large parking area they have between the ranch house and two of their outbuildings when she saw him. The morning sun was in her eyes and, according to her statement, she wasn't sure what she saw at first."

Trent pulled the photograph away from her face, placed it on his desk, then picked up the one next to it. He held it up for her to see as he had the previous one.

"Ethel went inside to get her husband, Bill, but he'd already headed out toward acreage they have at the base of the mountains. She found Morgan Reeding, one of Bill's ranch hands who's been there on Trinity Ranch since I was a boy. Morgan was probably the first to have a good look at Carl," he continued, his tone morose, as if he'd been the one to find Carl Williams.

Natasha took her eyes off the picture to look at him, but his attention was on the back side of the eight by ten, as if he was reliving every bit of it while going over it with her.

"Morgan was out in the barn overseeing some of the recently birthed foals when Ethel found him. He went with her around the barn and had his phone out calling me before they were halfway down the lane. That's when he stopped and ordered Ethel to turn around and go into the house." Trent exhaled and shook his head. "You see, Ethel is five months pregnant. Morgan couldn't control her hysteria when they both realized what they were looking at. He got her back in the house while calling me, then headed back for a closer look at the execution."

"Execution?"

Trent put down the picture he'd been holding up for her to see and picked up the next shot. Natasha's gut was turning. She'd had a heavier breakfast than usual; since it was part of the price of the room she'd taken advantage of the full breakfast spread Matilda offered her guests. At the moment, Natasha was regretting the sausage and cantaloupe that had tasted so good earlier that morning.

She almost gagged at the sight of the next picture. It was a head, or at least she was pretty sure it was, and it appeared to have been stuck on the end of a wooden post. As if knowing she didn't quite understand what she was seeing, Trent pulled that picture away, held up another of the head from a different angle, put that one down, then offered a third angle until Natasha had a pretty good idea of what had happened.

"Someone decapitated this man, tied his arms and legs to posts to stretch him out, then took his head and stuffed it on another post," she mumbled, not really making it a question but letting Trent know she got it.

Natasha slumped into her chair, forgetting all about trying to stay one up on the sheriff with his manipulative actions. She stared at the edge of the desk, ignoring Trent when he walked around the desk and stood next to her. She was too numb to get the images out of her head. And they were too grotesque for her brain to work around them.

"I'll get you some water." He spoke so gently his words didn't register for a moment.

Natasha continued staring ahead until Trent reappeared at her side, nudging her with a Styrofoam cup filled with tap water. She stared at it a moment, guessing it was tepid, and although she didn't want it, she had a feeling it would help settle her stomach.

"Thank you," she mumbled, accepting the cup and sipping. Natasha downed the water and set the cup on his desk, then dropped her head into her hands and rubbed her face. "What happened?" she began, then sucked in a breath and cleared her throat. "It's so terrible. Why would someone do that?"

Trent believed her father had done this. Just thinking about the fact that anyone might think her father would kill someone like this made her so furious, the nausea in her gut stilled. She was instantly filled with a cold, hard intent. It was absolutely imperative she find her dad, with whatever means possible. She turned slowly, staring up at Trent and wondering if he was as competent as she'd assumed he was when she'd first arrived in Weaverville.

"The news mentioned you had some evidence," she began, fighting not to shake with fury and an almost panicked sense of desperation.

Trent still stood alongside her. She didn't want to look at the pictures spread out on his desk any longer. So she stood and faced him.

"There is evidence," he said, watching her carefully.

If he thought she might do something stupid, like attack him for being an idiot, then let him worry. "Against my father?" she demanded.

"Yes."

She stared at him, waiting. He didn't say anything.

Trent watched Natasha's eyes turn a harder, flat tan shade. He'd barely known her a day and already saw how her eye color was a reflection of her emotions. Yesterday, when they'd sparred in the parking lot behind Pearl's, Natasha's eyes had glowed like gold. Now they were a flat, solid shade of tan, hard and piercing as she stared at him. She didn't break the silence but instead maintained eye contact. He got the impression she was trying to tear down his resilience. There was no way he'd comment on her father, though. There weren't any other clues pointing any direction other than toward George King.

Natasha worked in a law-enforcement line of work. She had to know Trent wasn't going to give her details on the case. He didn't ask her to come to Weaverville to brainstorm with her and work the case with her. Maybe she was used to her uncle talking openly about people who had bounties on them. That wasn't Trent's style, though. And it was especially not with a lady so gorgeous she could fog his brain with lust simply by entering the room.

He didn't trust himself around Natasha. Trent wouldn't jump her bones or put the moves on until she lowered her shield of resistance. Although the thought was definitely on his mind. If he spent too much time with this hot, sultry woman, he'd start sparring with her, or maybe some good old-fashioned flirting. Yesterday was proof he could do neither with Natasha. Not while working this case. Definitely not when he hadn't cleared her father's name, if he was innocent.

Trent needed to know where George King was. He was the only one who had disappeared after the murder. And he was the only one whose fingerprints were on the corpse once they pulled him down.

"Where's your father, Natasha?" Trent asked quietly, ready for her to explode the moment the words were out of his mouth.

Her expression shifted. It hadn't been what she'd expected him to say. That much was obvious. Her lips parted and she blinked. He'd give her this: Natasha was good at concealing her immediate reaction. Although she fisted and unfisted her hands, she gave no other indication that his question pissed her off. He'd bet a month's salary it did just that, though. What he needed to know was why it pissed her off. Was it because she believed she had him convinced she was completely ignorant of all details of this case, other than what she'd learned since arriving here? Or did she really not know where George King was?

"I have no idea," she told him, her body tightening. She moved her hands to her hips and narrowed her gaze on his. "I didn't even know he was here."

"Really."

She cocked an eyebrow. "I thought it was easier to see when a person told the truth when you spoke to them in person," she mocked him. "Try this on for size. You've known where he was in the recent past, which is more than I knew. But even I know he's not capable of an insane crime like this. Either you've never met my father or you're a really lousy judge of character."

Natasha shoved him out of her way. Trent stood to the side, watching her storm out of his office. He was tempted to believe she didn't know where her father was. As soon as Trent had a chance, he'd figure out why he was inclined to believe her. Other than her word, he had no solid proof as to what kind of relationship she had with her father. Trent couldn't ask her family, since they would probably cover for George King. So far, Trent hadn't found a neutral party who knew Natasha and her father.

For now, Trent would take her word. He had heard the pain in her voice when she told him she didn't know her father had been here. One thing he believed: Natasha cared for her dad. Trent would be curious to find out if her father cared as much for her. Until he had more answers, he wasn't going to let her walk out on him.

Chapter Five

"Natasha." Trent's boots made heavy sounds against the tiled floor as he came up behind her.

She was at the door, staring outside at the peaceful-looking town. The atmosphere of this quaint community was a direct contradiction to the grotesque scene he'd painted for her in his office.

When his hand came down on her shoulder, she realized she'd stopped at the sound of her name, her hand on the doorknob, yet she hadn't opened the door to leave.

"I'm sorry," he whispered, his body close behind hers.

Natasha looked over her shoulder and forgot to breathe. Trent was tall. Not as tall as her uncle or cousins, but a lot taller than her. A strand of black hair draped over his forehead, pushed the wrong way possibly in a moment of frustration. The cold determination that had made his gaze harsh was gone. In a different world Natasha would have easily reached up and brushed that strand of hair back in place. Sheriff Trent Oakley wasn't a man she could mess with, though.

Hell, she shouldn't want to mess with him, or even care about a single hair on his head. He'd more or less just suggested he believed her father responsible for Carl Williams' brutal murder. Worse yet, a moment ago Trent's cold glare made her think he believed she knew more than she was telling him.

Yet now he apologized?

"What for?" she asked, diverting her attention from those smoldering green eyes. He was back to being as dangerous as she believed him to be yesterday. And he was standing way too close.

"For upsetting you."

"You thought you could tell me you believe my father is somehow mixed up in that murder and it wouldn't upset me?"

He brushed his fingers over the length of her shoulder before dropping his hand. His scalding touch heightened too many sensations in her body. She almost exhaled in relief when he quit touching her. If he'd kept his hand on her she would have had to cry foul. Especially the way he was watching her now.

"I know he's mixed up with this murder, Natasha." Again Trent's voice was gentle, soothing, as if he knew what would trigger a beast inside her and manipulated her so she wouldn't strike.

Natasha turned and faced him. "How exactly do you know that?"

He studied her a moment, not backing up, which forced her to tilt her head in order to watch his face.

"There was evidence around the crime scene proving George King had been there shortly before we arrived."

"What evidence?"

He started to shake his head.

"Damn it." She fought the urge to shove him out of her way a second time. Somehow she knew putting her hands on him wouldn't be a wise move at the moment. "You asked me to come up here. I drove for over nine hours. Why do you want me here if you refuse to share what you've learned about this murder?"

Natasha lowered her gaze, which at eye level had her staring at the opening of his shirt and his tanned skin next to his collar. At the same time she let out a breath and when she inhaled dragged Trent's scent deep into her lungs. If they didn't put some space between the two of them, she'd do something she shouldn't. She wasn't egotistical and always considered herself rather levelheaded. She needed that matter-of-fact nature she used when brainstorming with her family to kick in now.

"Your being here has already helped me." He finally moved.

Natasha remained where she was, her feet planted and her back to the door. If someone were to enter the sheriff's office right now, she could go sprawling to the floor. Yet for some reason, she couldn't move.

"How have I helped you?"

"You've confirmed your father is a drifter."

"You didn't already know that?"

"I've faxed King's picture and the MO I worked up on him to every sheriff's office and police station in Northern California. No one has seen him."

It wouldn't surprise her if her dad was on the other side of the country by now.

"Natasha." Trent started toward her again. He had a way of saying her name that made her heart stop beating. She'd like to think he was all business, that solving this murder would consume his thoughts and he didn't have room to focus on her other than being George King's daughter. And maybe Trent was all business and she was simply torturing herself by thinking otherwise.

It would make all of this a lot easier if she only had to maintain her own desires. Unfortunately, she knew it was two-sided.

Natasha knew men. She knew when they were interested and when they weren't. When they were interested, she knew when they just wanted sex and when they were interested in a longer-term relationship. Trent's sexual desire for her was raw, hot, and stronger than anything she'd ever experienced with any other man. The carnal, almost savage lust sizzling in the air between them caused a tightening deep inside her that would swell dangerously out of control if she didn't get out of there soon. Because as well as she knew men, she also knew herself.

It sucked that this man believed her father was guilty. It annoyed her that he wouldn't share whatever evidence he'd compiled against her dad. It made her mad because in spite of his desire to find her father so he could bring him in on murder charges, Natasha still wanted him.

Trent stared at her and his green eyes darkened. His attention dropped down her body and her flesh sizzled as the ache for him swelled.

"You're talking about my father," she began, pulling her thoughts back in order and forcing his attention to her face. "I told you on the phone before I came up here I hadn't been in contact with him. Yet you needed me up here to learn he was a drifter?"

Natasha remembered the phone call she'd received previous to Trent calling her. "Why did you have someone else call me asking about Dad before you called me?" she threw out, watching for his reaction.

"Someone else called you?" The fogged look of desire in his eyes cleared. "What are you talking about?"

"Before you called me." She already suspected it wasn't Trent. The first caller had sounded older, and with more of an accent than Trent had. But if it wasn't Trent and he hadn't asked someone to make the call, who had called? And why would anyone else want to know where her father was?

"I only called you once." He turned away from her and walked around the desk, where he began searching through some papers. "Who else called you?" he asked, without looking up.

"He didn't identify himself." She was very professional, knew her job well, and had a good grasp on investigative methods. If there had been anything to learn from that first phone call, she would have reported it already. "He wanted to know if I knew George King. When I said I did, he asked where he was. When I said I didn't know, he hung up."

Trent was still looking through his papers. Natasha wondered if he had a dispatcher and, if so, had he given them the afternoon off so he could speak with Natasha privately? It appeared all there was to the sheriff's office was this outer room, Trent's office, and the short hallway that led to closed doors past his office. Maybe there were holding cells back there, or actual jail cells. If there was anyone in those cells either the walls were very thick or they were being quiet. She was pretty sure she and Trent were the only two in the office.

"When did he call?" He sounded distracted. "Would you know his voice if you heard it again? Did he sound old or young? What about an accent or anything about his vocal inflection that you'd remember?"

Natasha stared at the square tiles on the floor. The first phone call had annoyed her. She hadn't given her father a thought in ages. Work had been her life. Even after hiring Patty, she had to train her and there still hadn't been enough hours in the day for much else. After that first phone call, thoughts of her dad, where he might have been or what he might have been doing, had distracted her. She remembered Uncle Greg snapping at her to get the phone when Trent had called her. No one had ever needed to remind her to get the phone. She could, and had many times, answer the damn thing in her sleep.

"I wouldn't swear to being able to recognize his voice if I heard it again. I answer the phone to way too many callers. But he was older." She looked up and Trent was watching her, his expression fierce with clarity. "He sounded older than you do on the phone," she explained, and worked to hear his voice again in her head. "There was a slight accent."

"An accent?"

"Like a drawl. Maybe someone who lives in a rural area."

"A rural area where? This part of the country? Or did he sound Southern? From the Midwest?"

It dawned on her she was offering him his next clue in this case. Whoever called her could have been the murderer. Maybe they wanted to know where her father was so they could continue to frame him. She sucked in a breath, hearing the man's voice in her head.

"Not Southern. Not the Midwest. I'd say he sounded more like some of the people in the diner last night. It was a relaxed, softer drawl than other parts of the country."

Trent shifted gears and the subject without a blink of the eye. "If you were to guess, where would you say your father is right now?"

Natasha watched as he scribbled something on a pad while keeping his attention on her. Trent might be a small-town man, but he was an investigator. He just didn't look like the type of lawmen she was used to seeing. That didn't mean she couldn't switch gears right along with him.

"I don't know," she said, shaking her head.

"What's his current address?" Trent asked, giving her all of his attention now.

"I don't know," she repeated.

"So prior to me, or this other person, contacting you, you'd had absolutely no contact with your father in any way?"

"You're quick, darling," she said with a sardonic tone. "He might not be Father of the Year, but he's my dad. That's how he's always been," she added and her voice trailed off. She'd given Trent enough information for him to get the picture.

Trent left his pile of papers and came around his desk, tapping his finger against his lips as he focused on the floor and approached slowly. "There is caller ID at your office, right?"

"Yes." She watched him come closer, but when he began circling her as he continued tapping his finger Natasha stared ahead, only moving her eyes to zone in on him the moment he entered her peripheral vision from behind. "The number was blocked, Trent. We would have traced it and located the caller if it hadn't been."

"So you weren't incredibly bothered that someone called and asked about your father?"

She spun around and glared at him. "Yes, it bothered me having someone call and ask about my father. Just as it bothers me now that I don't know where he is. But from what I've gathered so far, that first caller could have been any number of people calling from this area code. You've already named him as the murderer."

Trent stopped circling her. He lowered his hand and returned her stare. "It was on the news, remember?" he said, his low baritone matching the dangerous look he gave her. "Reporters were on the scene. And I didn't invite them out there."

"We aren't accomplishing a thing," she snapped, turning and reaching for the door.

But she spun around again and stabbed her finger into his chest. It was as hard as steel and bent her fingernail backward. She ignored the quick jolt of desire that shot through her. "You think my father murdered that man," she accused, her heart pounding in her chest as she watched turbulence swarm in Trent's eyes. "You've already convicted him. Nothing I say is going to change that."

She spun around again, grabbed the door handle, and pulled open the door. Natasha half-expected Trent to grab her shoulder. She anticipated his touch and when it didn't come she hesitated before walking into the chilly afternoon weather. Then looking over her shoulder, she only half-turned, keeping her hand on the door. "Tell me you think my father is innocent until proven guilty."

She waited. Although she didn't expect him to respond, it still stung a bit when he didn't.

"Looks to me like the law in this land is rather jaded." This time she embraced the cold breeze when she stormed to her car. Getting aroused and getting pissed off at the same time never made for a good mix. Natasha knew men, though. She was smart to just go with pissed.

The following morning she checked out of the nice bed-and-breakfast. Her every move there was being logged and reported to the sheriff. In spite of not knowing why he'd really wanted her to come to Weaverville, she did know it wasn't to help clear her father's name. Natasha had to find a place to stay that wasn't under Trent's scrutiny.

Natasha dropped her luggage on the worn-out carpet of

the seedy motel. The small roadside motel looked like the kind of place that rented its rooms out by the hour. The heavy-set man at the counter never made eye contact but didn't turn her away when she offered cash for two nights.

Acorn, the unincorporated community just outside Weaver-ville, could also be described as locked in time. There weren't more than a couple thousand people living there. She'd been informed at the front desk that the closest shopping was in Weaverville, as well as the movie theatre and hospital.

More than likely the closest law enforcement was also in Weaverville. Natasha didn't ask and the guy at the front desk didn't offer. She stared at the lumpy-looking bed, the stiff armchair in the corner of the room, and the sticky-looking table in front of the window with heavy, lopsided closed curtains. Pearl's Bed-and-Breakfast had been a lot nicer.

And she'd been watched every minute she'd been there.

Why?

What had he hoped to learn by having Matilda spy on her?

After she unpacked her bathroom items she decided that although very little money had been put into the place, it was at least clean. The one towel in the bathroom was stiff, rough against her skin, and smelled strongly of bleach. But the bathtub was clean and the housekeeper had taken the time to wipe down the faucets so they shone.

Natasha opted against hanging her clothes in the very small closet. Besides, there were no hangers. Instead, she left her suitcase open to air out her clothes and tested out the bed. It could be worse. She wasn't in a sleeping bag on the hard ground. Memories of camping as a child with her cousins, aunt, and uncle popped into Natasha's head and she grinned.

"Where are you, Dad?" she whispered, and pulled her cell phone out of her purse. How many times over the years had she asked that question? For years during her childhood, some time after her mother took off, Natasha always believed her father being gone was a temporary thing. For a while she even fantasized about him searching the world for the perfect mother for her. He would return, with perfect mommy holding his hand, they would swoop her up, and the three of them

would make the perfect family in a perfect house somewhere.

"Wow. I'd forgotten about that," she muttered, letting the
childhood fantasy sink back where it had come from.

There weren't any complaints. Her father could appear
out of the blue, make her promises, and break her heart when
he left and didn't keep any of them. Even into her early adult-
hood he'd had that grip on her. Natasha would tell herself she
understood her father, accepted his free spirit and complete
inability to grasp how a parent should be. Then George King
would saunter into her world, wrap his huge arms around
her, and hold her close, as if he'd missed her more than she'd
missed him. Maybe as soon as he had her under his spell he
had taken off because so much unconditional love was more
than he could handle.

George King was about as flawed as a man, and father,
could be. But murderer?

"No way," she said adamantly. Then pushing the number
1 speed dial, she listened as the phone rang on the other end.
She recognized the change in rings when it rolled over to the
office phone number.

"King Fugitive Apprehension," a woman's voice purred
on the other end of the line.

Natasha rolled her eyes. "It's 'KFA,' " she informed Patty,
and enjoyed the moment of silence when she threw Patty off
guard. "I need to speak with my uncle, please."

"Greg King isn't available right now." Patty regained her
soft purr.

Lord, she sounded as if she were working for a phone-sex
business.

"Is there a message?"

"Yes. Tell him to call me immediately."

"May I take your name?"

"Patty," Natasha growled, not in the mood. "It's Natasha
and you knew that."

Patty's vocal inflection didn't change. "I'll give him the
message."

"Do that." Natasha sighed, picturing her uncle standing

nearby oblivious to her needing to talk to him. She she said good-bye, hung up, and left her phone on the bed as she stood and stretched.

She'd been up since 5:00 A.M., had headed out before the sun was up and with frost on her windows. She had driven south for two hours, just in case Trent was obsessive and compulsive enough to have her followed. Then pulling off to gas up the truck, she'd annoyed the tar out of her GPS as she wound along back roads, working her way north again, until she found Acorn. She wanted to be close to Trinity Ranch. Her father was definitely cut from a different cloth than the rest of his family, but nonetheless he was still a King. He was blood. And if Natasha had been in his shoes, accused wrongly of a grotesque crime, she'd go into deep hiding but not so far away she couldn't keep an eye on the developments of the investigation. In fact, if the tables were turned and it was her ass on the line, Natasha would do anything in her power to learn who the real killer was.

She stretched, twisted her torso a few times, flexed and unflexed her arms, then walked to the window, draped with the heavy curtain. The rod to pull the curtain back wasn't set right and got stuck in its tracking. Natasha pushed part of the curtain to the side and stared out of the fogged-over window. She squinted out at the highway and the occasional car zipping by.

Some kind of antique shop was across the street next to a gas station that desperately needed to update its pumps. The sign indicating its gas prices was the only indication given that the station was still open for business. Tall weeds grew up around the side of the building, and there were deep potholes at the entrance to the parking lot. A man left the station and walked to where his car was parked.

Natasha stared harder, trying desperately to capture details through a window that probably hadn't been cleaned in ages. Finally giving up, she moved to the motel room door and opened it far enough to see him before he reached his car.

He wore clothing that would be hard to describe, dark blue jeans and a pullover sweater that was a darker shade of blue. He was clean-cut, his most noticeable feature being his height. The man had to be close to six and a half feet tall, which was what grabbed her attention in the first place. It was a dead giveaway with all King men.

"Dad?" she whispered, her heart immediately swelling into her throat.

There was no way. It couldn't be this easy.

The man slid into his car, a Buick, dark gray. Natasha didn't catch the tag number, but she would. Racing for her purse, then the key to the room, which she'd left on the bathroom counter, she was out the door in the next minute, pulling it closed and waiting until she heard it click. Then she jumped into the Avalanche, and the tires spun over the gravel when she gunned it to keep up with the Buick that already had a decent lead on her.

"Is it you?" she asked out loud, gripping the steering wheel with both hands and dealing with sudden tunnel vision as she focused only on the rear of the car ahead of her.

It had been four years, but her dad had looked the same the last few times he'd swept into her life and out again. His hair was short, not quite a buzz but shorter than Uncle Greg's. It always had been. Her dad had told her once it was because Greg was the true rebel, not him.

He wasn't thin but definitely was not fat. Natasha had always thought him good-looking. She could see how any lady would fall for his King charm. He hadn't appeared concerned at the gas station. She hadn't noticed him checking out his surroundings. Certainly a man wanted for murder would be cautious about being spotted. They weren't that far from Weaverville.

Quite possibly she was chasing a ghost. But she had to know. The least she could do was find out where he was going. Then she'd regroup, get her thoughts organized, and come up with a foolproof game plan. At the moment, nothing came to her, other than pushing the speed limit to remain within view of the Buick some distance ahead of her. At least they weren't in L.A. with traffic closing in all around both of them. There wasn't another car in view from either direction.

Natasha hit the brakes too hard and jerked forward against her seat belt when the Buick's brake lights came on. It slowed drastically and for a moment she thought he was going to come to a complete stop on the road. Just when she was certain she would be forced into a confrontation with a man who wasn't her father and just happened to be almost a foot taller than she was, the Buick turned off the highway.

She wasn't going slow enough, which was just as well. If she turned off, it would be obvious she was following him. If this was her father, he'd panic that someone had discovered him. Natasha didn't have a clue where the narrow road went that was now lined with a cloud of smoke as the Buick disappeared into the rocky hills.

"Seven, K, five, eight, seven, nine, eight," Natasha said out loud, putting the license plate number to memory. She reached in her purse for her phone to enter the tag number so she wouldn't forget it. "Where's my phone?" She groaned when she realized where it was. "Crap, crap, crap!" she wailed, slapping the steering wheel. She'd left it on the bed in her motel room. "Hell of a lot of good it will do me there." If her uncle could see her now, witness firsthand her hunting skills under pressure and duress, he'd bench her until further notice.

She repeated the plate number, saying it over and over again as she spotted a county road intersecting the highway just ahead. Slowing and checking her mirrors, as she continued with her new mantra, chanting the tag number, Natasha pulled a U-turn in the road and headed back to where the Buick had turned off.

The cloud of dust the Buick left behind was dissipating in the cold breeze when Natasha turned onto the narrow road. It wound around the hills and, it appeared, led into the mountains. Natasha slowed, keeping it under thirty miles an hour as she glanced back, searching the highway in both directions. She'd rather no one see that she left the highway. If she was following her father, she didn't want to give up his hiding place, at least not until she knew what had happened.

Would she turn him in if he told her he'd committed murder?

Natasha shook her head, immediately seeing how preposterous her thoughts were. Her father wouldn't kill anyone. It would take up too much of his time and he simply didn't dedicate that much of himself to anyone. And he sure as hell wouldn't commit a murder as heinous and disturbing as Carl Williams'.

She heard several loud pops at the same time her steering wheel yanked to the right. "What the—!" she cried out, holding the wheel with all her strength to keep the truck on the road.

There wasn't anyone around her. She checked her mirrors, strained to see as far as she could in all directions. The hills were more intense out this way than in Weaverville, and closer to the mountains.

Had someone seriously just shot out her tires?

"God." It was a hell of a lot of work just to navigate the Avalanche to the side of the road. It was obvious she was driving on rims when she brought the truck to a stop, then glanced around again.

A dark Suburban turned off the highway and started toward her.

"What the hell?" Her fear leaped over to irritation as she glared at the approaching SUV. "Why did you shoot out my tires?" she yelled, jumping out of the truck and ready to take on the sheriff in or out of his vehicle. He was seriously out of line for disabling her like this.

Natasha had barely taken a few steps when she came to a halt and looked at the ground. Among the gravel on the narrow road was a spew of spikes, like screwdrivers, stuck in the ground and facing upward, their small pointed edges just enough to take out a tire, or two, or four.

And she'd almost stepped on one of them. Edging back toward her car, she took a better look at the road. It had been booby-trapped. Then how did the Buick get past this? One look off the road and she understood. There were tire indentations cut deep in a wide curve, giving berth around the sabotaged section of the road. Whoever had driven down this road ahead of her knew the spikes were in the road and knew exactly where to turn off the road to prevent sabotaging their vehicle. Had the driver of the Buick put this trap here to prevent anyone from following them?

Was that something her father was capable of doing?

"Whoa!" she yelled as the Suburban grew closer, creating a cloud of dust behind it as it moved along the road toward her.

Natasha started waving her hands over her head and leapt to the side of the road, running along the embedded tire tracks and continuing to wave her arms.

"Stop!" she cried out, grabbing Trent's attention. "There are spikes in the road!" she yelled, running toward him.

Trent rolled down his window, then came to a quick stop when she yelled her warning a couple more times. She ran to his car and came to a stop, fighting to catch her breath as she realized she wasn't used to this elevation.

"There are spikes in the road," she said breathlessly. "They blew out my tires."

Trent opened his truck door, forcing her back a step, and got out of the truck, taking his time to zip up his jacket against the cold wind as he squinted toward her truck.

"What are you doing out here?" he asked.

"What are *you* doing out here?" It should have been her question first.

Trent gave her his attention for only a moment but didn't answer. Instead, he left her standing there and started toward the booby-trapped section of the road. When he reached the first spike he kicked it with his boot, then squatted down and slipped on black leather gloves before pulling it out of the ground.

"Interesting," he mumbled, standing and tossing the metal spike in his hand as he looked around at the rugged, undeveloped land. "Someone laid a trap for you."

"I don't know that it was for me," she began, staring at the Avalanche. She couldn't see the front passenger tire, but the driver's side front and back were torn to bits, the rims of the wheels on the ground with the black tires hanging off of them. It was bad and her uncle would be pissed when she told him about it.

"Who do you think it was for?"

She shook her head, not really having a clue until she could confirm who she'd been following. "I have no idea. My guess is someone doesn't want anyone else going down this road."

He gave her a look. "Good detective work."

Natasha stared up at him. His comment might have been light, but his expression was dark and foreboding. If she had to guess, she'd say he was rather pissed.

"Why are you all bent out of shape?" she demanded. "You aren't the one who is going to have to buy all new tires."

"Not to mention the tow bill."

"Right." She swore his features hardened further, and if she were the type of woman who got nervous that a man might hurt her now would be the moment. Trent was livid. "Why are you so pissed?"

"Why am I pissed?" Trent took a step toward her but then stopped and blew out a breath as he turned away. "You're out here in the middle of nowhere ignoring my calls."

"I wasn't ignoring your calls," she snapped.

"Then why didn't you answer?"

She didn't want him realizing she had rushed out of her motel room and forgotten to grab her phone. Then she would have to explain what would have distracted her so much that she would have left it behind.

"Because I was turned around," she said, exasperated, and threw her hands up in the air to ensure she pulled off the level of frustration she should be feeling after being lost. "Because I hate getting lost. And because the only thing worse than getting lost is having it rubbed in my face that I'm lost. And why the hell are you following me?" She was shouting by the time she'd finished.

If the man in that car was her father and if he had grown creative enough to sabotage the road so no one could find him, then possibly he was watching this little interaction between her and the sheriff. If he was far away, he might not be able to tell what they were saying, but at the least she hoped he'd recognize her voice if she yelled. And if he was watching, her yelling at the sheriff would assure her father that the sheriff wasn't with Natasha.

Trent stared at her, his lips together, searching her face. Natasha wasn't sure he bought her story. But it really didn't matter. With her truck down, she couldn't exactly search more for her dad. Instead, turning this on Trent, making sure he knew she would not tolerate being followed or watched, no matter what his reasons, would keep the conversation away from more sensitive areas, primarily her father.

"I wasn't following you," Trent said, his voice calm, relaxed, as he once again glanced around them.

Not that there was anything to see. Natasha had lived her entire life around law-enforcement men. She knew that look when she saw it. Trent was focused, believing he was narrowing in on something.

"Is that so?" She crossed her arms over her chest, feeling the chill in the air for the first time since hopping out of the truck, dosed high on anger and adrenaline. "You just happened to be driving along this backwoods highway at exactly the same time I just happened to be out here?"

"What looks like a back-hills highway to some is actually a commuting road to those who live out here. Which happens to be land under my jurisdiction, which makes the people out this way my responsibility. So yes, darling, I did just happen to be making my rounds at the exact time you decided to take a turn down a road you probably have no business being on and ended up falling victim to a malicious booby trap." He gave her a curt nod. "And you're quite welcome. No need to thank me."

Natasha blew out an exasperated sigh, deciding to take her time surveying their surroundings as well. The ground looked rough, with large rocks protruding from the ground surrounded by tall, wild grass. There were hills in the direction her truck was pointed and high, stretched-out meadows on the opposite side of the highway. Another time, she might have better appreciated the incredible beauty from this raw, undisturbed land surrounding her. At the moment, though, she worked to put her emotions back in order. It would be smarter to remind herself of the many reasons why she didn't pursue dominating, cocky, aggressive men. Maybe if she did, it would stop the sudden throbbing between her legs from standing so close to Trent.

"Thank you," she said, although she wasn't sure she believed his story. It was one hell of a coincidence that he showed up the moment she was stranded, for a second time. Although if he hadn't, she'd be walking back to that seedy motel or sitting out here for God only knew how long until help showed up. "Would you mind calling a tow truck for me?" she asked.

"Hm," Trent grunted, and pulled out his phone. But instead of heading back to his Suburban, he started along the tracks embedded in a half circle along the road, around the sabotaged section.

Natasha hugged herself against the biting cold and hurried after him, watching her footing over the uneven ground and deep ruts created from a vehicle continually driving around this part of the road. If only she had noticed the deep grooves in the ground when she had first headed this way. Possibly she would have made it into the hills ahead of them where the road headed before the sheriff had spotted her. She shook her head and tucked her hair inside her thin jacket to keep it from blowing in her face. That is, if he hadn't already been following her. When she realized she was staring at Trent's hard ass as she followed him, she made herself look away. If only repeatedly telling herself the real reason he would be following her was because he thought her father a murderer would make the heat swelling between her legs go away. What was it about this man?

Trent started talking on the phone before he reached the road again. Remaining behind him, she listened as he described her truck, then gave its location. She caught herself staring at his ass again when he told the dispatcher that it was a charge to his account.

"Hey," she complained when he instructed they should tow the truck into Weaverville.

Trent kept walking until he reached the end of the Avalanche. He hung up his phone, slapped it to his belt, then squatted next to the rear tire.

"Damn shame," he grunted. "Looks like these were new tires. And now you'll need a new spare, too," he added, straightening and kicking the destroyed tire she'd put on the truck the night before last.

She remembered when Uncle Greg had new tires put on this particular truck. "They were new," she admitted. He would be mad and demanding answers when he learned all four tires, and the spare, were completely destroyed.

Natasha glanced up the road, which disappeared into steep rocky hills that stretched along the horizon ahead of them. She wondered where it went and how soon she'd be able to find out. With how much it would cost to replace all the tires on this truck, Natasha decided she'd definitely earned the right to find out.

When Trent walked to the front of her truck, bent over and ran his gloved finger over the sliced tire, then moved around to the other side, Natasha hugged herself, burying her hands inside her sleeves as her hair once again blew around her face.

The low-hanging sky was a heavy, dull gray. The air was growing moist, and when she exhaled she swore she saw her breath. It had been years since she'd been in temperatures this cold. And she knew in this part of the state it got a lot colder.

Trent stood with his back to Natasha next to the passenger's side rear tire. His hair also blew around his face, but when he turned slightly, she saw how pinched his expression was.

"Do you know how lucky you are?" he whispered, turning dark, turbulent eyes on her.

Natasha looked up at him, forced to pull a hand out from the warmth of her sleeves and grab her hair so it would quit slapping her in the face. "Let me guess. I'm lucky because you showed up. And had you not been here, it's certain I would have suffered some deadly peril."

She swore he growled. Trent's body grew before her, his muscles hardening as he curled his gloved fingers into fists.

When he blew out a few expletives, his breath was visible over the cold air. Trent stalked away from her. He was around the Avalanche and opening the driver's side door before Natasha realized what he was doing.

"Hey!" She hurried around the truck, grabbing his arm when he was backing out of the cab, her purse in his hand. When he turned on her she noticed he also had taken her gun out of the glove box. "What the hell are you doing?" she demanded.

He pushed her purse against her chest and thrust the truck keys at her. "You don't have to wait for the wrecker since it's a charge. Come on. We're going to find out what someone went to such desperate means to hide. Or are we still going to play like that wasn't what you were out here trying to find out?"

The last thing she wanted to do was drive with Trent into the hills and find out who was hiding back there when he was this pissed off. But if she insisted on staying with the Avalanche, Trent would investigate on his own. That wasn't acceptable, either. She followed him back to his Suburban without saying anything and let him open the passenger door, hold it for her, and close it once she was sitting on the bench seat.

She put her purse on the seat between them, made quick work of checking her gun, confirming it was still loaded, then securing the safety as Trent hurried around the front of his truck.

He brought the cold in with him when he climbed behind the steering wheel. Roped muscles bulged against his jeans as he accelerated and left the Avalanche behind, heading off the road and making a large circle around the embedded tire tracks before driving back onto the road right before the hills began. He turned on his headlights, hit the high beams, and drove cautiously around sharp curves. Rocky, steep inclines swept higher than Natasha could see as they worked their way through the hills in silence.

The road went along farther than she guessed it would.

Apparently, the trap had been set for all unwelcomed visitors before the hills began. Natasha was pretty sure they were heading north and knew at some point, by definition, these would no longer be hills but the Trinity Alps.

"Why don't you trust me?" Trent asked after driving for a few minutes.

"What makes you think I don't trust you?"

"You left the bed-and-breakfast and tried to make me think you were heading home. Gas is really too expensive to drive south a few hours before pulling a U-turn and heading north again."

She quit looking ahead at the tunnels of light the headlights made on the road and looked at Trent. "How do you know that's what I did?"

Instead of answering, he grinned. The look on his face warmed her entire body by several degrees.

She shook her head. "And you're asking why I don't trust you?"

"What do we have here?" Trent was looking ahead out the windshield.

Natasha did the same and stared at a rugged-looking log cabin. They hadn't been driving on a road but a long, twisted driveway. The dark gray Buick was parked in front of the cabin.

Chapter Six

Trent turned off his headlights before they swept over the rustic cabin. As he braked to a stop, the wind shook his Suburban. They'd barely made it into autumn and already the temperature was plummeting. Natasha wouldn't make it through the night if they had to explore the scene with it this cold outside. And she was probably stubborn enough to refuse to stay in the warmth of his Suburban.

If she caught her death of foolishness in the form of a nasty cold or flu, it would serve her right. Thoughts of nursing her back to health in bed, or better yet, chaining her to his bed were going to distract the hell out of Trent if he didn't stay focused.

"Who lives here?" he asked, ready for the same look Natasha had given him with every question he'd asked since finding her out here off the highway.

"Sheriff, I didn't even know Acorn was here until a couple hours ago. How the hell would I know who lives here?"

Natasha's tan eyes were hooded by thick black lashes when she shot him a defiant glare. Her full, tempting lips pressed into a disapproving scowl. He stared back at her, tempted to believe she was telling the truth.

Something deep in his gut made him cautious. She might not be lying but that didn't mean she might not be holding back crucial information. Natasha was stuck with him for the time being. They were going to do some serious bonding, whatever it took to get her to open up to him. And he did mean whatever it took.

He studied the branches bending over the gray Buick in front of the cabin. It was conveniently parked at an angle so someone pulling up couldn't read the license plate without getting out of their vehicle first.

"Is that the car you were following?" he asked, trying another angle.

Natasha rolled her eyes. She shoved her gun into the back of her jeans and tugged her sweater over it. Then zipping up her flimsy jacket, she reached for the car door handle.

Trent grabbed her wrist. Natasha spun around, causing all that long black hair to fly over her shoulder. "Let go of me," she hissed.

"Where do you think you're going?" He didn't let go.

"I think I'm going to get out and take a look around," she hissed. She focused on his hand holding her wrist. "The tracks on either side of the road around those spikes look too wide to have come from that car. Maybe you should check that out. I'm going to knock on that door and ask if this road is their driveway.

"Because if it isn't, that makes it a public road." She tapped her thumb against her window. "And those spikes over there look damn familiar. Someone owes me new tires."

"I didn't even know this cabin was here," he muttered half to himself.

He hadn't noticed the spikes and had to lean around Natasha to look out her passenger window and see them. There was a small pile of metal spikes alongside the edge of the cabin. "I'll be damned," he muttered.

Natasha grinned triumphantly. Then she stared at his fingers wrapped around her narrow wrist and tried tugging free once again.

"Nope," Trent said, shaking his head when she looked ready to protest. "You're going to be frozen within minutes with that thin L.A. blood of yours. Stay here. I'll be back in a few."

"I'm not staying here." She tugged to free her wrist.

"You're staying in here if I have to handcuff you to the steering wheel."

"I dare you to try," she snarled.

His insides hardened. Trent didn't do dares.

The thought of handcuffing Natasha, forcing her to do his will, submit to him, damn near got him hard as a rock. He imagined pinning her down, preventing her from moving while he took his time exploring that hot little body of hers. The sexual tension between them was burning off the charts. If he tried to fuck her, she wouldn't fight for long. Her curiosity was at least as strong as his.

Natasha didn't trust him. And she was withholding information from him. He didn't know what it was yet but until he did, making love to her would only end in her resenting him. One way or another, he would gain her trust. Pushing her when she challenged him might help crack that tough exterior of hers.

"Since you insist." Trent kept a firm grip on her wrist and enjoyed the hell out of her shocked expression when he reached behind him for his cuffs. "I'm always up for a good dare."

"Like hell," she snapped, then tried her hardest to free herself from his hold. "Let me go, you back-hills Neanderthal," she hissed, although to her credit she didn't yell or do anything to draw attention to them.

"Back-hills Neanderthal?" Trent dropped his cuffs between his legs, where he seriously doubted Natasha would try grabbing them. Then pulling her up against him, he moved fast, capturing both of her hands in one of his. "Enough, Natasha," he whispered.

Long, silky black hair fell across the side of her face when she shot him a scathing look. "You're right. Enough. You're following me around as if I were a suspect in a crime I knew nothing about before arriving here."

"You aren't a suspect." He tugged on her wrists, causing her to fall forward, then wrapped his arm around her.

Their faces were inches from each other and he saw the moment her anger dissipated and lust, raw and on fire, made her cheeks flush and her eyes glow with passion he ached to explore.

"Handcuff me to anything in this car, Sheriff, and I swear I'll scream so loud it will ruin any investigation you try to do without me."

Trent smiled and she stiffened. When he let go of her wrists, though, she didn't try to move. Her hair was smooth and soft when he brushed it away from her face.

"Alright," he whispered. "We'll check this place out together," he decided, willing to call a truce before the sexual sparks in the air between them began exploding. Natasha was becoming too much of a distraction. He needed to keep his hands off her. Since he seriously doubted she would return to L.A. when she didn't know if her father had committed a crime or not, he might as well keep her by his side while he investigated this murder.

She blew out a breath, her hair wild around her face. Something had changed in her expression, and Trent was pretty sure he knew what it was. They were inches apart. It would take nothing to kiss her. She wouldn't fight him if he did.

"The only way I'm working with you is if you admit my father is innocent."

Trent nodded once. "Innocent until proven guilty."

"Uh-huh." She didn't believe him.

"I'm accepting your terms," he pointed out, but then brought her closer. Close enough he could breathe in the smell of her shampoo on her hair and watch darker flecks of gold dance around her pupils. Trent lowered his attention to her lips, which were moist, full, and slightly parted. "You're here for a reason, darling," he drawled, watching her lashes flutter over her eyes when she studied him as he spoke. "Whatever your reasons, you aren't telling me everything you know. You're withholding information, and I don't know yet if it's pertinent in solving this case or not. So in order to prove you can trust me, I'm going on a leap of faith that I can trust you, too."

"Leap of faith," she murmured. After a moment she nodded and relaxed. "Okay. We'll try it your way. But you let me worry about freezing to death. I'm not as fragile as you think. Let's go."

"Okay," he said slowly, let go of her, but then put his arm on her shoulder when she turned again for the door. "But you are going to make me a promise."

"What's that?"

"This is my territory. I know this land and I know these people. I call the shots. Do you understand me?"

She looked at him only a moment longer. "Yes." When she reached for the door this time, he let her open it.

Trent hated having to worry about her safety and keep an eye on their surroundings. He met her at the front of his Suburban, and when she stood next to him, hugging herself and searching the rugged, undeveloped land around them, he noticed her teeth were chattering. Trent slid out of his coat and wrapped it around her shoulders. Where she came from chivalry might be dead but she would learn quickly it was alive and well where he came from.

When she looked up at him, startled, he put his fingers against her lips. "You're welcome."

She smiled against his fingertips. "Thank you."

Although only a minute or two had passed inside his truck, Trent felt as if they'd just jumped over one hell of a hurdle. Not to mention, just now when she grinned up at him Trent swore he saw her true nature for the first time. Natasha still grinned when she looked around her, checking out their surroundings. This fiery-natured, willful, and sexy little woman loved a good investigation.

"Let's see who's home," he said, and started toward the gray Buick. "And I want that tag number," he told her under his breath.

"I can remember it."

"Photographic memory?" he asked.

"Something like that."

There were two windows on either side of the cabin door, both of which seemed to be in dire need of cleaning. With no sun and heavy cloud cover, Trent couldn't tell if there were curtains over the windows or not.

"Warm," he said under his breath when he put his hand on the hood of the Buick.

He glanced over his shoulder at Natasha. His coat dwarfed her. It hung to her thighs, which made her slender, trim legs appear even longer. She'd slid her arms into its sleeves and her hair was partially tucked under the collar while several thick strands tumbled past her shoulders. She looked up at him, her expression more nonresponsive than it should be. She was still holding out on him. That was about to stop.

"Okay," she said slowly, moving in next to him and also touching the hood. She didn't appear surprised, concerned, worried, or even curious about who owned the car, and he knew she had turned off the highway onto this road for a reason. And it wasn't because she was lost.

There was no way he was buying her being out this far because she got turned around. If it wasn't for the tracking bug Trent had Matilda drop in Natasha's purse, which he guessed was what Natasha caught Matilda doing, he never would have found her. This was part of his territory. He hadn't lied about that. But he seldom drove out this way unless he got a call or a complaint.

If it wasn't for that tracking device, Natasha would be in serious trouble right now. The people who lived out this way weren't exactly the kind to lend a helping hand to strangers. Folks in Acorn lived among the seclusion of the hills because they valued their privacy. Trent knew some of the farmers out here were borderline legal with the crops they grew. Unlike in his father's day when the law was cut and dried, today a farmer might be able to legally grow marijuana. Trent left the farmers alone unless there was trouble. Putting spikes down on a road, though, definitely constituted someone with something to hide.

Trent glanced around, unable to shake the sensation that they were being watched. It might be whoever was inside. But he'd had the same sensation while driving around the curves in the hills. Trent didn't bank on skin crawling, or tingles up the spine, as indication from a more higher-developed part of his brain that something was about to happen the way some investigators did. He relied on hard facts and his gut.

Trent started around his Suburban, watching Natasha as she stared hard at the cabin.

"There's definitely someone inside." Natasha cleared the distance between them, speaking under her breath, barely moving her lips. Their arms brushed against each other when she stopped next to him and didn't move.

"Let's go find out who," he said, and put his hand on the middle of her back, then guided her alongside him toward the rickety structure.

It didn't have a porch as much as someone had built an awning-type overhang against the front of the cabin, which protruded a good five feet out from the rustic-looking log walls. The door to the place looked solid, possibly newer than the rest of the structure. Trent noticed not only were the windows dirty, but also the glass had aged, which would have made them difficult to see out of even if the panes had been scrubbed clean.

He wondered how long this cabin had been here. It possibly dated back to the gold-mining days during which time many took up camp in the Trinity Alps determined to strike it rich panning for gold. These hills led into the mountains, and there were a lot of creeks that ran down them, which at one time were known for bedding gold.

Trent rapped against the door, knocking firmly, although, with his gloves on, the sound was somewhat muffled. He left Natasha standing behind him as he stepped to the side of the door and peered in the window. Something crashed inside and Natasha shrieked.

Trent reached for her just as Natasha reached under his bulky coat for her gun.

"Stay close," he muttered, although he wanted to order her back to his Suburban. If he thought it would do any good he would have. "We've got probable cause to enter without a warrant now," he told her.

"Bounty hunters don't need warrants," she said, whispering, and was right on his heels when he turned the doorknob.

It wasn't locked. "You aren't a bounty hunter," he reminded her, also whispering, and turning the doorknob.

Neither of them said anything else when he pushed open the door and stepped into the dark cabin. It wasn't any warmer inside. At first glance he guessed the fireplace hadn't been used in ages. Possibly it was useless, with a dilapidated chimney. A quick survey of the one-room structure and he could tell someone had been staying here.

Trent walked around the small cabin, his gun pulled and pointed down in front of him. Natasha moved in alongside him, her gun in both hands as she searched the room. She walked to the far wall and pushed at something with her boot; then, squatting, she nudged at it with her gun.

"Sleeping bag and food wrappers," she announced, looking over her shoulder at him. "Lovely accommodations," she added, wrinkling her nose. "Do you know who owns this place?"

"No, but I'll find out." He stood over her, noticing she wasn't touching anything with her bare hands. "There might be a pair of spare gloves in the glove box."

Natasha stood and when she looked at him they were once again standing close. "Now you tell me."

The way she puckered her lips made him want to kiss her. He looked away first, keeping his mind on his job. "There isn't anywhere in here to hide."

"I thought there was someone in here, too."

She moved to the back side of the cabin at the same time he did. Anyone staying in this place was definitely here out of necessity. He couldn't imagine anyone staying here by choice. It was one hell of a hiding place, though. If Natasha hadn't been on this road it never would have crossed his mind to drive through these hills looking for King. There were at least a couple dozen remote locations closer to Trinity Ranch.

And he'd explored all of them. Trent could have kicked himself for not expanding his search sooner.

"Look." Natasha pointed with her gun. "I think this is a trapdoor of sorts."

She nudged at part of the back wall and Trent moved closer. Then bending down in front of her, he ran his finger along the back wall. Someone had cut out a portion of the wall, in the shape of a small door, then put the part of the wall they'd cut out back with hinges. He pushed against the part that had been put back, and it fell to the ground outside.

Natasha jumped. "That's what we heard," she said, sounding excited as she bent over next to him, then started crawling forward.

"Let me go first." But when he touched her, his hand landed on her rear end since she was already crawling outside through the hole in the cabin wall. Instinctively his hand curved around her soft bottom. For a moment every inch of him was hard as he fought back the urge not to let his fingers slide between her legs.

God, this woman was hot. She was also feisty, daring, and definitely not panicking considering their circumstances. Not many women would crawl through a hole in a wall when they had no idea who might be waiting for them on the other side.

She turned the moment she was outside and pulled her legs through. "Whoever was in here probably ran up this back hill. We would have seen them otherwise."

Before he could crawl through after her, Natasha was bounding up the hill. Trent cursed under his breath, not taking time to put the wall back as he sheathed his gun and took off after her.

Natasha agreed it was a good idea to put a level of trust in each other and work together. It put one hell of a burden on her, though. Trent Oakley was by far the sexiest man she'd ever met. She'd damn near frozen while crawling through the cabin wall. Her body still sizzled from when he'd touched her ass. In spite of telling herself it was a reflex and that he hadn't cupped her rear end on purpose, Natasha still felt the pressure between her legs as she reached the top of the hill. He had held her in a tight grip back in the Suburban. She imagined he might even be capable of holding her down. Not many men could. Natasha liked the rough-and-ready type. None of the men she'd gone out with in the past, though, had truly been able to force her to submit. During foreplay, if things got rough, which she loved, she was always able to outmatch the man she was with. Half the time that turned them on, in which case she was done. The other half of the time, her date got bent out of shape because she was stronger and more adept than he was, and still, they were done.

Now, with Trent, she caught herself holding back. She easily could have freed herself when he threatened to handcuff her. It might have caused a bit of a commotion, however, and they hadn't parked so they could fuck. They had come here to see if her father was here. Trent didn't know that. Or at least she hoped he thought they were simply after whoever trashed her tires.

Did her ability to hold her own turn him on? Or did it create a need inside him to pressure her to submit? She wasn't sure why but the thought of Trent completely overpowering her sexually got her so wet she stumbled on the hill.

"Damn it," she cursed under her breath and quickly rubbed her hands on her jeans. "Stay focused," she ordered herself. It would have been nice to have those gloves he had mentioned were in the Suburban.

Natasha continued up the hill, falling to her hands and knees once again when another thought hit her. If they found her father, if he was hiding out here, it would imply one hell of a large amount of guilt. Regardless of how he'd sworn to presume innocence, Trent would haul him in. She would have helped Trent find him.

"Crap," she hissed, and damn near flew over a fallen log half-buried in the ground.

Trent's coat protected her from more than just the elements. It prevented small protruding sticks from ripping at her skin when she climbed over the log, which was more like a fallen tree.

Natasha stared at a piece of fabric tangled in branches on

the other side of the log. Someone else had tripped over the log. They hadn't been as lucky. It had torn their shirt.

"Natasha!" Trent was right behind her.

She shoved the torn piece of material in her coat pocket. Trent leapt onto the fallen log behind her and jumped to the ground next to her.

"Are you okay?"

"I'm fine," she said, slightly out of breath. "Although I didn't take that log as gracefully as you just did."

Trent braced himself on the uneven ground. With the extreme tilt in the earth as the hill grew steeper, they were almost eye to eye.

Natasha caught herself admiring how well the great outdoors appealed to him. His plaid flannel button-down revealed enough chest hair to almost make her drool. His shirt was tucked into his jeans, which showed off a hard, flat waist. And the way those well-worn jeans hugged his muscular legs almost made her forget why they were out there.

Almost. If her father were hiding out here, she had to throw the sheriff off his scent and come out here later, alone. Natasha needed to talk to her dad before Trent got his hands on him.

"I'm fine," she repeated, forcing herself to look away. She scanned the hill for any signs of life other than the two of them. "Let's see what we can see at the top."

"Alright, but I'll lead." Trent held up his gloved hand as if he expected her to argue. "You don't know the kind of people who live out here and I do. If they don't recognize me, they would know my name if I call it out. Gives us less of a chance of getting shot."

She nodded, willing not to argue since he'd just filled her with hope. Maybe the sheriff didn't believe they were chasing her father. He possibly thought whoever was out here was simply another drifter, or that this land was part of a bigger piece of property and whoever owned it just happened to want to camp out in that dilapidated cabin. Maybe they were trailing a criminal wanted for another crime.

Natasha really didn't care as long as Trent didn't have his

thoughts on her father. Besides, following him up the remainder of the hill gave her one hell of an ass shot. Thankfully, he moved fast. Natasha raced up the hill after him.

The need to burn off energy hit her hard. Adrenaline pumped through her body. Her breasts were swollen and her nipples were hyper-sensitive, growing even more so every time she moved and they brushed against her bra. She took on the hill, fighting it and the demons growing inside her, making her acutely aware of how close Trent was as she continued hiking to the top.

Trent was eventually right next to her, pointing out broken branches, or a partial footprint in the soft dirt that suggested whoever they were chasing had taken this same path.

"Shit," Trent grumbled when they finally stood at the top of the hill and stared at the endless hills and valleys spread out in front of them.

The mountain range was barely visible on the cloudy, gray horizon. Patches of fog had settled in a the valleys below them, and she and Trent stood staring down at it now.

Continuing on would be ridiculous. Natasha squinted through thick sections of trees, stared at large boulders in the ground on the other side of the hill. She saw no easy way to continue hiking. Someone had come this way minutes ahead of them, and disappeared. Whoever had been in that cabin apparently knew this land fairly well. Maybe she hadn't seen her father at the gas station after all. Maybe they were chasing some back-hills person, who for whatever reason was camping out in that old cabin . . . and had put spikes in the road so no one would drive out this way.

That's when she spotted him. Already down the hill in front of them, a man in a plaid shirt wearing what appeared to be a down-lined winter vest was moving through the trees alongside the bottom of the next hill. It almost appeared he was trying to do a wide circle, track his way back to watch the cabin, and spy on her and Trent until they left. Then he might return to his cabin, although Natasha seriously doubted Trent would leave this place alone. Whoever was running had to know their hiding place had been compromised.

She stared hard at the man. He was well over six foot. His long legs made quick distance over the rough terrain he was traveling. There was no hiding or mistaking the King men. All of them were giants. And all of them were muscular, incredibly handsome men, including her father.

"Natasha," Trent whispered, turning so the breeze, which was sporadic through the trees, wouldn't help his voice carry in the direction of the man down in the valley. "There he is."

"I see him."

"Is that your father?"

Trent didn't know if the man was George King, or not. For the first time, she saw a different side to the sheriff. Natasha looked at him, stared into his green eyes. Gone was the cockiness and arrogance. Trent met her gaze, but continued shooting his attention in the direction of the man hurrying back around the base of the hill beneath them. He wasn't as worried about whether she would lie to him as he was keeping an eye on whoever the man was. He trusted her. She trusted him, too, to do his job.

"I don't know," she whispered.

Trent reached up underneath her hair and rubbed the side of her neck just above the coat's collar.

"You don't know?" He sounded surprised. "It would really help if we knew if it were him, or not."

Trent didn't believe her. Something constricted in her chest. She didn't feel caught in a lie since it had been four years since she'd seen her father. Natasha didn't remember her father's hair being as gray. This guy was pretty far away. She could be wrong. Maybe it wasn't him. So she wasn't lying when she said she didn't know. Searching Trent's face, she willed the hardened expression now there to go away. She preferred the glow in his eyes when he believed the two of them were working together.

"It's been four years since I've seen him," she reminded him.

"But it could be," Trent pushed.

"It could be," she admitted.

That spark returned to his eyes and a slow grin formed at

the corner of Trent's mouth. His fingers dragged along the collar of the coat before he dropped his hand to his side. "Find out," he whispered. "Yell to him."

Natasha's heart started thudding in her chest. If the man below were her dad, he probably would know the sheriff, especially since Trent was looking for him on murder charges. If she yelled at him, her dad would think she was helping to turn him in. She told herself she didn't care if Trent believed her trustworthy. But the truth was, she did care. Just as she cared for her father.

Damn it. Nothing good could come out of this.

Natasha spun around, turning her back to Trent.

"Dad!" she yelled. Her voice echoed back at her.

The man beneath them froze in his tracks and Natasha's heart stopped beating. "No," she whispered, the one word barely audible to herself. She was pretty sure Trent didn't hear her, although he was so close behind her she swore she felt his body heat combatting the frigid cold around them.

"Dad," she continued, wishing her father, wherever he was, could hear her. "I know you didn't do it."

The man didn't call back to her. Instead he turned slightly, shifting his weight; then he pulled his hand out of his pocket.

"Down!" Trent yelled in her ear at the same time he tackled Natasha and flung her to the ground.

The man below pulled a large gun out of his vest pocket, raised it, aimed directly at her and fired. The loud explosion echoed repeatedly off each of the hills. It sounded as if he fired again and again.

Natasha went numb. In that final second before Trent bulldozed into her and sent the two of them sprawling over rocky, uneven ground, she had stared straight into the eyes of the man who tried to shoot her. They'd glowed with so much raw, unadulterated hatred, it had chilled her blood. Although she'd never seen him look that way, she swore he was her father. George King had just tried to kill her.

Chapter Seven

Trent adjusted himself on top of Natasha's body. He was all too aware of her soft curves underneath him but at that moment he was more satisfied that with his weight on her she couldn't get up and get hurt. He pulled his gun out and aimed at the man fleeing into the trees.

Goddamn, if he didn't look like George King. Trent had seen King a few times in town at the diner and out at Trinity Ranch. It had never crossed his mind that he'd have to put the man's face, or body type, to memory, though.

Trent aimed and fired. His gun exploded just as loudly as the man's below had.

"God, crap! Trent," Natasha hissed, suddenly squirming underneath him.

If asked at any point in time later, Trent would swear the hardest shot he ever got off in his life was the one at a murder suspect with Natasha underneath him, twisting and rubbing her hot, round ass against his dick.

"Stop." He ground out the order as he tried for a better angle, keeping his eye on the man who was still running as fast as he could away from them.

Trent fired one more shot just as the man disappeared into trees on the other side of the valley below. "Damn it."

"What the hell are you doing?" Natasha freed her arm out from underneath him and grabbed his firing arm.

Trent lowered his weapon. "What do you think I was doing?" he demanded, then tried to catch another glimpse of the man, who, of course, now was gone.

"Quit shooting. Why are you trying to shoot him?"

Trent laid his gun on the ground, securing the safety. "Because he just tried to kill you," he hissed, barely able to contain the growing rage in him. If that wasn't his murderer who just escaped him, there was another equally unstable, enraged motherfucker running around in his jurisdiction. Neither thought sat well with him.

Pushing himself to his feet, Trent grabbed his gun and Natasha. He kept a firm grip just above her wrist as he marched down the side of the hill they'd just climbed. Maybe he dragged her alongside him a bit more fiercely than needed. Her black hair flew loose around her face and in his peripheral vision. Natasha complained, he thought. He wasn't sure. What he did know was if he said a word, he would start screaming and yelling. He was so damned pissed.

"I swear, if you manhandle me one more time," she snapped, digging her heels in and tearing her arm free from his grasp once they were at the bottom of the hill.

He turned on her. "You'll what?"

Natasha took a step closer and lowered her voice. "Don't do it and we won't have to find out."

"Did you follow your father out here?" he demanded, asking the one question that was rubbing him raw at the moment. "Is that why you turned off the highway?"

"I already told you why I turned off the highway." Natasha walked away from him, rubbing her hands and stared at the cabin. "Maybe we can figure out who he was by looking around some more in there," she said, and nodded at the cabin. "Got any flashlights?"

Trent stared at her a moment when she looked over her shoulder at him with the question. Maybe she was telling him the truth. Maybe she had driven south, cut back, and headed back up north to throw him off her trail. He guessed she

nt noticed she'd referred to the man she'd called Dad
hort bit ago now as "whoever had been staying here."
eved she loved her father. And unlike when he had first
her in L.A., Trent now accepted that she hadn't seen
several years. He didn't know what type of relationship
with him prior to that, or if George King was a good
was clear he was a pretty crappy father. Trent decided
ush the matter for the time being.

t's get out of here."

straightened and looked around the cabin. "What
he sleeping bag and clothes over there?" she asked.
ave them. I have a few items in the truck we're going
here as well."

eyes lit up when she looked at him. "Spy toys?"
toys?" he repeated.

grinned and looked away. "That's what I call them."
ugged. "Surveillance equipment. It's pretty much my
part of the job. There is some really cool stuff out
the market."

thered the evidence bags while Natasha put the wall
ether. When she was done he could hardly tell where
artment was. Then leading them out to the truck, he
bags in a small tote he kept in the back of the Sub-
d opened a side hatch.

, I admit these aren't my favorite part of the job," he
ing out a small leather black box.

a almost grabbed it out of his hands. "What do
"

ome listening devices."

lready opened the box and was fishing through the
bugs he'd purchased almost a year ago but never

you formatted them to your computer yet?" she

of answering, she held the listening devices in her
ared ahead. "You feel like someone is watching
ispered.

wanted to find her father and talk to him first. And maybe she
had turned herself around so that not even her GPS knew how
to straighten her out.

"Why did you not want me to shoot him?" he asked, feeling some of his temper wane.

He watched all the air deflate out of her as she exhaled.
She reached for her hair at the back of her neck and twisted it
so it wouldn't blow around her face.

"I don't know," she said, sounding defeated. She looked
at the ground between them instead of at him. "He looked
like Dad but I wasn't sure. And well, if he was, I sure as hell
didn't want you shooting him." Her eyes were a flat shade of
tan when she finally met his gaze.

"Let's search that cabin." He would let it go at that for now.

It was completely dark and their beams of light bounced
off the dilapidated walls once they were inside the old cabin.
After hiking up and down that hill, having his adrenaline and
his temper spike and recede, and with it getting colder, Trent
was feeling rather stiff.

"I think I found something."

"What?" Trent turned from where he'd been inspecting
the weak floorboards, checking to see if any of them might
be intentionally loose.

She was on her knees with her back to him. His coat still
hung on her small frame, drowning her but probably keeping
her warm. She sure as hell had been hot when all those curves
had been snuggled underneath him. As crucial of a moment
as it had been, and he'd performed within the letter of the law,
he'd swear to it, Trent was also aware of how well their two
bodies had fit together.

After going over every inch of the cabin, inside and out,
for any clues that might let them know who had evaded them
and shot at Natasha, Trent planned on confirming how well
their bodies fit together. She might not have thought it through
yet, but when they were done, he was taking her home with
him. Her truck would be in the shop getting new tires and
she'd checked out of Pearl's. Whatever motel room she had
reserved for the night, they would stop and get her things,

then head back to Weaverville. He also planned on getting her to talk. She would open up to him, if it took seduction to do it.

"What did you find?" he asked when she grew silent again. Trent crossed the small, dimly lit cabin and stood over her.

Natasha had twisted and neatly knot her hair into a bundle at the back of her head. Trent was fascinated by how easily she was able to pull it away from her face. He wondered if it would be just as easy to untie it and watch it tumble back down her back and over her shoulders and down her front.

"The wall here is hollow." She looked up at him, made a face, then tapped the wall with her fingernails. "I mean, there isn't much to the walls anywhere in this cabin, but right here the sound is different."

"Learn this from watching detective shows?" He grinned at her as he knelt alongside her.

When she glared at him there wasn't any hostility in her eyes. "I don't watch a lot of TV," she offered. "But my uncle and cousins have found clues in hidden compartments in walls before. It seems to be the most common place people hide things." She shook her head and the knot on the back of her head slipped a little. "You'd think if someone was going to make a conscious decision to break the law they would at least do the research and learn to do things unlike the way every convicted criminal has done before them."

Trent tried not to laugh. Natasha's face was wrinkled into an almost comical expression as she shook her head. He believed she had some insight into the mind of a criminal. Natasha was the product of a law-enforcement family, raised by a cop and his loyal wife, then graduated into the family business of bounty hunting. She knew no other life. Which explained a lot. Natasha couldn't comprehend her father being anything than low-abiding the way the rest of her family was.

"Right here." She ran her fingernails through a seam in the log wall, then dug in and gripped one of the logs. "I've got it."

"Let me help." Trent reached for the log just as Natasha pulled it free from the wall. For a moment he thought she'd

broken the wall and that a rush of frigid a[ir] them and make the cabin even colder. "Da[mn]" when he instead stared at a compartment [that ap]peared to be a fake log.

Natasha reached inside, but Trent g[rabbed her] "Wait," he instructed, jumping up and hu[rrying] cabin. He was back in a second and Natas[ha was kneel]ing facing the wall. She'd turned to wat[ch him and] moved to the side, giving him room, whe[n]

"There's a key," she said, pointing at [something] loose among the other objects Trent bega[n to re]hidden compartment and place in eviden[ce]

"I got it." He held it up between his [fingers] she aimed the beam of her flashlight at it[.]

"I'd say it's a safe-deposit key."

"Interesting," Trent muttered, and dr[opped it in a bag] by itself.

He'd brought in a marker as well, and [was able] to use, writing on each bag as he filled [it. Besides the] key there were several individually [wrapped rolls of] money, which appeared to all be in sma[ll bills.]

"That's all the money," he said, and li[fted out a box] that looked to have been a bit too weath[ered, and it crum]bled in his hand. "Be careful with this," [he said, handing] it gingerly to Natasha.

She let it slide into a bag, then s[aid, "This one] looks just as old," she said, picking u[p a box that was] already sealed. "Those are some old [   ]

Trent lifted the last item out of t[he wall.] "What] in the hell is this?"

Natasha took it, keeping her ha[nd under it as] she held it out in front of her. Tre[nt reached for a] bag and opened it, but whatever it [was]

"I think it's a stuffed animal." [She laughed.] Look. There are two button eyes [on this very] old, worn-out teddy bear. I wonde[r how long it's been] here before whoever was using th[is cabin for smuggl]ing ever came here."

He'd been attentive to the darkness around them every time he'd left the cabin and while moving around inside it. He hadn't seen, or heard, anyone.

"He's come back," she whispered. "He's watching us."

"Fascinating that he'd come back," Trent also whispered. "Must be something in that cabin worth dying for."

"Everything we found looked old and forgotten. Maybe he doesn't have anywhere else to go," she suggested, her eyes wide as she focused on his face.

Trent saw clouds covering her pretty tan eyes. She looked haunted, confused, and willing to go to any means to fix things.

"Let's get in the truck." Before she could answer, Trent took her arm and turned her, then guided her to the passenger door, which he opened for her. "We'll talk inside," he added under his breath when she looked at him like she'd protest.

The moment he closed his driver's side door, Natasha started speaking. She was leaning forward, long black strands of hair already fallen free and preventing his ability to see her face. The black leather box with his unused listening devices he'd bought over a year ago with grant money the county had qualified for was on her lap, and she fingered it delicately, stroking the leather with her thumbs and index finger.

"I don't know if that is my father out there or not," she mumbled.

"I know."

"I know you have to go on the assumption that he is George King." She sounded resolved and defeated.

More than anything Trent wanted to pull her hair back, see her pained expression. He knew he'd see ghosts she'd kept hidden possibly most of her life. Maybe knowing her father was a criminal yet keeping that knowledge stuffed in some forgotten dark corner had allowed her to believe he was good, like the uncle who might have been more of a father to her than her biological father. She didn't want Trent to see the pain she was enduring any more than she wanted to feel it.

"We're supposed to ride on knowledge that all men are

innocent until proven guilty," she continued, tracing invisible lines over the top of the box. "And you haven't told me all of your insurmountable evidence that points toward my father being a killer, but the man out in those hills . . ." She paused, blew out a loud, exhausted breath, and straightened, staring straight ahead.

There wasn't a thing Trent could fault about Natasha. If she had a boyfriend, or several men, down in L.A., she'd made no show of calling anyone or sending calls to voice mail. Natasha was one of a kind, a woman unlike any he'd ever met before. It created a tightening in his heart, spreading through his chest, just staring at her and acknowledging the depths of her complicated nature. The more time he spent with her, the more he wanted to know her.

She patted the box in her lap. "These have to be formatted on your computer, or a laptop," she said, changing the subject. And when she glanced at him her expression revealed none of the pain she had to be experiencing. "It isn't hard to do and only takes a few minutes. I don't suppose you have a laptop here in the truck?"

He shook his head, skeptical that doing anything with those listening devices involving a computer would be simple or only take a few minutes. He should have known the advertising was misleading when it said the devices were simple and could be installed with one simple step.

Natasha grinned, grabbing his attention.

"Old school," she grumbled, rolling her eyes. "You have no idea how much easier your job could be if you kept a laptop at your fingertips."

He returned her grin. "You're full of shit, King," he informed her, then nodded at the box. "Let me install those in the cabin. We'll get out of here and go check on your truck."

"Working together isn't going to last too long if you don't believe me." Her eyes flashed with that glow that made her entire expression flush with a vibrancy he'd love to untap and explore. Natasha nodded at the phone on his belt. "Call KFA right now and ask them about my computer skills. I know what I'm talking about."

"I'm sure you do." he said slowly. "It would be smarter to plant them now and you can show me all your formatting skills once we're back at my place."

She narrowed her gaze on him at the mention of going to his place. "Okay. We'll do it your way. But I'm planting them in the cabin. If that is my father out there, and I am saying 'if,' he won't hurt me."

"No way," Trent said, reaching for the box. "He's already shot at you once."

Natasha didn't try to stop him from taking it. "Trent," she said, saying his name with a soft, alluring tone. "My father is possibly a better shot than my uncle. Always has been. My grandfather was a hunter and believed his boys should know how to use a gun as well as they could use a pencil or pen."

"You aren't going to convince me he missed you, or me, on purpose. The man didn't have to shoot. He could have just kept running."

When she stared at him and didn't continue arguing, Trent slipped his hand out of his glove and cupped her cheek. In spite of how red her cheeks were, her skin was soft and warm. He rubbed his fingertips over her cheekbone.

"My father believed the same thing, darling," he whispered, unable to keep his voice from sounding raspier than it had before. The urge to kiss her damn near overwhelmed him. "I'm one hell of a shot and you can call anyone in Weaverville and ask them right now if you don't believe me."

When she smiled, he swore the inside of his truck got a hell of a lot warmer. Trent stared into her incredibly unique eyes and the silence grew between them. It wasn't uncomfortable. Natasha could piss him off, pick a fight with him, and challenge him in ways that if any other woman tried, he would never tolerate. Maybe once he fucked her, his strong attraction toward her would subside. He hoped so. Trent had no desire to get all wrapped up in any woman. He had the biggest case of his life to solve and wished Natasha weren't distracting him so much.

"Now stay here. And I mean it this time." Even as he stepped out of his truck, he worried sleeping with Natasha wouldn't take his mind off her. He was fooling himself thinking otherwise, but whatever it took to work this case.

Trent held the bugs in his hand as he turned an eagle eye on his surroundings and made himself focus on the night instead of the beautiful woman in his truck. The icy chill in the night air helped clear his head. It was imperative he remain focused. If King wasn't staying at this cabin, Trent needed to face the possibility he might have a second case on his hands.

He didn't have several deputies, or dogs, he could scour these hills with. Nor did he use computers. It didn't bother him being called old school. He would study everything they'd bagged and labeled from inside the cabin. Then if he learned anything substantial after planting these bugs, he would take it from there. If a manhunt came into play it wouldn't be difficult to round up volunteers to help lure whoever was out here in.

He walked across the uneven ground to the old, dilapidated cabin with the flashlight weighing down in his coat pocket. His gun hand was free and his fingers twitched, ready to pull his forty-five. More than likely whoever had set up camp in this cabin would steer clear of it for awhile.

Trent entered the cabin and set the black box on the unstable-looking table in the middle of the room. He pulled his small notepad out of his pocket and jotted down a quick note, ripped it from the pad, and left it on the table. Then grabbing the black box he headed back to the Suburban.

He might be foolish in buying into the haunted look he'd seen on Natasha's face. The evidence against George King was pretty strong. But Trent was going to give Natasha this one chance. So he'd written: *Don't hurt your daughter. She's here for you.*

Trent's home was surprisingly cozy, even with its strong masculine edge. Natasha got the impression a woman hadn't put her mark on this place in a long time, if ever.

She'd set up shop with her laptop at his couch. Trent had

disappeared upstairs after building a fire, which she now stared at instead of doing the work online she'd planned on doing. It was nice being alone to regroup, get a handle on her senses, but being in Trent's home was making it more difficult than if she'd been alone in a motel room somewhere. Or at least that's what she told herself as she was continually aware of every creak in his home as Trent moved around upstairs.

"It's just a bad case of lust," she mumbled, returning her attention to her laptop and trying to get her eyes to focus. Now wasn't the time to fall for a guy. She managed a chuckle. Especially a guy who was a good day's drive away from where she lived.

"What's funny?" Trent asked.

Natasha started and grabbed her laptop to keep it from sliding off her legs. She hadn't noticed him standing in the doorway leading from his hall into the living room.

"I was just thinking about the new girl we hired at the office not too long ago," she lied.

He nodded and started toward her. "The place going to be in shambles when you get back?"

Natasha wouldn't be surprised if Patty rearranged the entire office to her liking while she was gone. "I wouldn't be surprised."

"Your truck will be ready in the morning," he told her, stopping at the edge of the coffee table and tilting his head as he stared at her laptop. "What are you doing?"

She'd been doing a lot of things in the hour or so she'd been sitting in his living room, but mostly being acutely aware of how everything around her breathed of Trent Oakley. Whether she'd leaned back on the comfortable couch or sat forward, stood and stared out the large window behind the couch or paced the length of the room, feeling the braided oblong carpet under her bare feet, or the smooth, cool hardwood floor around it, every sensation she'd experienced brought Trent front and center in her thoughts.

"Well, I haven't been formatting your listening devices,"

she said, leaning back and making a face. "Bring me the box. I need their serial numbers and the brand name. I don't remember it."

"Okay," he said slowly but didn't make a move to go get the box. "What else have you been doing?" he pressed, starting around the coffee table to see her laptop.

"I've been checking out the serial numbers on these bills." Even going over the items they'd found at the cabin made her think of Trent, when they should have been guiding her thoughts around what the hell they were doing in the cabin and, more so, whoever put them there.

Trent sat on the couch next to her, resting his arm on the back of it and moving in close enough to see her screen. "Learn anything?" he asked.

His leg pressed against hers. Her insides quickened and instantly she was wet. She was being ridiculous. They were both adults. He was a sheriff and she had plenty of law enforcement training. She'd done research to help find someone or solve a mystery plenty of times. Trent wasn't the first good-looking man she'd worked with before. She didn't remember it ever being this difficult to focus on work when any other man with strong sex appeal had sat next to her.

"Actually, yes." At least her fingers didn't tremble when she pointed at her screen. "This site allows you to see circulation patterns of bills. It's a highly regulated site, but my uncle has access to it. Therefore, so I do, since I work for him," she explained, and grinned, hoping when she looked at him her expression was playful, yet relaxed, and that she looked indifferent to how close he sat. Because she was sure that was how she looked whenever she explained something to any of the men who came into the office back home. Although at the moment, even a couple of the men who came to mind, who occasionally worked with her uncle, didn't hold a flame in the good looks department compared to Trent.

He nodded, those green eyes of his searching her face for a moment before returning his attention to her screen. "So what did you find?"

He was all business. It sucked. She sighed loudly and

inched away from him slightly when she leaned back on the couch. "Nothing," she told him.

"Huh?"

"That's just it." She donned the latex gloves she'd worn while handling the money and picked up the first evidence bag. "None of these bills have been in circulation for sixty years."

"Really?" He picked up the other evidence bag full of money and stared at the stack of twenties inside. "Can't tell you when I've last seen a twenty from the forties," he commented. "Did you count it?"

"Forty-five hundred dollars." She dropped the bag she'd been holding. "This stack of bills is mostly one-hundred-dollar bills. I haven't entered every serial number, but all of the bills were printed before 1950."

Trent stared for a long time at the bag in his hand. She wondered what he was thinking.

"Forty-five hundred bucks was a lot of money that long ago," he said.

"Not a bad stash by today's standards, either, but definitely not enough to kill someone the way Carl Williams was murdered."

"If the two are even connected." He looked at her, searching her face. "These things haven't been stashed in the wall of that cabin for sixty years. Someone put them there recently. There were no cobwebs or dust on any of them."

Natasha looked at the bags with the cash in them. Maybe her computer skills ran circles around Trent's, but he had spotted something obvious, like no cobwebs, and in the dark. She was a long way from being the investigator in the field that her uncle and cousins, and Trent were.

"I didn't even notice that," she mumbled.

"I was moving spider webs and layers of dust off the walls and in the corners all over the place in that cabin."

She nodded. She had been, too.

"When you spotted the section of wall that was hollow, the first thing I noticed were no cobwebs or dirt along the panel we pulled out."

"I'd been wiping dust off the walls, too," she admitted, and had still missed the obvious.

"You aren't at a lot of crime scenes."

He didn't sound accusatory but more as if he defended her missing an obvious clue.

"We don't really have that many crime scenes. They are more like manhunts."

She looked at him, and his attentive expression almost made her lose her train of thought. Before she looked away, his focus dropped to her mouth. She looked at her computer screen, then at the other evidence bags on the coffee table.

"I don't know what to think about the teddy bear, but I can probably find out who currently owns the land if you'll help me by saying exactly where the land is." Natasha flipped over to another screen she'd opened earlier, a site for Trinity County. "You can find any property owner here."

"I already found that out. It's Piney land."

"Piney land?"

"Ethel Burrows used to be Ethel Piney."

"Jim and Ethel Burrows own Trinity Ranch." She flipped to another screen and pointed, showing him where she'd confirmed the owners of Trinity Ranch.

Trent glanced at her screen and nodded, then leaned back, stretching his legs so they were on top of her feet under the coffee table. He made no attempt to adjust his position, nor did he seem overly interested in her ability to learn who owned what property in his county. Natasha flipped to another page, determined to prove her usefulness and keep her mind off the long, muscular body threatening to distract her until all she would be able to think about was how soon, and where, they would have sex.

"When was she Ethel Piney?"

"Her maiden name was Piney. Ethel was married to one of the Popes, a ranch hand on a ranch south of here. She hooked up with him shortly after high school," he said in a slow, lazy drawl, sounding as if explaining all this to her didn't bother him. But he didn't sound as if any of it mattered, either.

Natasha frowned, trying to follow what he'd said. "So Ethel was a Piney. She married and her last name became Pope. But she left that guy. Now she's a Burrows and lives on Trinity Ranch and apparently owns it along with Jim Burrows."

"That's right."

"So she wouldn't have any connection to that land we were on today."

"It's not her land. The deed isn't clear which Piney owns it and they're a fairly reclusive family. I don't know any Pineys around here but I'm going to look into it."

"Oh." Maybe there was a connection between the items in the cabin and Carl Williams' murder. At the moment Natasha didn't have a clue what, or how any of this tied in with her father. "We need to find out what this key is. My aunt and uncle have a safe-deposit box at their bank. I've accessed it before. Their key looks like this. But I guess if it's as old as everything else here, it could be for something else."

Trent leaned forward on the couch. He took the bag she'd lifted with the key in it and placed it back on the coffee table. "Give it a rest for now," he said, his voice turning soothing.

Natasha didn't want soothing. She wanted answers. If Trent turned gentle on her, she quite possibly would melt in his arms. And God, she wanted to feel his muscular arms wrapped around her. She wanted to know what his naked body would feel like pressed against hers. She wanted him buried so deep inside her the pressure that wouldn't quit swelling, and throbbing, would finally go away.

Fucking Trent would be pointless. As soon as she figured out how to get her father out of this mess she would be returning to her life in L.A. Trent would continue his life here. They would never see each other again. As much as hot, mind-blowing sex with Trent sounded wonderful, he wasn't the one-night-stand type. Or maybe she couldn't be with him.

"No. I can't," she snapped, snatching the bag up again.

"We'll think better if we take a break."

"I'm here for one reason, and one reason only," she informed Trent, moving so she faced him, and put distance between them. "I'm going to prove my father's innocence.

Even if that was him at that cabin, he's probably hiding only because you think he committed murder."

"Natasha."

"No," she yelled, letting the one word slice through the air between them. She jumped off the couch, putting her laptop on the coffee table, then moving around it, needing away from that virile body so she could think.

Trent moved just as fast, coming around the coffee table from the other side and cutting her off in the middle of his living room. When he gripped her arms, his touch created a heat too strong to ignore. She damn near sagged against him from the affect of it.

"Your father's fingerprints were found all over Carl Williams' body."

She couldn't have heard him right. Natasha lifted her gaze and stared into eyes so beautiful, at features so perfectly chiseled, at black hair that bordered his manly features, and wished they could go back in time just a few moments, to just before he'd uttered those words and ruined the perfect man for her.

"All over Carl Williams' body?" Her voice didn't sound right, as if her vocal cords had constricted too tight in her throat. Tears she wouldn't ever allow to fall for her father again had receded and left her eyes dry. Her eyes burned.

Trent nodded, sucking in a breath. His thumbs rubbed against her bare arms. Moments ago his touch made her sizzle with need. Now she felt empty, unable to feel a thing.

"Williams was found spread-eagled, bound—"

"I saw the pictures." She wouldn't cringe against the image of the dead young man when he appeared in her mind. Her father wasn't capable of such a horrendous act. He wasn't.

"King," Trent began, and the pained look on his face, as if it hurt him as much as it did her to lay the facts out before her, made his expression darker, almost vulnerable looking. "Your father," he amended. "His fingerprints were around the man's wrist, on his torso, his neck." Trent shook his head. "I know how to do my job, darling," he said, lowering his voice until his words were a rough whisper, brutally honest and at the same time brushing over her like pin pricks against her skin. "The positioning of fingerprints, where the pressure points are, show how a person grabs something, which direction his hand is coming from. I'll show you."

Before Natasha opened her mouth to tell Trent she knew how to read fingerprints, he'd left the room. His solid footsteps seemed to match the heavy beating of her heart. He was next to her again in a moment, holding a file. Suddenly he was willing to tell her everything.

What had changed? Natasha wouldn't let her thoughts go there. Not now. Not when it didn't matter if anything had changed between them or not. This man standing next to her was definitely the sexiest, most perfect man she'd ever met—yes, she'd admit it. Why the hell not?—and was also as wrong as a man could be for her. She wanted him more than she'd ever wanted another man in her entire life. Yet he was telling her that her father had committed a heinous crime. Worse yet, he would be the man who would arrest her father and make sure he was sent to prison, or worse.

"Take a look at the fingerprints found on Williams' body." Trent opened the file and positioned a couple printouts but then slapped the file shut and pressed one hand in the middle of her back. "It will be easier to see here."

"I know what you're talking about." There wasn't a lot of protest in her voice and her legs were wobbly when he walked with her into his kitchen.

"I want you to understand why I'm taking the angle I am on this case."

Natasha looked at him as he focused on the contents of the file, spreading them out on the table and positioning them where he wanted them. There was strength in his profile, in the way his jaw was set with determination, in his incredibly focused nature. She imagined Trent to be the type of investigator who when he took on a case lived, breathed, and slept it until he had the thing cracked wide open and solved. Uncle Greg was the same way. God, was that why Trent seemed so perfect to her? He was just like Uncle Greg, like the man who'd raised her. She was falling for this man because he was just like the man who raised her.

The thought was so incredibly warped she almost laughed, which was insane. She should be crying. Yet she couldn't cry.

"Here are prints on Carl's wrists," Trent told her, and angled his hand on top of the photograph to show how the aggressor's hand would have been positioned. "Those prints were made before Carl was spread-eagled and bound to the poles."

"How do you know they weren't after?" Natasha studied the gruesome pictures. They weren't as gory as the full-body shots had been. These pictures had been altered to show the fingerprints on Carl's skin. "It looks like he was gripping Carl's wrist, which he couldn't have been doing if Carl was hanging. In order to hold his wrist the way this picture implies, the person would have had to have been standing on one hell of a ladder. You showed me the other pictures. He was up in the air. Maybe my father was trying to get him down."

"Natasha," Trent began, and faced her. His hands were on her arms, caressing them before he started speaking. "Carl was hanging, his wrists and ankles bound to those two poles when I showed up at the scene. He remained in that position until the medical examiner arrived at the ranch; then we cut him down. Once he was down, he was in the ambulance and removed from the property. I promise you, no one touched him once he was cut down without wearing gloves. The ladder used was cast to the side of the barn by the house. There was blood on it but no prints. The only way those prints could have been put on Carl's body was before he was hung on the posts, or as he was being hung on those posts."

She stared at Trent, managed to nod, then lowered her attention to his chest, unwilling to lose herself in his compelling gaze. His palms ran up and down the outside of her arms, brushing over her skin, consoling and arousing but, worse yet, distracting.

Her world was crashing in around her. The constants she

knew in life were dissipating before her eyes, with the simple validation of where fingerprints were found, in what position, pressing down from what angle. She could see the forms on the table Trent hadn't bothered pointing out to her. Natasha had printed off fingerprint analysis before many times. The printouts at the edge of the table were the damning evidence that the person who'd grabbed Carl Williams while he'd still been bleeding, held on to his wrist firmly, and pulled upward, as if lifting the blood-drenched hand up into the air to that post, had been her father.

"Natasha, it's all there."

She backed away from him and he let her go. Natasha didn't shake from anger, pain, or regret. All the emotions that should be bombarding her simply weren't there.

Turning, she returned to the living room, picked up her shoes and socks she'd taken off earlier, once the fire had warmed her, then sat stiffly at the edge of the couch and put them back on. Her luggage was in the corner and her laptop on the coffee table. All she had to do was gather her few belongings and head out the front door. This wasn't her world. Trent Oakley would never be her man. She didn't belong here.

My father isn't a murderer!

The small voice screaming at the back of her head was easily ignored. Natasha wouldn't endure any more pain because of her father. All her life she'd adored the man who helped give her life. Her mother had given up on the both of them when Natasha was four. Natasha had told herself, and her aunt and uncle told her the same thing most of her growing-up life, that her father adored her, loved her with all his heart, but wanted her growing up in a family environment. She grew up with her cousins, in their home, with Uncle Greg and Aunt Haley as parents because Natasha's father couldn't be both mom and dad at the same time.

Other parents raised their children by themselves.

The little voice in the back of her head usually annoyed the crap out of her. It screamed the brutal truth, demanded she see the reality of being a child not cared about and not loved by the two people who brought her into the world. Yet once again it failed to pull off its mission. Natasha wouldn't let her father hurt her again. That would require feelings. There was no lust for Trent, worry for her father, pride over her computer and detective skills. Nothing had room to creep back in around the numbness consuming her.

"I don't blame you for thinking him guilty." She looked at Trent as he stood in his living room watching her.

Natasha walked over to her laptop, and shut it down.

"I want you to understand why I'm investigating this murder the way I am."

She smiled when she looked at him, but there wasn't any happiness inside. The void filling her left her dull, almost lifeless, with an emptiness that would hurt like hell if it weren't for the fact that her emotions couldn't get around the black hole taking over her insides.

"Of course."

"Natasha," Trent spit out, lunging at her and yanking her laptop from her hands. "Did you think I was such an inept sheriff I would go after a man for a crime simply because he wasn't from here? You didn't come up here simply because I demanded it. You believed in your heart, before knowing anything about why he was in trouble, that your father was an innocent man."

"He's on the run. There are places my father could go for help. His family has never turned him away, no matter how many years passed without seeing him. He saw me earlier today. I know that was my father. Yet he shot at me. His message was clear. He doesn't want my help." Natasha listened to herself talk and managed to register the meaning behind the words she spoke rather mechanically. "If he hasn't gone to Uncle Greg but has sent me a rather harsh message, I need to face up to the obvious."

"What's that?" Trent reached for a single strand of hair bordering her face and brushed it behind her shoulders.

Less than an hour ago, possibly just minutes ago if he'd touched her like that Natasha would have melted; the pressure that continued building the more she was around Trent quite possibly would have erupted. Yet now all she felt were his calloused fingertips that were neither too warm nor too cold. She didn't blink when he ran his fingers down the side of her face, nor did she look away.

"My father killed that young man. If he hadn't, he would have let me help him."

Chapter Eight

The next morning Natasha walked briskly into the shop, with its familiar smells of oil and gasoline. "I'm here to pick up my Avalanche," she told the man standing behind the counter.

A thin woman with gray, bristly hair sat with her back to the counter, facing a computer. She looked over her shoulder, giving Natasha an appraising look over the rim of her glasses.

"The Avalanche is a charge," she announced.

Natasha wasn't in the mood for people to explain or discuss anything. She just wanted the truck and to drive. Drive until the void inside her dissipated, go far enough away from this picturesque town lost in time that the terrible things that had happened here wouldn't affect her. She wanted to keep going until her father wasn't on her mind any longer.

"It was," she explained, even though she just wanted to snap at the woman that she was a bad businesswoman to insist on getting paid next month when she could have the bill settled today. "The sheriff believed he was doing me a favor when he found me stranded at the side of the road."

The woman turned around farther. "He was doing you a favor, honey. Sheriff Oakley is a good man." She stood, tugged on the oversized T-shirt she wore that advertised the Powell gas station they were standing in, and moved in next to the man who still stood at the counter. "If he takes care of you it's because he believes you're good people."

"I *am* good people," Natasha insisted, and realized the urge to knock the woman down a few notches for getting snappy wasn't there. After a sleepless night on Trent's couch, she was even more numb. "Which is why I would rather pay cash for your work and quick service in repairing my truck. I don't want to be in debt to your good sheriff."

The door opened behind Natasha and a rush of cold hair hit hard enough she hugged herself against its brutal lashing. The woman behind the counter humphed. Then she lifted her hand and slapped an invoice in front of the man at the counter. He'd been looking incredibly busy with paperwork in front of him, more than likely used to the woman giving customers tongue-lashings and wanting no part of it. Natasha didn't blame him.

"Mary, are you giving Natasha grief?" Trent asked as he entered the shop, and leaned against the end of the counter. Trent had an amused grin on his face as if he knew the moment Natasha had leapt out of the Suburban, anxious to clear the bill before Trent could inform the shop owners he had it covered and she could pay him later, what she'd be in store for once she walked into the shop.

"She wants to pay cash." Mary shrugged and returned to her computer, turning her back on all of them.

The man took the invoice and looked it over. "Can't say I ever had a truck, or any vehicle, come in here with all four tires lashed up like yours were, miss."

"It's Miss Natasha *King*," the woman informed him, looking over her shoulder. She shot Natasha a look that could only be described as hateful. "You got any family in town, Miss *King*?" Each time she said Natasha's name there was emphasis on her last name, as if "King" was a derogatory word in the woman's mind.

"I did," Natasha answered truthfully, her tone flat.

Mary humphed again and shot Trent a look as if demanding to know what he would do about Natasha's presence in town. "Carl never did a soul wrong," she muttered under her breath. "And her daddy killed him."

"Mary," the man at the counter snapped.

"What?" she hurled at him. "What did I say? You know damn good and well who she is. She's that demented murderer's kin."

"That's enough," the man warned Mary.

"I can't believe you put such good tires on that truck. She'll probably use it to get her daddy across the state line." Mary pointed a finger at the sheriff. "Don't let her looks fool you. If she's in town and she's his blood, it's as plain as the nose on my face what she's doing here."

"God damn it, Mary!" the man bellowed.

"It's okay." Natasha reached over the counter and took the invoice from the man's hands. Seventeen hundred dollars. She blinked. Then swallowing, she looked at Mary, who was standing behind the man with her arms crossed against her skinny frame and glaring at Natasha. "For the most part, Mary, you're right."

Her confession didn't cause Mary's features to relax. Trent quit leaning against the counter. He was by Natasha's side before she continued speaking. Fortunately, he didn't touch her. She wasn't sure she could handle his hands on her right now. She'd never had to defend her family name before, but the words came out anyway.

"I heard my father was in trouble and drove up here. I can't find him. And although it's not in his nature to do something so incredibly horrendous as what happened to Carl Williams, I'm sure your sheriff will sort through the evidence and find the killer."

Mary glared at Natasha a moment longer, then turned on her heels and stormed out of the small office, disappearing into a back room and letting the door she'd gone through slam behind her.

"You know Joanna Williams, Carl's mama, is a good friend of Mary's," the man explained, not looking at Natasha.

"Yup." Trent took the invoice out of Natasha's hand. "Are

you sure you can cover this right now? I can charge it to my county account and bill KFA for it."

"I've got it." She took the invoice back from Trent and placed it on the counter in front of her, then pulled her wallet out of her purse. It would max out one of her credit cards, but she didn't want any ties to this town, or reason for Trent to stay in touch, once she left.

Never knowing what it would be like to have sex with Trent, never knowing if he was truly as perfect as he appeared, would be better than longing for what she gave up. She pulled her credit card from her wallet and placed it on the invoice, then rubbed her suddenly moist fingers down her jeans.

She couldn't wait to get out of Weaverville. Signing the credit card printout, she then took her receipt, stuffed it in her purse, and mumbled her thanks. She should have shown more gratitude in spite of Mary's outburst. It wasn't the older lady's fault Natasha was George King's daughter, and Mary had every right to be upset over her friend's son's death.

Natasha walked out of the shop to her Avalanche, which had been parked on a narrow one-lane road with no sidewalks. The road was under a canopy of trees, and led into a peaceful looking neighborhood. All the homes in this town were well-kept and of an era gone by. This was definitely not a place where terrible, disturbing crimes ever happened. She'd hauled her luggage out of Trent's Suburban to her uncle's truck before paying the bill. Now all she had to do was get behind the wheel and leave.

"Where are you going?" Trent didn't touch her, kept a few feets' distance, and squinted in the morning sun that shone against a perfectly blue sky. "You might as well tell me. I'll find you no matter what."

"Home." Natasha started the truck, feeling as numb about returning home as she had since Trent told her that her father's fingerprints were all over Carl Williams' body. Trying to release a dead, mutilated body didn't fit her father's nature any more than him committing the despicable act. "I'm sorry I wasn't able to help you."

Trent studied her a moment. In spite of her insides being null and void of all feelings, she was still aware of how incredibly handsome he was. The slightest twinge of regret rose from deep in her belly, and she looked away, gripping the steering wheel. Her fingers tightened around it when he stepped closer. Trent held on to the top of her car door and leaned forward, his face close enough she smelled the soap he used and his unique, intriguing smell that was all man.

"I know we haven't known each other that long, but I didn't think you were a quitter."

"Who the hell is quitting? I came here to prove my father hadn't done anything wrong." She sucked in a breath, unwilling to let go of the black void keeping all emotions at bay. "I'm not quitting. I just lost."

"So just like that you think he's guilty?"

"Do you suddenly think he's innocent?" she countered.

Trent's green eyes were darker than the tall pines in the mountains and clouded over with thunderous emotions that almost made Natasha shiver. "I've never assumed he was guilty," Trent informed her, barely moving his mouth when he spoke. "I've told you the evidence was damning. There are enough clues pointing toward your father that it merits bringing him in. It's my job to lay out the facts and confirm the accuracy of every minute from the point when Carl was attacked to when he drew his last breath."

Natasha nodded once, stiffly. "I know," she muttered, unsure what else to say.

There wasn't anything else to say. She could reach for the door handle, but not without touching Trent or making one hell of a show of trying not to touch him. Once again she was feeling the air between them singe her skin with charged energy filled with desire. The numbness was going away. The sooner she got out of there, the better. Instead of trying to close the door, she put her hand on the gearshift.

"I'm sure I'll hear the details in the end."

"Don't leave."

The intensity of his lust slammed up against her. Where

"Yup," he said, his eyes peeled to the road ahead. "Nope. Nothing is wrong. Just wanted to make sure I'm covering all bases."

He was serious, although his expression was relaxed. Natasha could barely make out a man's voice through the earpiece, but she couldn't catch what he said. She fidgeted in her seat, studied her nails, which she hadn't done since arriving in Weaverville, and stared at the road ahead. It was impossible not to eavesdrop on the conversation with Trent right next to her, but the way he'd closed down on her since leaving the office, she felt as if she shouldn't.

"You heard right," he said after another brief pause. "No, nothing like that." For the first time there was a brief chuckle, or was it a snort?

Natasha found herself watching Trent. Not only was he captivating, by far the best-looking man she'd ever laid eyes on, there wasn't anything else in the truck to look at other than him. And damn it, she was in the truck with him, by invitation she reminded herself. So what if she listened to his call? If he didn't like it, he could take her back to her truck. She'd go see the Burrowses on her own.

"Sounds good. I know where you are. We'll be there in less than ten minutes." Trent didn't say good-bye but hung up, pulling the Bluetooth from his ear and dropping it back in the cup holder.

We? She definitely picked up on that word. "Who were you talking to?" she asked the minute he hung up. If he'd said "we," then whoever it was knew she was with Trent.

"Jim Burrows." He slowed the Suburban and pulled off to the edge of the road.

"What are you doing?"

"Turning around. He's out dealing with some cattle and suggested we come talk to him there. You don't have a problem trudging through a field, do you?" For the first time since they'd left, Trent's eyes glowed when he looked at her.

He thought she wouldn't be able to handle getting a bit dirty.

"Bring it on, cowboy," she slurred, giving him a harsh look. She'd show him she could handle his world as well as she handled hers.

The wind blew hard on the high grounds and Natasha grabbed her hair at her nape, twisted it, and tucked it into her coat. Trent kept a pretty good clip as he worked his way over uneven ground, around gigantic cow patties, and up a hill. All he'd done when they'd finally parked was ask if she was ready. When she nodded, he had taken off. Natasha would be damned if she let him leave her behind. And something told her he would, too.

At the top of the hill, Natasha forgot about keeping up. She paused, gulped in the frozen air filled with a mixture of livestock smells, the earth, and something carried down from the mountains that made breathing this air all worthwhile. She stared, awestruck, at her surroundings. The Trinity Alps were breathtaking, rugged and dangerous looking, and looming closer than she'd seen them since being here.

Trent had started down the side of the hill and she turned, following him, although not as concerned about returning to his side. Once again the tranquil beauty of the land around her in this part of the world settled her insides. If he wanted to be grumpy, that was his business. She watched her footing, following him, but continued glancing at the mountains around her.

When she reached the bottom of the side of the hill, Trent had joined several other men. She could only imagine what directions he'd been given for him to know exactly how to find these men. Two men leaned against a low wooden fence that ran across the high meadow and disappeared around another large hill on the other side of a bunch of cattle.

What was a bunch of cattle called?

They had exchanged greetings before she reached them. Natasha watched Trent shake hands with a large man wearing a cowboy hat. He nodded to the two other men, each of them wearing a ball cap and standing on either side of the man in the cowboy hat.

"I'll keep you posted on that one," Trent said, and the look he gave her when she paused, stood next to him, and stared back, then looked at the other three men curiously, could only be defined as mischievous.

One of the men coughed, covering his mouth quickly, and looked down at the ground. She couldn't see the other guy's face because he pulled his ball cap low. But the man in the middle, with the cowboy hat, tipped it back and gave her an appraising once-over.

"Good day, little lady," he said, nodding. "Looks like you were enjoying my land."

"This is the most breathtaking view I've ever seen in my life." She grinned at him and gestured toward the mountains. Trent hadn't lectured her about remaining quiet as he had before going to the bank. When he narrowed his gaze on her she turned away before he could deliver the silent warning. "I take it you're Jim Burrows." She held out her hand.

"Yes, ma'am. And you're George King's daughter."

"That's right." His hand was calloused, large, and cold. But his expression seemed focused and his pale blue eyes danced as if he laughed a lot. "I'm Natasha King," she told him.

"Well, I sure hope your daddy is found innocent," he said, sounding as if he meant it.

"Me, too." She lowered her hand when he released it but already felt good vibes off the large rancher. He didn't seem to be the type of man she pictured would plot and carry out such a terrible murder, and that of his son, illegitimate or otherwise, if what she'd been told was true. "I'm very sorry about what happened to Carl Williams," she added.

Natasha swore she heard a low growl coming from Trent but ignored him and kept her attention on Jim. The man's face sobered immediately.

"Most god-awful thing I've ever seen done to another living creature, man or animal, in my entire life." He cleared his throat and adjusted his hat on his head. Then, looking at Trent, he said, "I don't want you stopping until the son of a bitch who killed my boy burns in hell for his sins. You hear me, Sheriff?"

"I plan on finding him," Trent said just as seriously. "There were just a few things I wanted to clear up with you. You're busy. I see that. This won't take time."

"Don't rush any part of your investigation on my part, Sheriff," Jim said. Then looking at the men on either side of them, he grumbled under his breath, his words barely audible, as he instructed them on what to do with the cattle.

At least Natasha was pretty sure that was what he told them to do. Both men nodded, grunted good-byes to Trent, and tipped their hats at Natasha; then they were heading along the length of the fence in the direction of the grazing cows.

"Got herds grazing on each other's land," Jim muttered to Trent, who nodded in understanding.

Natasha wasn't sure what he meant, but she now remembered what a bunch of cows were called—a herd. That's right.

"Post is a good neighbor, best a man could ask for. Hell, I've known him most of my life." Jim had started walking along the fence in the direction the men had gone, and Trent fell in line along side him. Natasha wasn't sure she liked following behind, as if she were tagging along and not meant to be part of the conversation. She smiled, though, when Jim paused and turned, looking over his shoulder at her. "And I know you'd be surprised to hear it," he added, winking at her. "But that is over sixty years now."

Jim was a natural flirt. That was her definition of someone who flirted with everyone, it just being part of their nature. Now if he graduated to "serious flirt" he'd be the type of man who might follow through on the attention he bestowed on a lady. She thought of his two bastard children and decided Jim probably definitely qualified as a serious flirt. Possibly he wasn't showing his true colors because she was young enough to be his granddaughter and because she'd arrived with Trent. She was fairly certain Trent wouldn't have given any indication they were together.

Which they weren't. Not really.

"I've never had a problem with the Posts over at Excelsior Ranch. Dan Post and I have a situation and we're going to have to work it out. His cattle keep ending up in with mine, and mine tend to get through the fence and mingle with his. Gets to be a problem when you've got a bull mingling in with each other's cattle." He glanced at Natasha again, giving her a sly grin.

She wasn't positive she got his meaning but guessed it might mean his and his neighbor's livestock might breed with each other.

"You guess what that problem might be?" Jim paused and turned, which forced Trent to do the same, and when he looked at her so did Trent.

She might as well go for broke. "My guess is you have to decide who claims the newborns."

Jim Burrows had a deep, resonating laugh. "Told you," he said, and slapped Trent on the shoulder. "That's right, little lady. And like I just said, we don't want the problem of deciding who owns which calves."

Natasha wondered what Jim had told Trent, but when she looked at him he was squinting at the fence. "Looks like your property line is held up well with the fencing," he said, making it sound as if he'd heard this dilemma discussed before. Was part of his duties as sheriff making sure ranchers didn't try claiming each other's cows or calves?

"We'll get it worked out." Jim squinted under his cowboy hat, facing Trent. "Now you didn't come out here to check on our property line issues. Talk to me about Carl. What have you learned, Sheriff?" Jim's voice had deepened and his demeanor sobered.

Natasha saw the charming side of the older rancher but also saw the man who could run and maintain a ranch this size and earn it the reputation of being the largest and most successful cattle ranch in Northern California, if not the entire Northwest. She wasn't sure about the latter but suspected Jim Burrows would give any other rancher a run for his money.

"Why didn't you tell me Carl was your son when I was here last week?" Trent asked, not allowing a moment to pass before firing out the question.

"A man gets set in his ways," Jim said, and adjusted his hat on his head. He tilted it against the afternoon sun, then kicked at the ground with his boot before focusing on Trent. "After years of keeping a secret it doesn't come easy talking about it."

"So you didn't think of him as your son?"

"Now wait a minute, Sheriff." Jim held up his large, work-worn hand. "I provided for that boy and his mama since the day he was born. Carl was my flesh and blood, and don't think for a second it didn't tear me apart seeing his life ended like that. Whoever killed him will pay dearly. You've got my word on that," he said, his voice having turned hard and fierce sounding. At sixty-some years old, Jim Burrows still looked like a man who would dish out a threat and see it through and didn't mind telling the lawman as much to his face.

"Whoever did this will be prosecuted to the full extent of the law," Trent said calmly.

"Damn right!" Jim barked, then reached for his hat. "Excuse my language, little lady."

"Did your wife know you were supporting Carl and his mother?" Trent asked.

"Which wife?" Jim didn't smile, but he certainly didn't appear ashamed to be on wife number two.

"Either," Trent said, his expression and gaze on Jim never wavering. "Did either wife have a problem with you sending Carl and his mother money?"

Jim didn't answer right away. When he did, all humor was gone from the man. "No, Sheriff. Neither Sandra nor Ethel had a problem with my supporting my boy."

"Boys, right?" Trent pressed.

"Of course I have more than one son. This isn't news, Oakley. You've known my boys all your life," Jim growled. "Don't sneak in from the side, boy. If you got a question, let's hear it now."

Trent didn't so much as blink. "Are you Pat O'Reilly's father?"

Jim Burrows stared at Trent, and a peculiar expression

crossed over his face. Natasha watched all color drain from the man's face and swore the good-sized rancher seemed to deflate before her eyes. It didn't happen in the blink of an eye, but within the few moments that she and Trent waited out in silence the color slowly returned to Jim's face. He started looking flushed, then pulled his cowboy hat from his head and ran his fingers through coarse dark brown and gray hair. He turned from them, staring at the men down by the cattle. Natasha guessed he probably wished he were with them instead of answering Trent's questions.

She looked up at Trent when he quit watching Jim and turned to look at her. Trent's expression looked strained but determined, which didn't surprise her. He was one hell of a determined man. The dominating, aggressive nature of his beast was quite likely what made him a good sheriff. But it might be why he was still single, as well. Although she didn't miss the looks the ladies working at the bank had given him, and her, when they'd first entered.

The thick waves in his dark hair bordered his hardened features. Sunlight pulled out a trace, here and there, of auburn strands she hadn't noticed before. His height and broad shoulders, his muscular and perfectly fine-tuned body, were only the half of what made Trent so damn appealing. It was his personality. Natasha saw how any woman who took the time to know him would see the hard edge, his no-nonsense mannerisms, and an unbreakable will to protect and provide for all who mattered to him. Probably women had tried to rein in all the aggression and sheer willpower welled up inside the man. And each of them had failed.

Natasha relaxed, exhaled, and continued staring into his compelling green eyes. Even when she was positive every bit of his thought process was focused on Jim Burrows right now, Trent still watched her like a hawk. Natasha understood this was how he took in all his surroundings, all of which were land and people he'd been sworn in to protect.

The moment Jim shifted his weight, Trent snapped his attention in that direction. Which proved Natasha right. If she were to make a quick movement, whether it be drastic or barely detectable, she didn't doubt for a moment Trent would snap his focus back to her. Although knowing what she did about Trent so far, he probably wouldn't look but would simply reach out, grab her arm, and tighten his fingers around her like a vise.

He might be a brooding son of a bitch and have an inclination to throw tantrums when his authority was challenged, but he wasn't fully ignoring her. For some seriously warped reason, that heightened her spirits.

Natasha returned her attention to Jim when Trent did. The rancher adjusted his hat on his head before looking at Trent.

"Where the hell did you hear that?" Jim hissed, his tone almost demonic. He sounded seriously pissed.

Trent did a good job of standing up to the rancher, who probably ran his business with confidence that he could bend any man's will in his direction if necessary. Natasha would bet her uncle and cousins wouldn't flinch under this man's gruff nature either. She straightened, knowing Jim thought of her only as a little lady, but didn't fear him either. She'd take him on, and probably win.

Were all Trinity County men dominating and built out of stubborn pride and a misguided belief that women needed to be protected and trained to sit, heel, and obey?

"Is that a 'yes'?" Trent asked.

"Now you listen to me," Jim snarled, pointing his finger at Trent's face.

"I am listening," Trent said coolly. "Is O'Reilly your son?"

"Damn it, Oakley. I want to know right now where you heard that."

"Answer the question, Jim."

Jim glared at Trent, his face so fiery red Natasha started worrying he might grab his chest and fall over from a heart attack.

"Yes!" he bellowed, his voice echoing off the rough, uneven land around them. "Yes," he repeated, a bit quieter a second time. "He's my son, too. Now tell me how in the hell you knew that," he demanded, barely giving Natasha a look when he waved his hand in the air briefly in her direction. "Why did you bring her along to hear a conversation like this?" he asked, this time just honestly sounding confused.

"Because Trent heard the information about your illegitimate sons from me," she explained.

"Natasha," Trent roared, although his voice didn't echo; instead it sliced the air wide open between them and hit her hard with fierce aggression.

"Really," Jim said, still somewhat confused, possibly that she'd entered their conversation when he'd just implied it wasn't a proper exchange for her to hear. A noticeable wariness appeared on his face as well. "Now where in the world would you hear information like that?" Jim asked her.

"Not another word," Trent whispered.

The look Trent gave her was harsh enough he might as well have told her she'd be walking to her truck if she kept speaking. She pursed her lips, confident she could take Jim Burrows on and hating being curbed the way Trent just did to her. But she wouldn't challenge him in front of this old-school rancher who would definitely think less of Trent if she did. She doubted it would change Burrows' opinion of her one way or the other.

"There really better be a better explanation for why you didn't tell me about Pat than the reason you gave me for not telling me about Carl," Trent said, speaking just as harshly to Jim as he had to her.

"The reason is the same." Jim's voice was cold and he straightened, puffing out his chest, and didn't look away from Trent when he spoke. "I never knew about Pat until he came to town after he'd finished high school. His mama took him to Sacramento and never told me I was his daddy. And Pat isn't a result of misguided thinking. I've done my penance for Carl and have no regrets today." Once again the proud rancher stood before them, puffed out like a peacock. "Pat is almost your age," he said, still looking at Trent. "I was with his mama before I married, or even proposed to, Sandra."

"He's your oldest son," Natasha said under her breath, and looked up when both men looked at her.

Trent cleared his voice, getting Jim's attention once again. "Your shock over my question makes me think very few people know you're his father."

"No one knows," he emphasized. "Not a damn soul, until now. And if word of this gets out . . . ," he added, waving that finger again.

Trent looked like he might yank it off Jim's hand if he didn't put it down. "I don't do threats, Jim," Trent stated dryly. "I've only got one more question for you; then we'll let you get back to work. Tell me about Nellie Burrows."

This time Jim's hand did go to his chest. He staggered backward as his mouth fell open and his complexion turned ashen.

"Wh-h-at . . . wh-h-at . . . ," he stammered. Then trying again, "Who have you been talking to?" he said, whispering. His expression then turned wild, angry, and pretty crazed looking. "You!" he said, snapping at Natasha. He turned his fierce look on Trent. "You sent King's daughter to my ex, didn't you? Set her up for some little-girl chat." He spit out the accusation, then looked at Natasha. "Did you have tea with my ex?" he snarled.

Trent grabbed Natasha before she could respond and yanked her to him, then shoved her behind him. If it weren't for the incredibly uneven ground, she probably would have maintained her balance better. As it was, she ended up grabbing Trent so she wouldn't fall.

Jim started chuckling, although the well-humored man they'd met when they first walked out here was gone. "Nellie Burrows is a myth, a ghost conceived out of jealousy and in an effort to rob family of the fruit of their labors. And I'd be real careful if I were you, Sheriff. It might not do well for your career if word gets out you've captured yourself a killer's daughter."

"Why, you," Natasha snarled. She was instantly pissed.

"Enough!" Trent ordered, holding Natasha against him

so she couldn't move. "Nellie Burrows isn't a myth. I have a picture of her in an evidence bag, along with her dress and a rather large amount of cash that once belonged to her. Now you're going to tell me everything you know about her so I can determine if she is linked to your son's murder or not."

Chapter Sixteen

Trent moved alongside Natasha as they headed down the hill toward the Suburban. He had a pissed-off woman, whom he happened to be sleeping with, ready to attack the father of his murder victim. Trent also had a prominent citizen in his community, who'd already been traumatized by the death of a son he could never really claim due to his own morals and convictions, now further traumatized through Trent's questioning. A dull headache began throbbing at his temples.

"I want to be there when he tells you about Nellie Burrows." Natasha continued marching down the hill, balancing herself with her hands held out in front of her.

"I don't think that's a good idea." Trent couldn't afford for her to explode on Burrows. Not that he thought the man was guilty of anything, other than infidelity, but because he didn't want to have to deal with pulling the two of them apart if Natasha and Burrows went at it full force.

She spun around, slapping long strands of hair that had slipped free from her coat away from her face. At the same time, she stepped on a clump of ground, losing her balance.

Trent told himself he wouldn't touch her. He had a serious murder investigation to focus on, and Natasha was distracting him. They needed to talk. Now wasn't the time, though. So he'd told himself he would keep clear of her until there was time for the two of them to hash it out. They would start with Natasha admitting that submitting wasn't synonymous with failing. It meant trusting, something Natasha would learn to do with him.

When she started to fall, instinct kicked in. Trent grabbed her. She fell against his chest, her hand immediately pressing against his shoulder to stabilize herself.

Then she froze, turning stiff as a board.

Trent stared down at her wide eyes and her lips pressed together into a firm line. "Should I have let you fall?" he asked, still holding her.

"Huh?" She was looking past him.

Trent turned and looked at the truck parked next to his Suburban; then he looked back at Natasha. She blinked and looked up at him, her expression haunted.

"What is it?" he whispered, concerned with how pale she was.

When she remained quiet he gave her a slight shake. "Damn it, Natasha, talk to me. Would you accept we're together on this and trust me?"

She blinked again and this time shook her head as if trying to knock some unpleasant thought out of her head. "What?" she asked, looking dazed. But then her expression transformed and she backed out of his arms. "I never said I don't trust you."

Now wasn't the time for that argument. "Why did you just freeze?" He looked at the truck again. "Do you know that truck?" He studied it some more, but it simply looked like an old work truck. They were a dime a dozen on any ranch. It did mean someone had shown up since they'd arrived here, and Trent hadn't seen anyone. He looked past Natasha back up the hilly meadow, but Burrows and the other men were still over the hill and out of sight.

"The tag." Natasha pointed and cleared her throat.

"The tag?" Trent asked, looking at her, then staring at the license plate. "Do you recognize it?" Then it hit him. Before he could comment, Natasha filled him in.

"That's the truck my father drove when I found him out

at the cabin in Acorn. It's the same tag number." She looked at Trent sheepishly. "I memorized it."

"Come on," he said, grabbing her hand and marching back up the hill, this time holding on to her firmly so she wouldn't trip.

Natasha didn't fight him but held on tightly, her small, cool fingers intertwined with his. They stopped when they neared the top and stared at Burrows, who was with two of his ranch hands.

"That's him," Natasha whispered, as if the men across the meadow would hear her. She turned, facing Trent, and pointed into her palm. "Over there. That's him."

"Who?"

"That's the man who was with Rebecca Burrows when they were on horseback and ran into me at that cabin where the clothes were."

"That's Pat O'Reilly."

"Pat O'Reilly?" She stared at him as if something didn't make sense.

"Yup." Trent watched her frown. "You're sure it's the same man?"

"Positive." Her gaze had faltered, but she shot it back up to Trent's face. "And I'm positive that's the truck my father was driving. But why would they both be driving the same truck?"

"Good question." He took her hand, leading her back to the Suburban. "Burrows has a couple of those trucks, I think. His ranch hands use them."

"But my dad isn't working here anymore."

He looked down at her and she looked up, searching his face. Maybe he wasn't working here, but he was close by, very close. Natasha looked as if she was thinking the same thing.

"Let's head over to the ranch house. We'll meet Burrows there." Trent followed her to the passenger side of his Suburban and opened her door for her.

Natasha was lost in thought, running her teeth over her lower lip, when he climbed in on his side. She looked so damn hot, and she wasn't even trying. Her hair was windblown, half tucked into her coat and half out. Although her coat was tailored to show off her slim figure and wouldn't keep her warm at all once the temperatures really dropped, her blue jeans and boots helped her fit in more to his world than her leggings and shoes she'd worn when she'd first arrived a week ago.

Trent started the truck, curious what had her lost in thought. He didn't ask but instead pulled his seat belt around him, then backed out onto the road and headed toward the Burrows home. He had a few things bugging him, as well, one of them being Natasha's father. It wouldn't have been easy for him to simply obtain one of Burrows' ranch trucks. And if one had been stolen, Burrows would have reported it stolen.

"Do you know Pat O'Reilly?" Natasha asked after a moment of driving. Her eyes were exceptionally light today, although her mood wasn't obvious. If anything, she was reserved, being cautious around him. Her outburst toward Burrows was wrong. She knew that. Natasha didn't appear the type of woman who would fall over herself apologizing, though.

"He's a few years younger than I am and didn't move here until after high school, but yeah, I know something of him."

"What do you know about him?"

He glanced over at her. Natasha was watching him intently.

"We've never been friends, but we know each other."

She sucked in a breath, held it, stared at him. "So you don't like him?"

O'Reilly was an asshole, which was probably why Burrows had been so adamant about keeping knowledge of him being his son a secret. O'Reilly was nothing like Williams or any of Burrows' legitimate sons.

"Let's just say O'Reilly has never been too crazy about me."

She nodded, as if that bit of information fit into whatever thoughts she was mulling over in her head. Trent followed the highway around toward the Burrowses' ranch house. It was going on late afternoon and a thin layer of clouds had turned the skies gray. Trinity Ranch was on higher-elevation land, rich bountiful meadows cut thick with gullies left over from gold-mining days. It was beautiful land, closer to the mountains than his place, and land that had been coveted by more than one neighboring rancher over the years. Burrows and Post seemed to have been on a friendly basis when Trent had shown up. He hadn't been called out to settle any disputes lately, but back in the day when his father had still been alive there had been some doozies between the two neighboring ranches.

Burrows had mentioned twice while Trent and Natasha were talking to him how good a neighbor Post was. Did he think Trent wouldn't remember the disputes he and Post had had in the past? Or was there another reason why Burrows wanted them to think he was such a good neighbor?

"Do you think it's possible it might have been Pat O'Reilly who shot at me when we were at that cabin earlier this week?" Natasha's question came out of the blue, and Trent looked at her, wondering if that was what had been nagging at her since they'd left the far end of the ranch.

"I hadn't thought about it. Why?"

"When I saw him just now, across the meadow," she began, adjusting herself so her back was at the passenger door and she faced Trent. She pulled one leg up and rested it on the seat, causing the denim to stretch and accentuate her long, slender legs. "I couldn't help thinking I could have mistaken him for my father. He wears a hat, but his hair is sort of gray sticking out from under it. But he's tall. The men in my family are really tall and big."

Trent was six feet, two inches. He gave it some thought. O'Reilly might be close in height to him.

"Burrows is a big man. Most of his boys are good sized."

She shook her head. "I'm just talking about O'Reilly. He was with Rebecca when I was riding Midnight. He kept glancing over at the cabin. What if they knew those clothes were in there? Maybe they were coming to take them and I prevented them from doing it."

"Why would they leave clothes in a cabin? I'm all for speculating and brainstorming, but we need facts."

"Do you have O'Reilly's prints or DNA on file?" she asked.

"Actually, I might have his prints. I did book him quite a

few years back when he first moved here. He isn't quite as wild as he was when he was young and just out on his own."

"Maybe you and I should take a look at that cabin I found," she said, facing forward once again and letting her voice drift off as she spoke.

They were nearing the Burrowses' or he would have discussed everything with her further. Natasha's eyes lit up when she speculated, tried to fit random clues together. He didn't doubt it was in her blood. The thought of brainstorming together, weighing the pros and cons of every clue they had on this murder, and figuring it all out together had an unusual, strong appeal. Now wasn't the time, though. They had other matters on hand.

His phone rang as the entrance to the ranch came into view. Natasha's eyes were peeled to the entrance instead of him when he accepted the call.

"Oakley," he said, holding the Bluetooth in his ear as he adjusted the volume, then slowed and signaled to enter the ranch.

"Trent, this is Burrows," the older man said. "My wife wants to talk to your little lady when you get to the ranch."

"Ethel wants to talk to Natasha?" Trent frowned and was very aware of Natasha shooting her attention his way.

"Why?" she whispered.

"Yup. I just talked to her, let her know I was heading that way and bringing you two on in with me. Before I could even tell her why I'd invited you over, she asked to speak with Miss King."

Trent thought about it for a moment. He prayed he wasn't making a mistake. Natasha had strong investigative skills and a yearning to uncover the truth in a mystery. He saw that easily. But she flew off the handle too damn easy. If Ethel said anything to her about her father . . .

"She didn't say what she wanted to talk to her about?" Trent asked.

"Nope. As soon as I told her we'd be over that way soon, she hurried to get off the phone. Probably picking the place up for you," he added, chuckling. Burrows apparently didn't seem to think there was an issue, and he'd seen a peek at Natasha's fiery side.

"All right. We're pulling in now."

"Trent, do you really have proof Nellie Burrows existed?" Burrows' voice had changed, softened somewhat, as if he were suddenly discussing something almost reverent.

"I'll show you as soon as I see you."

"I'll be damned," he muttered.

Trent pulled the Bluetooth out of his ear. Burrows had sounded completely in awe. Trent was real curious why the man didn't think Nellie was real but figured he would know soon enough. After pulling up to the ranch house and parking alongside the wraparound front porch and behind two ranch trucks Natasha was staring at shrewdly, he cut the engine and studied Natasha.

"I don't know why Ethel wants to talk to you," he began slowly.

She turned her head and looked at him, making a face as she spoke. "You've told me the woman is pregnant. Like I would strike out at a lady in that state, in her home. You don't think much of me, do you?" she sneered, although that bite she could put in her words when she was pissed wasn't there.

He was afraid he thought a bit too much of her. When Natasha opened her truck door and got out on her side, Trent hurried around the front of his Suburban, meeting her in time to close her door for her.

"It's nice to see chivalry isn't dead," she muttered under her breath.

"Act like a lady and I will always treat you like one," he informed her, lowering his voice as well.

Natasha looked up at him, not saying anything but giving him an odd look. Since he'd spoken the truth and would never be anything but a gentleman when they were out in public, Trent let it slide. Natasha probably wasn't exposed to good manners by many of those city men she'd spent time with.

Just thinking of her with any other man rubbed him wrong. Another surefire indication he was getting too close to her. He had to accept it as the truth, though, or what she'd said at the office wouldn't have upset him the way it did. Unfortunately, there wasn't time to dwell on where his relationship was going with Natasha. As long as she didn't go anywhere. He had a murder to solve.

Natasha watched the woman facing her look back and forth between her and Trent as he and Jim Burrows talked. Ethel Burrows was sizing them up, deciding for herself if they were having sex, since she probably would never ask. Not that Natasha would tell her if she did.

Natasha couldn't remember what the paperwork had said, but Ethel looked to be in her early to mid-forties. She had short platinum hair that curled around her face in soft waves. Natasha doubted it did that on its own, which meant Ethel spent a fair amount of time making herself look pretty every morning.

Ethel's nails were painted a pretty pink and fairly long. This woman didn't do a lot of physical labor on the ranch. That much was obvious at a glance. She wore tight blue jeans and high heels and didn't look very pregnant to Natasha. Some women didn't show until their sixth month or so. Natasha had read somewhere that Ethel was five months pregnant. Either way, those blue jeans couldn't have been that comfortable.

Jim pulled out two imported beers and held up one to Trent as he came around a long, narrow island in the middle of the kitchen. The room was impeccable, but Natasha didn't see Ethel as the fresh-apple-pie type of ranch wife, either. Natasha wondered what the woman did do with her days while Jim was out with his cattle.

"You two men run along," Ethel said, sidling up next to Natasha and wrapping her arm around Natasha's. Ethel began guiding her across the kitchen. "Go do your men talk. Us ladies will visit out here." She waved Trent and Jim on, watching until they'd disappeared behind a dark mahogany wood door and closing it.

"You've got a beautiful home," Natasha said once the women were alone. She accepted a chair at a round kitchen table. Running her hand over the smooth, nicely polished wood, she didn't feel a single crumb. Either they had one hell of a housekeeper or there weren't a lot of family meals conducted here.

"Thank you." Ethel beamed. "I spent the first year I lived here completely remodeling the place. You can't have another woman's mark on your home," she added, giving Natasha a knowing nod. "Now, what can I get you to drink? I can't have alcohol these days," she said, patting her tummy and grinning. Crow's-feet and fine lines around her mouth showed off her age, which Ethel otherwise appeared to be hiding rather well. "But I do have fresh iced tea."

"That sounds fine."

Ethel poured two iced teas out of a glass pitcher, then joined Natasha at the table. "Now honey, tell me about your daddy."

Natasha bristled in spite of the broad grin on the other woman's face. She'd anticipated Ethel bringing up her father, but not like this. There was a gleam in Ethel's eyes. Her face glowed. She couldn't wait to hear every detail Natasha might offer about her dad. And it was a look Natasha had seen way too many times during her life. Ethel Burrows had been having sex with Natasha's father!

No wonder her father disappeared when Carl Williams was murdered.

Damn it, Dad!

"I'll tell you anything you want to know if you tell me where he is," Natasha said coolly.

Ethel straightened, giving her a wary look. Natasha waited it out. Ethel was starving to know about the man she was sleeping with. The rerun was so old it was almost boring. Natasha waited out the moment of silence knowing it wouldn't take long for Ethel to break. She was in love with George King, as all the women in his life had been, and would do whatever Natasha wanted for information on the man who never had opened up to any of them since Natasha's mother had left so many years ago.

Jim Burrows stopped talking when the door to his den opened and Ethel pranced in and up to his desk. Natasha followed slowly behind, her face flushed but not appearing upset. If anything, Trent wasn't sure he'd ever seen the look she had on her face right now before.

"How dare you not tell me about Nellie Burrows." Ethel sang out, her voice too much forced cheer.

He turned and stared at her, with her body stuffed into jeans at least a size too small. Natasha snapped her attention to Ethel as well. When Trent glanced at Natasha, she met his gaze.

She looked stressed. But also almost amused. He could definitely tell she was holding some emotion back. If she was pissed, if Ethel had raked Natasha over the coals for being George King's daughter, Natasha was doing a better job than Trent ever would have guessed her capable of keeping her anger under lock and key. He'd obviously misjudged her.

At the same time, she appeared awkward, uncomfortable. He watched her shift her weight from one foot to the other, then mess with her hair, combing it with her fingers. Natasha didn't know what to do with her hands or whether to stay where she was, just inside the den door, or move closer. Seeing her like this would have been comical if he hadn't sensed some level of pain, or other dark emotion simmering just under the surface.

"All this time the legend was true?" Ethel was saying. "And everything in the coffin? Do we have it? How much money is there?"

"Forty grand," Jim said.

Ethel plopped down in an expensive, leather-backed chair next to Jim's desk. Her ass hit the wood hard enough to make a slapping sound. Trent was sure he heard her jaw snap open and shut as she sat there stunned.

"You're kidding. Forty thousand dollars?" It was hard to

tell if Ethel was going to laugh or cry. It was a reaction similar to the one Jim had when Trent answered his questions about what he'd found, which Jim seemed certain were the contents of Nellie's coffin. "All of the feuding was over a mere forty thousand dollars?"

"Hush, Ethel." Jim used a tone with his wife Trent hadn't heard out of the man. It was soft, nonaggressive. Jim reached over his expensive desk for Ethel's hand. "Don't get yourself upset. If you wish to listen to our conversation, that's fine, but please don't get all worked up."

"I'll try," she said sulkily.

Trent caught Natasha rolling her eyes and dared gesture for her to sit in the chair next to him. If she made a show of not listening to him in front of the old rancher, it would be something Trent would never live down with the good old boys in the area.

"It really would help to hear what you know about Nellie Burrows," Trent pressed, getting Jim to look at him and not the women. "I need to rule out any connection between these items and Carl's murder."

"What items?" Ethel scooted to the edge of her seat.

Natasha slid into the chair next to Trent and pressed her hands in her lap. She hadn't said a word since entering the room.

"Nothing of importance, sweetheart," Jim said, using that doting tone of his again as he smiled at her. It didn't look like Jim smiled often. His expression was almost unnatural. "Just some old clothes and a picture."

"Huh." Ethel inched back in her seat and began checking out her painted nails, her grunted response and mannerism showing her sudden lack of interest.

Obviously, anything not of monetary value bored the probably already-bored housewife.

"You were saying . . . ," Trent encouraged, nodding for Jim to continue with what he'd just started explaining before the women entered his den.

"Yes," Jim said, once again using his deep, raspy voice.

"Back in 1850, I believe, two brothers, Stephen and Jericho Burrows, came to Northern California from Chicago. They were after gold, just like everyone else. And they found some, struck it rich. These two brothers saw their surroundings in a way most didn't. They took a good look at this land, and although it was being torn to pieces from all the mining, it was good and wealthy land. They used their gold and purchased a good chunk of it. The Trinity and Excelsior ranches were born," he said dramatically, then took a drink of his beer.

"Eighteen-fifty?" Ethel said, wrinkling her nose. "Now I've heard the legend of Nellie Burrows from my grand-mamma and even some of the folk around town. It didn't start until around the depression, I think."

"Now sweet pea, no interrupting." Jim used that nauseating soft voice again.

Ethel blew him a kiss and resumed checking out her fingernails.

Trent managed a side look when Natasha looked at him. Her face was so void of expression, reaction, of anything. It was damn weird. As much as he wanted to hear this story, he really wanted to know what had been said out there. Whatever it was, Ethel certainly didn't act as if she'd just chewed Natasha out. If anything, Ethel seemed in higher spirits than usual. On the few occasions Trent had seen her with Jim she was sullen and moody and seldom smiled, as if she was absolutely miserable.

"We'll skip a few generations, just for you, my love," Jim said, although this time he was back in his deep presentation voice. "And I don't have to tell you both ranches flourished. The land was rich. The railroad was nearby. Trinity Ranch and Excelsior Ranch made the two families very wealthy." He paused, but this time to tap his finger on his desk, looking down, as if trying to remember the order of the story.

Trent sat, anxious, although not sure why. Maybe he really wanted a strong lead to pop out for them. He glanced at Natasha. Her hands were folded in her lap and she was glancing down, her hair partially blocking her profile. When Jim began speaking again, she focused on him, her placid expression making it impossible to know if he was boring her to death or her mind was just hundreds of miles away.

"The ranches remained in the family. Always have," he added proudly. "Trinity Ranch was passed down to sons, sometimes daughters. Excelsior Ranch did the same, although there were a couple who passed on early in life along the way, leaving the ranch to their spouses. Eventually, with in-laws taking possession, then leaving the ranch in their will to a relative they'd felt earned it, there came a point when the neighboring ranches weren't owned by blood relatives anymore. And as my beautiful wife just said, in 1920 a young boy and a young girl from each ranch fell in love. They had a daughter, Nellie."

"So the story goes," Ethel said, giving Trent a knowing wink.

When she also gave him an interested once-over, letting her heavily made up eyes travel up and down his body until she looked at his face and grinned, Trent swore Natasha straightened, grabbing the armrests of her chair, as if to keep herself from flying out of it.

"Sweet pea, we now know it's a true story," Jim reminded her.

"Oh yeah," Ethel said, switching her longing look from Trent to Jim.

Jim continued with the story. "Neither ranch approved of this courting going on between these two young people. But young folk being what they are, they didn't listen. As the story goes, they ran off and got hitched. When they come back, she's pregnant. Now when that baby girl was born, it was obvious she wasn't quite right. Sheriff, I don't have to tell you how stories get blown out of proportion. I've heard everything from little Nellie being blind, to just being too slow for school, to that little girl looking like a monster."

Trent hadn't mentioned the picture being of Nellie. Natasha looked at him but apparently was as anxious as he was to hear the story out. She remained quiet.

"I heard she was so ugly she scared the cows," Ethel said,

her eyes wide as she whispered to them. "They couldn't even take her off the ranch."

"Now this is when the parents of this young man and woman come forth and tell the two of them that they are actually more related than anyone had let on before. And I don't have to tell you, when that young man found out he had married and birthed a daughter with his own kin, he was mortified. The way of it is he ran off, joined the army, and never returned home," Jim said gravely.

This time when he paused his wife didn't interrupt. He downed a good portion of his beer, then placed the bottle on a coaster and leaned back in his chair.

"Whatever was wrong with that little girl, it was real. She didn't live long. Her tombstone is worn out to where you can hardly read it, but I've been told it says she was born in 1920 and died in 1950. Her mother buried her on the property line between the two ranches in honor of her mixed blood."

"So you know where this grave is?" Trent asked.

"Yup. Can take you there myself if you like."

Trent nodded and Jim continued.

"It wasn't long after that the rumors started about an unknown amount of wealth being buried with Nellie. Now, I will say, when her mama had her buried, she did it privately. Through the remaining days of her life, she never told a soul where her daughter was buried and her ranch hands were loyal. Each of them that helped her bury her daughter took the secret to their grave."

"So how do you know where she was buried?" Trent asked.

"Now Sheriff, when I took over this ranch, I knew a good business is run by not buying into speculation. Something is, or it isn't. And we don't make money on the isn'ts."

"That's why you're so rich," Ethel said, grinning at him.

"I found that grave myself, set my men out to take on the property line. We were having issues with it anyway, if you remember. Our cattle get across the fence from time to time today, but back in the day it was bad. Your daddy came out more than once to resolve disputes with my dad and Excelsior Ranch folk."

Trent wasn't positive things were as calm as Jim claimed they were right now. Trent just nodded and let Jim continue.

"My Jimmy wasn't going to have anything to do with that nasty curse."

"Curse?" Trent asked at the same time Natasha did.

Everyone looked at her. Ethel looked smug and rather satisfied that she knew something they didn't. Natasha nodded at Jim. "Go on," she prompted.

"It's a good story." When he smiled at Natasha, Ethel scowled, obviously not liking her husband giving anyone attention but her, in spite of how she behaved.

Jim didn't notice his wife's praise, or he didn't care. "Yes, they called it Nellie's curse. Within years of her dying, if not sooner, both ranches began having unexplained difficulties, things that just hadn't ever happened on either ranch before. There was a bout of bad feed on Trinity. That was back in the late fifties, I think. Lost almost a hundred head of cattle. Excelsior experienced their fair share of woes, too. Then there was the feuding. All of a sudden the two ranches began quibbling over water rights. One year there were quite a few calves birthed that Excelsior claimed, yet it was apparent they were the offspring of one of Trinity Ranch's bulls. It went on and on, decade after decade. Even when I was a boy, when something went wrong my daddy would blame it on Nellie's curse."

"What did you do with the contents of the grave once you dug it up?" Trent asked, pretty sure Jim knew there were laws protecting graves.

"Oh no," Jim said immediately, leaning back and smiling as he held his hands up in defense. "I never dug up the grave. I told you I found it. And I did. I found a hole, freshly dug up and deep and long enough to be a grave site. Since we went over every inch of the property line and that is the only thing remotely resembling a grave, I knew it was Nellie's. Of course, up until today I thought someone had dug it up to play a practical joke. I honestly didn't think the young girl ever really lived."

Ethel remained focused on her nails and crossed one foot

over the other, rocking it, as if really bored. Jim watched her a moment before shifting his attention to Trent.

"Where did you find the items buried with Nellie?" he asked Trent.

"In a cabin on Piney land," Trent told him, and watched for Ethel's reaction. "Then some of it was in a safe-deposit box over at the bank. That was in MaryAnn Piney's name."

"MaryAnn Piney is Ethel's great-aunt, isn't she, sweet pea?"

Ethel looked up, nodded, and grunted, then resumed her attention to her nails.

"Yup, the Piney's are my wife's kinfolk. Guess that really makes the contents ours by law, right, Sheriff?"

"Right now all of it is labeled and in evidence bags."

"Sweet pea, didn't you tell me a couple weeks ago you were going to close out a safe-deposit box for your great-aunt?"

"Yup." Ethel looked up quickly, her hair bobbing around her head when she nodded. "I guess I never got around to it." When she looked at Trent her eyes were wide and her smile plastered to her face. Trent narrowed his brow and frowned, curious about her going to the bank for her aunt when Mary-Ann Piney hadn't remembered having the box.

Ethel jumped up, almost causing her chair to teeter backward. "If you'll excuse me. I need to go to the little girls' room."

Chapter Seventeen

Natasha watched until Ethel had walked out of the room. She exhaled with relief when Jim got up, excused himself, and followed his wife out of his den, leaving the door open.

"She looked a little flushed, didn't you think?" Jim asked, but then disappeared into the rest of the lavish home before either of them could respond.

Natasha flipped herself around, damn near jumping to her feet. Another time she might have grinned at Trent's astonished look, but there wasn't time to waste and she knew it. She knew exactly why Ethel left the room, and as long as Jim was with her Ethel wouldn't be able to call Natasha's father and warn him. A lot more made sense now, although it was still jumbling around in her head so fast it was difficult to grasp it all.

"We've got to go," she said urgently, and grabbed Trent's arm.

He didn't budge but looked up at her, his brooding expression showing he was still taking time to digest everything they'd just heard.

"There isn't time," she hissed, tugging on him harder.

Trent stood slowly, coming to his full height, then tugged on his shirt. Another time, maybe when all of this was over, Natasha might remember to ask him if he even owned a sheriff's uniform. At the moment it didn't matter. All that mattered was getting to her father before he ran again.

"Come on, damn it." She was getting pissed. Jim and Ethel might be back at any moment. "We need to go to my father," she whispered.

"What?" That got his attention.

"I'll explain on the way."

"What did Ethel say to you?" Was that concern on his face?

Natasha's heart warmed in spite of the urgency of the moment. "I'll tell you once we're out of here. Let's go," she commanded, then started toward the door. "Tell them you got a call. Anything. I don't want Ethel alarmed."

Ethel might guess Natasha would run to her father the moment she left the ranch, although she wasn't the smartest woman Natasha had ever met. They stood a good chance of reaching her father if she and Trent left right now. Trent started following her but not as fast as she'd like. If she had it her way, they would be bolting out of the house and spinning tires as they peeled out of the driveway.

"I've got it all figured out." It wasn't completely the truth, but it got Trent moving.

"I want every detail. No holding back this time!" he barked, but was on her heels. Jim was at the other end of the room, hunched toward a closed door, more than likely talking his sickeningly sweet talk to his wife.

There was no excuse for infidelity. None whatsoever. But Natasha could see how Ethel had grown weary of the man who'd provided her with the lifestyle she so obviously adored. Sacrifice for so many material possessions often came with a high price.

Not her problem. Her problem was shacked up in a motel room in Redding and might just still be there if they hurried and got to him before he got tipped off by Ethel.

"Jim, I'll be in touch soon." Trent was all business and placed his hand on Natasha's shoulder as he escorted her to the front door.

"Oh." Jim turned around, took a few hesitant steps toward

the two of them. Then he looked nervously back toward his wife. "I do apologize. A man should have more control of his own household," he sputtered, appearing seriously distraught. "She's suddenly under the weather."

"I hope she will be okay." Trent had reached the front door and opened it.

Natasha almost ran to the Suburban, taking time to glance around the wide-open area leading to the highway. There were outbuildings behind the house. One of the two work trucks that had been parked in front of the house was no longer there. Had there been anyone else in the house with them? She hadn't heard anyone, but that didn't mean anything. The house was not only huge but also very well built. She doubted a floorboard squeaked anywhere.

Natasha didn't hear the rest of Trent's parting words to Jim Burrows, but she didn't care. She was in the passenger seat, seat belt on, and tapping her fingers against the dash when Trent came around the front of the Suburban and entered on the driver's side.

"What the hell was that all about?" he barked, sliding his key into the ignition. He fired up the motor and put it in drive.

"How fast can you get to Redding?"

"What?" Trent cursed under his breath.

"How fast? Head there now. I'll talk. You drive." She looked urgently at the highway, not even sure which way they needed to turn but checking both directions for oncoming cars. There weren't any. "Go, go!" she demanded.

"Slow down right now," Trent snapped, turning onto the highway, then accelerating. He appeared to be putting his foot into it.

Natasha would have to accept he'd hurry as fast as possible. "I know where my father is," she said, turning and focusing on Trent. "Ethel told me. She's been hiding him."

"What?" Trent shot Natasha an annoyed look. "I don't like being in the dark. Talk. Talk now and don't leave out even the slightest detail." Then as he shot her another side-glance, his harsh expression softened only a bit. "I'm heading to Redding. Where in Redding is he?"

"He's staying at the Holiday Inn."

"There are two. Which one?"

"Crap."

She must have looked horrified, because Trent cursed again, white-knuckled the steering wheel, and brought the Suburban up to the speed limit as he worked his way along the two-lane highway.

"Tell me what you found out," he said, his voice calmer. "You said you've got it all figured out. Did she confess to the murder? Or say who killed Carl?"

So it was the second little white lie Natasha had told this afternoon, the first one being a cross-her-heart promise she wouldn't take the sheriff to her father. Ethel had been convinced, as apparently was Natasha's father, that Trent would take him in immediately on suspicion of murder. Ethel also seemed to know his fingerprints had been all over Carl's body.

Instead of answering Trent, Natasha started at the beginning. It was the only way she could get it all out of her and have it make any sense.

"I was pretty nervous to be left alone with Ethel," she began, forcing herself to take slow, deep calming breaths in between sentences to help calm down. "It was bothering me a bit too much that she was being so sweet. And it didn't stop when you two left the room."

She needed to think straight right now. An overwhelming sensation that everything was unfolding around her, all the facts, the truth about what had happened, and it was slipping around her in a world of treachery and deceit. That made it harder to grasp ahold of the truth, especially in a world where so many of those possibly involved lied on a daily basis.

"Go on," Trent said, staring ahead at the road.

"The moment we were alone and sitting at the table, she gushed, wanting me to tell her everything I could about my father."

"She wanted to know about George King?"

"It was more than the question. It was how she asked it," Natasha said, wishing she could calm down. "Like I said, she was gushing. She poured us tea and sat down opposite of me with a grin so big you would have thought I'd brought her favorite gift to her. And I had."

When Trent gave her an odd look she bit her lip, knowing once she dove in there was no turning back. She hated how all of this would make Trent think less of her father. Maybe her dad was a player, but she loved him. Once they got to him, and after Natasha killed him for being the biggest idiot in the world, she would prove that love and clear his name.

"I brought her me. She was ready to do anything if I would just share with her everything I could about my dad. She wanted to know his favorite food, what he liked to do in his spare time, how many girlfriends he'd had over the years, what he'd done before he came here." She paused, caught her breath, but knew she'd gotten her message across.

"You're kidding me." He looked shocked.

Natasha nodded. "I knew the moment we sat down. It's bad, terrible even, but unfortunately it's the truth."

"What is the truth?" Trent snapped, suddenly frustrated. "What are you talking about?

"She looked and behaved just as so many women in the past have looked who have fallen in love with my father. Once they had me alone they hounded me for information about him." She took a deep breath and continued, staring out the window instead of at Trent's disgusted expression. "My dad kept his private life private. Women were always falling for him and tried getting him to open up to them. Then he would saunter out of their life. Too often he would leave a desolate lady clinging to me and demanding to know where he went. I hated not knowing any more than they did. When I permanently moved in with my aunt and uncle the parade of women stopped. I agreed to appease Ethel's curiosity if she told me where Dad was."

"And she knew." Trent didn't make it a question. He loosened his grip on the steering wheel, then tightened it again.

"Oh yes. She knew. She's been hiding him since all of this mess, as she put it, happened on the ranch. Ethel was worried when Carl was murdered there would be so many questions asked and that George would appear suspicious when he wasn't where he was supposed to be at the time of the murder."

"Crap," Trent hissed. "Do I want to know where he was?"

Natasha cringed. It was as bad as she thought. Trent might be a wild lover. He was aggressive and demanding. But when it came down to what was right and what was wrong it was a line he would never cross, no matter what. In spite of Natasha telling herself it was all for the best, long-distance relationships seldom worked, a heaviness weighed down on her she couldn't shake.

"He was with Ethel." It was harder to choke out the words than Natasha had thought it would be. "But on the plus side," she added without taking a breath, "he didn't kill anyone. He's got an alibi, but a very reluctant one for obvious reasons."

She snuck a look at Trent and he took his attention from the road and stared at her a moment. His gaze was dark, calculated, and very pissed off.

"Did she say anything else?" he asked tightly.

That weight descending on Natasha began pressing against her chest. "She said something about getting money together. She told me it was just to protect my dad, but I think she has something bigger planned. I think she was planning on taking off with my father."

"She got a bit spooked when we started talking about the money found in the cabin and in the safe-deposit box."

"Jim is so in love with her he didn't notice."

"I think he's in love with having children," Trent said, a sour edge to his tone.

If the baby was even his. Natasha didn't voice her fears, but the unspoken possibility hung between them.

"And that's everything she said to you?" Trent asked after a few minutes of silence passed and they continued along the highway. It was starting to get dark and the drivers of the occasional cars passing them flicked off their high beams as they approached. Trent did the same, then turned his high beams back on once there was no oncoming car. "What made her hurry into the den?"

"Oh. Well, she'd been pushing for any personal information I could offer her about my father, and honestly, I was getting tired of talking about him with her." Natasha stared out the window. Talking to Ethel had resurfaced too many old memories, and the emotions that had gone along with them.

"Sounds like fun," Trent said dryly.

"No, it wasn't fun."

"I was being sarcastic."

She shot him a pensive look. Dark shadows crossed his face, making his features appear even more restricted. This was the exact reason why not to let a man get under her skin. She'd been foolish enough to think she might be willing to give Trent a chance. That simply would never happen. Let him look at her as he did now, not quite with disgust but definitely shut down. Natasha stared at a stranger, a man she thought she was getting to know and, damn it, even open up to, but that wasn't the case. They were from different worlds.

"No, it's okay," she said, remaining calm even with her insides twisting in painful knots. "My father is now, and always has been, in love with women. Or better yet, the idea of loving women." Maybe she was clinging to childhood beliefs, but she always thought he'd only loved one woman, her mother.

"Which is why you have gone to so much effort to never fall in love with anyone," Trent said, his voice rough, tight, a raspy whisper, as he looked away from her and returned his attention to the road.

"What?" she gasped.

He didn't elaborate. Instead, he changed the subject. "Better find the numbers of those two Holiday Inns and find out where your father is. We'll be in Redding soon."

Natasha fumbled with her phone, called Information, then wrote the first number down and pushed the button to put the call through on the second number. The first Holiday Inn confirmed George was staying there, and she jotted down the address.

"Got it," Trent said, nodding when she told him which motel. "Now tell me again why we are rushing in here to see him?"

"What?" she asked again, feeling as if she and Trent were suddenly existing on two different planes. "To let him know he doesn't have to keep hiding!" she exclaimed, almost shouting. She threw her hands up in the air, then let them fall to her lap. Her palms slapped against her legs. "He's got an alibi. We know he didn't kill Carl." Natasha shot Trent a focused glare. "You aren't going to arrest him, right? Because if you are, just turn around right now. I wouldn't be able to live with the knowledge that I was responsible for bringing my father in."

Trent didn't look at her. "I'm going to talk to him."

Natasha reached out, touched Trent's arm, then pulled her fingers back. "Please, just let me talk to him first." It was sickening knowing she didn't have a voice in this matter. Trent was the sheriff of Trinity County. She couldn't interfere with an investigation, no matter who was being hunted down.

"We'll talk to him together."

Less than ten minutes later Trent pulled into the Holiday Inn parking lot. Natasha immediately scanned the cars parked there for any sign of someone loading up and getting ready to leave.

It made no sense. When she and Trent had left Trinity Ranch, her mind had been whirling with bits of information that all just needed to be pieced together, now it was more like a tornado. Her thoughts were running rampant in her brain, leaving her feeling dizzy and exhausted.

She wanted to threaten Trent, warn him he'd better behave around her father. She had brought a lot of information to the table with this case. He owed her this. He owed her time with her dad, to talk to him and to hear what he had to say.

When had her father ever shared his thoughts with her?

Damn. Natasha fought the urge to drop her head in her

hands and have a good cry. All those wonderful pieces of the puzzle were being slam-dunked at her, and she was dodging them, or at least felt as if she was. Maybe all of this was just too damn personal for her to see the picture accurately in order to piece it all together.

"Dad!" Natasha sat up straight, all her jumbled thoughts dissipating the moment she saw her father crossing the parking lot.

"Where?" Trent demanded, but then saw George without Natasha having to point. "Okay. We're both going to be cool here, all right?"

Natasha wouldn't be able to handle Trent informing her yet once again how she should behave. It was her turn to inform him a thing or two. But then, it was her turn to take the lead in several areas when it came to her sheriff.

Her sheriff?

Natasha wasn't going to go there right now.

"You be cool," she snapped, and opened her passenger door before he'd put the truck in park and jumped out.

Her coat was loose on her, since the heater in Trent's Suburban worked so well. She immediately yanked it up over her shoulders as she darted around cars toward her father.

"Dad!" she yelled.

George had a suitcase in each hand and was walking away from her toward a group of parked cars. Natasha didn't recognize any of them. He looked over his shoulder, saw her, and she swore he cursed. Then he turned and moved faster toward the cars.

He was not going to walk out of her life, yet again, this time before speaking with her.

"Dad!" she yelled louder, her voice fierce when she called out to him. "Don't you dare run," she shouted, not giving a damn at the moment who might hear her. Although she hadn't seen anyone else in the parking lot.

Her father reached a small green Honda and adjusted his suitcases so one was under his arm and he held the other by the handle. Natasha wasn't sure what he dished out of his pocket. She hauled ass, though, coming up behind him just as the Honda beeped and its headlights and taillights flashed once as he unlocked it. The trunk popped open, and George carried the two suitcases to the back of the car.

Natasha stopped, placing her hand on the roof of the car as she stood on the driver's side. She wasn't a child anymore and her father wouldn't get into the car without moving her out of the way, which she just dared him to try to do.

"We need to talk," she said, meeting his gaze over the top of the trunk when he placed the bags inside and began lowering it.

"Why did you bring the sheriff, Natasha?" George sounded reserved, worried.

"We were together." She shrugged. "We were at Trinity Ranch," she specified. "When I found out you were here I knew I didn't have time to get the Avalanche and drive here." She nodded at the trunk as he closed it. "And I was right."

Trent walked up to join them, his body stiff, his movements cautious. He looked ready to pounce if needed, once again the dangerous predator and, with or without the uniform, a sheriff to be reckoned with.

Natasha returned her attention to her dad, who was also watching Trent and looking as if he might pounce as well any moment. Lord, it was a male showdown, testosterone at its peak. Her father was in better shape than he'd been in years.

"Dad, he isn't here to arrest you," Natasha offered.

Her father looked at her, then returned his attention to the sheriff. "Are you here to arrest me?" George asked.

"I guess that all just depends," Trent drawled, his voice a few notches lower than usual.

Natasha gave him a scathing glare. Trent kept his attention on her father.

"Dad," Natasha said, taking a step toward him.

Her father looked at her but continued shooting cautious glances toward Trent as if he didn't trust what the man's next move might be. Natasha wanted to yell at her father to relax. She wanted to order Trent back to the Suburban. Neither man would listen to her though, which made her want to scream. But she was here, her father stood in front of her, and it was do-or-die right now.

"Dad," she repeated. "Where were you the morning Carl Williams was killed?"

"What?" Her dad looked at her as if he wasn't sure he'd heard her right.

"Tell me where you were," she started. "Dad, look at me. Just me!" she barked, taking a step to the side, closer to her father, and forcing him to turn his head in her direction and not at Trent. "He's not going to leap through the air!" she cried out when her father continued watching Trent. "I told you, he simply brought me here. He isn't here to arrest you."

"And I suppose he always has handcuffs looped to his jeans and a gun strapped to his side." Her father pointed at Trent.

Natasha looked at Trent. It hit her then. She'd broken into a full run, darting across the parking lot to stop her father before he could leave without talking to her first. Trent easily could have outrun her and reached her father before she had. But Trent had been more than a few paces behind her. She stared at the handcuffs clipped to his jeans and, on the other side of his waist, a gun in a holster he hadn't been wearing earlier. He'd held back for a few seconds to put those things on before following her over here.

Trent's expression was hard, calculated, and when he slowly shifted his attention from her father to her Natasha stared into the eyes of a man determined to see his job out to the letter of the law. How many times had she seen that same hardened glaze in her uncle's eyes, even her aunt's and her cousins'? It was the look of a lawman, sworn to uphold the law under all circumstances. And Trent would do just that, based on what her father said now and regardless of how she felt about it.

As much as Natasha wanted to hate Trent at the moment, in her heart she knew she didn't, which somehow made it hurt even more. Regardless of what he might be feeling toward her, he accepted that his job came first.

She looked away from him, her eyes burning. Her family

came first, and for the life of her she never thought in a million years that would create a conflict.

"Dad," she said softly. "If you aren't guilty, there's no reason to arrest you, right?"

"My fingerprints are all over Carl's body." Her father did look at her now and she saw the desperation in his eyes. For weeks now this had been his nightmare, fear, panic, that he might go down for a crime he didn't commit.

"Why were your finger prints all over his body?" she asked.

"Because I tried to take him down," her father hissed. "That boy hanging up there," he began, and his large body shuddered. "You didn't see it. And pictures don't hold a flame to how he looked, how he smelled," George stressed. "To how his body swayed, or to how blood continued dripping to the ground, one repetitive drip after the other."

Natasha hugged herself, feeling the pain the sight of that boy had brought to her father. At the time he'd had no clue his life would get any worse than it probably had been seeing the mutilated body and reacting to it.

"I know it must have been horrible."

"Horrible?" Her father laughed, although there was no humor in it. His light brown eyes, a shade or so darker than hers, were glassy when he looked down at her. " 'Horrible' doesn't define it. Ethel wouldn't quit screaming. The ranch hands were barely awake and can't figure out how to zip up their own trousers in the morning before they've downed at least several cups of coffee."

He shook his head, grunted, and Natasha wanted to walk into his arms. She wanted to hold him, assure him the pain of it all would pass. But she had a job to do, it fell on her shoulders, and since neither man would budge, Natasha wasn't going to stop until she'd done it. She was going to prove her father's innocence.

"Dad, I believe you. You tried to get him down. But forensics show the angle of your fingerprints on him weren't right." She hesitated, trying to figure out how best to explain what the tests had shown.

"I see." He straightened, his expression hardening. "My sweet little girl, you're in over your head, baby. Go home. This isn't your fight."

"I'm not a little girl anymore," she snapped. "There's no more sending me home, or to my room so you can slip out without seeing me cry because my father has left, once again."

Her words might as well have been a slap across the face. Her father's expression tightened, and he looked at her as if she were someone he didn't know. Natasha forged ahead, having said that much. If she didn't finish this out, she would just look stupid for complaining she didn't have the picture-perfect father.

"And since you won't fight, it becomes my fight," she informed him, dropping her hands to her sides and squaring off, stepping closer to her dad. "Because that is how a family is. You're going to explain and you aren't going to quit talking until you've satisfied me, and the sheriff over there, that you aren't guilty of anything that can get you arrested."

Her father narrowed his gaze on hers, and for a moment she thought he would shoot her down, as he always had. Instead he sighed, shook his head, and gave her what might have been a smile, except there wasn't much to smile about at the moment.

"You're one hell of a lady, Natasha," he said, meaning it. "Perfect in every way. Not like your old man. Not a bit. But sweetheart, these guys are too good. They've washed away their tracks, played all their cards right. And I've always been a man to know when it's smarter to fold than to press on and go broke. Maybe that is one thing I can teach you."

"How to be a coward and give up because the road ahead is too rocky? No thanks, Dad. I'll pass on that lesson. Who is so good they've covered all their tracks?"

"I'm not sure," he admitted, and looked from her to Trent. "There were some things going on and I'm afraid Carl was simply a distraction from the true crimes happening. Damn shame, too. That boy didn't deserve to die. He wasn't in their way and wouldn't have done a thing to stop them."

"Dad, who?" Natasha shouted, quickly losing her patience

with her father talking in circles, especially when his life depended on clearing things up. "What was going on at that ranch?"

"A few of them were getting ready to take old Burrows down, baby. But there isn't any proof," he added hastily, turning to Trent as he continued. "There's no way I can verify a damn thing I'm telling you. I know what I know from hearing them talk. Ethel was scared." He stopped then and looked at Natasha. "I know what you think of her, sweetheart, but she isn't a bad lady. She had it rough and an extra bit of security is important to her."

"I don't want to hear you defend her, Dad." Natasha sliced her hand through the air. "She's *Mrs. Burrows,*" she stressed.

Her father actually looked appropriately chastised. "You're right," he whispered.

"Cut the crap, Dad. You are who you are. I prayed every night when I was growing up that you'd change, want to be a family man, to be my father," she snapped, but then pressed her fingers to her head. They were surprisingly cold, especially since her head felt as if it were on fire. This wasn't about them or their lack of a family unit. Her father was who he was. "The past is just that, Dad. But today, tonight, right here, I will not walk away from you. I will stand here and remain here until there is no doubt in anyone's mind that you're innocent." She walked into her father, slapped her palm against his chest.

Her dad flinched, tried to take her hand in his. Natasha pulled away.

"What were those things doing hidden in the cabin?"

Her father frowned. "What things?"

Natasha studied him, unsure how far he'd go to protect Ethel. "Why did Ethel use her great-aunt's security box at the bank?" She tried a different angle. "Did you help her dig up the grave?"

"Grave?" Natasha's father took a step back, his eyes widening. "No one dug up any grave," he insisted, slicing his hand through the air. "Ethel isn't guilty of a damn thing."

Natasha shook her head. "Why are you defending her?"

She nodded at the trunk. "You were going to leave her, too. Take off like you have on any woman the moment she wanted to know what your favorite meal was," she spit out sardonically.

"I was leaving here to go get her, Natasha." Her father's expression turned grave. "Shit's going to hit the fan on that ranch. I told you this isn't your fight. Well, it sure as hell isn't my or Ethel's fight, either. Yes, before you ask, she did call to let me know the two of you had just left the ranch. She wasn't sure if you were coming here, but I knew. You'll always fight until your last breath, sweetheart. I just hope someday you learn to look around and see some people aren't meant to fight but to love."

His voice had grown quieter as he spoke, and Natasha found herself staring into his eyes, seeing wisdom there she hadn't seen before. Maybe years of running, of heading out the moment any relationship got serious, had finally taken their toll on him. It might be too late for her and her father, but there was someone in his world he cared about. And apparently he cared enough to go back into the fire and pull her out.

"Wait a minute, Dad," Natasha said, waving her hand in the air to shove aside all the meaningful advice. It was clouding the issue and making her think about things she couldn't afford to think about right now. "How is this not your fight? Don't you care if you go to prison?"

This time George's laughter sounded a bit more sincere. "Sweetheart, I would love very much to never see the inside of a prison. And, if it came down to it, I have a bit of a nest egg put aside. If the good sheriff sees fit to haul my old ass back to Weaverville, I can spring for a pretty decent lawyer. But that isn't what I'm talking about. Like I told you, Carl Williams' murder was the fireworks. A crime of passion is often violent and bloody. But a crime of the heart is worse. It's sinister, destructive, and too often backfires and wipes out not only those you once loved and now despise but those you still care about, too."

Chapter Eighteen

"I need a room." Natasha returned the stare from Matilda at Pearl's Bed-and-Breakfast until the woman came to her senses and realized she had a guest wishing to spend money at her establishment.

"Oh. Of course." The hefty woman fluttered her hands in front of her, seeming for a moment to have forgotten how to do the check-in process. "Do you wish the same room as . . . er, before?" She managed to remember the process and began hustling through the check-in.

"That's fine." Natasha didn't care where she stayed as long as it was in Weaverville and close to the jail where Trent had taken her father.

It still wouldn't sink in. How could she have read Trent so wrong? What in the hell had he been thinking? He had stood there the entire time Natasha had spoken to her father and had heard every word he'd said. George King did not murder Carl Williams! Plain and simple. End of story.

Anger and pain still coursed through her veins. Even after standing there, listening to Trent calmly inform her father he was going with them back to Weaverville for further questioning, she hadn't realized Trent's intentions. What questioning? She had run her father through every single detail of the case, had asked him questions using different angles. Maybe she didn't have a badge or piece of paper certifying her as a professional investigator, but damn it, she knew the process!

"May I see your credit card, please?" The way Matilda asked, it sounded as if she'd already asked once and been ignored.

"Yes." Natasha gave herself a mental shake. "I'm sorry. It's been a long day."

"Of course, dear."

If Matilda Patterson knew George King was down at the jail with the sheriff undergoing interrogation, the entire town would know. A mean chill flashed through Natasha, causing her to shiver and almost drop her wallet when she pulled it out of her purse. She managed to open it and pull out her credit card. Her brain was fried, clogged with too many pieces of truths and facts. She was hurt from believing she knew someone when apparently she didn't. All she wanted to do was climb into bed, any bed, as long as she was alone, and fade away into a dreamless sleep. If she were prone to using sleeping pills, tonight would be the night for several.

"Here we are," Matilda said, holding up the credit card printout. "If you'll just sign here."

Natasha scribbled her signature. "Thank you," she murmured when she accepted the key and pamphlets about Weaverville along with a printed list of curious facts about Pearl's Bed-and-Breakfast she'd received the first time she'd stayed here.

Natasha didn't wait to be offered an escort but walked around the counter and pushed through the door to the kitchen. For a moment she thought of informing Matilda she'd better not drop a bug in her purse this time, but what was the point? Obviously, Sheriff Trent Oakley ran this town the way he saw fit. Everyone fell into line and did things his way or he bulldozed them over. Natasha still felt the pain and bruised pride from his bulldozer.

She worried she would toss and turn, with Trent's impassive expression frozen on his face when he'd dropped her at his house and at her truck. Her father had been in the backseat, silent, brooding, a giant of a man known and loved by everyone for his gallant nature and playboy charm, reduced to a suspect in a murder investigation, a crime he so obviously didn't commit. It had been the worst drive of her life.

Her father's look of betrayal, Trent's cool, incredibly attentive eyes watching her even when she didn't say a word but got out of the Suburban and traipsed across the drive to the Avalanche. Trent's dark, forbidding stare, his arm relaxed casually on the rolled-down window of his truck, waiting as she started the truck, turned on the headlights, and finally, when it was clear he didn't plan on leaving until she did, turning his head and keeping his gaze on her as she pulled out in front of him and headed into Weaverville. Natasha was sure she would toss and turn. But as she blinked, peeled the thick, fresh-smelling quilts down to her nose, and peered out at the bright sunshine causing dust motes to float around in the air across her room, she realized she'd gotten her wish. She had slept soundly through the night without so much as a tiny dream.

After showering, and putting the same clothes on she'd worn the day before since her suitcase was in Trent's house, Natasha grabbed her phone from her charger and placed the call home. She unloaded on her uncle, then her aunt. After hanging up with them and more worked up than she'd been last night, Natasha called Marc. She called Jake. Her aunt called Natasha back. She put in another call to Jake when she heard he'd called Uncle Greg, concerned.

"More than anything, I just want to know how many times you've fucked him," her younger cousin had said, his deep baritone ornery sounding even though long-distance and several states away.

"None of your damn business," she'd shot out at him. Jake was the youngest and the tallest of all the King men. Natasha had told him more times than she remembered all that meant was that it would hurt more when he fell.

"That much, huh?" he said, the laughter in his voice simply annoying her further.

"Jake, you don't get it. I trusted him. I took him straight to Dad."

"I do get it."

"Yeah? Mind sharing this incredible insight you have?" She was getting a headache.

"He took Uncle George in for further questioning. Has he arrested him?"

"I don't know," she admitted. "I thought talking to all of you would help me calm down and then I'd head into town to see what happened between the two of them."

"You sound so cool and relaxed."

She wanted to punch him in the nose.

"If you want, Natasha, we can come up there. Angela and I can catch a flight and be there before this evening."

Natasha suddenly wanted to cry. "That's not necessary. And you're a sweetheart, Jake, to offer."

"Anything for my brat of a cousin," he said, but then turned serious. "Dad says Uncle George is innocent. You do, too. That is good enough for both of us. Angela can't find a lot of details about this online."

Natasha laughed, but it came out sounding more like a snort. "Weaverville is small town, Cuz. Not to mention, you aren't going to find a Web site, or blog, about Trinity Ranch."

"Someone up that way has a computer. And if this is local gossip and the happening item of the moment, you might be surprised who could be sitting in their bedroom blogging away about it as we speak. Oftentimes you can learn more than you think that way."

Natasha thought of Rebecca Burrows and all the anger welled up inside her. The young woman could write one of those blogs that ended up with a million hits from people feeding off her rage.

"Good point." Natasha glanced at her laptop. Her temples were throbbing, and another cup of coffee would probably kick off a full-blown headache. "I haven't eaten," she announced, but felt silly for doing so.

"Go eat," Jake stated the obvious. "Angela did just get a few hits for Trinity Ranch," he added.

Natasha pulled her laptop out of its case and plopped on

her unmade bed, opening it. "Are any of them connected to Rebecca Burrows?" she asked, half-joking.

"She's got a blog."

"Are you kidding me?" Natasha waited impatiently as her laptop loaded; then remembering the bed-and-breakfast only had dial-up, she cursed, then cursed more when her cousin laughed at her.

"I can't believe my cousin, computer geek Natasha, is in a town that lives off dial-up." He laughed long and hard.

She struggled with the phone cord she had in her laptop case. At least she came prepared for everything. "Go to hell, Jake."

"Sounds like you're already there."

She yanked the phone cord for the telephone in her room out of the wall, plugged in her cord, connected it to her laptop, then tapped the edge of her laptop with her fingernails while waiting for it to connect.

"Actually, Weaverville is the most beautiful town you could ever imagine," she told him truthfully. "The Trinity Alps are breathtaking. I should have taken pictures. None of you will believe I've hiked across a meadow where cattle graze so I could speak with the rancher who owns Trinity Ranch."

"Huh," was all Jake said. "Natasha, you should read this woman's blog. She hates Trinity Ranch and Jim Burrows. That's the owner? Damn, and she is his daughter? Wow. There is some rage going on up there. Why isn't she a suspect?"

Natasha wanted to scream. The dial-up was taking forever. "Paraphrase it for me."

"She's going on and on about how men suck for leaving loving wives for skanky younger bloodsuckers."

"Oh yeah. I got that one firsthand." Natasha stood, stretched, and gave up on her laptop. "I'm going to go find food. Thanks for letting me vent."

"Take care of yourself and be careful," Jake advised, his voice softening with sincere concern.

It made Natasha want to cry. She needed to get out of there. "I always do."

"I know."

She said quick good-byes and hung up. Her stupid cousin, whom she loved so much, would have a field day if he knew he'd brought tears to her eyes.

It was cold outside, but the sun was bright. Natasha opted for stretching her legs a bit and walked across the street to the Nugget, leaving the Avalanche parked behind the bed-and-breakfast. It hadn't surprised her that Trent had made no effort to call her or check on her since leaving her at her truck last night. But it hurt. She admitted she had feelings for him. Accepting them was the only way to get over them, then get them to go away.

Natasha forced the scowl off her face, focused on the ground, and hurried across the street. If she looked up at any car driving by or any passerby on foot, she'd have to endure the stares she knew were being thrown her way.

They would look at her, laughing. *Who was she to think she could prance into this town and sweep the sheriff off his feet? None of our women have been able to do it. Little city slicker thought she had skills better than all of them. Looks like the sheriff showed her.* Not to mention, Natasha was positive they were all labeling her the daughter of a murderer by now.

She thought of retreating, running to the safety of her room. Natasha wasn't sure if anywhere delivered in Weaverville. Probably not. She hurried across the parking lot to the door of the diner.

Two men were leaning against an old pickup truck parked behind the diner. Natasha immediately identified it as being identical to the two that had been parked in front of Jim Burrows' house yesterday.

"I didn't see it coming. I'll tell you that. Ethel Burrows doesn't seem smart enough to pull off a heist right under her husband's and the sheriff's noses."

Natasha froze in her steps, her bare hand wrapped around

the cold metal of the handle on the door to the diner. What had she just heard?

"Never underestimate the power of sex," the other ranch hand said.

Both men started laughing.

Natasha let go of the handle, balled her hand in a fist, and stuffed it in her coat pocket for warmth. Her cell phone was in the way. Reaching in her other pocket, she pulled out her gloves, put them on, then grabbed her hair and twisted it before stuffing it inside her coat. She looked around, searching for a good spot to stand, listen, and not be overly obvious.

"I heard she lost all the money, though. Doesn't the sheriff have it as evidence?"

"Evidence to what? It doesn't have anything to do with that murder. I heard she's already down there signing paperwork to have it all turned over to her, or Trinity Ranch, as I'm sure she'll tell him. She's picking up her lover boy while she's down there."

Natasha's eyes damn near bugged out of her head. There was nowhere to hide. She pressed her back against the side of the building, looked down, and hoped she appeared to be waiting for someone before going inside. The two men didn't appear to notice her as they continued.

"I don't get women. She goes to all this trouble to snag fifty grand when her husband is worth ten times that much, at least. Why would she run off with some penniless ranch hand when she has the master of the ranch wrapped around her finger?"

"Ethel Piney, or Pope, or Burrows, call her what you want, is addicted to the adventure of it all, not to the catch. Trust me. She'll take off with that King fellow and drop him like a hot potato before winter is out. I'll bet my next paycheck on it. Within a year she'll be married to some millionaire and doing his butler." Again both men laughed. "But I'll tell you one thing: she's getting the hell out of Dodge before the fireworks do go off. Carl Williams' murder was just a cover for the real crime on that ranch. I know I won't be around when the wrath comes down on Jim Burrows. If he weren't so goo-goo eyed for his wife he'd see the danger for himself. His death will make everyone quit talking about Carl, the poor boy. He didn't deserve to get caught in the middle of all that rage."

A cover for the true crime going down out at the ranch? Hadn't her father said something very similar? Natasha stumbled away from the diner, reached in her pocket for her phone, and raced across the street to her Avalanche, not bothering to see if anyone was watching her or not.

Trent picked up his phone on the first ring. "Oakley," he grunted. It was only noon and already felt as if it should be well after five.

"Trent, this is Helen Pratt over at the Nugget."

Trent leaned against his desk, rested his forehead on his free hand, and forced himself to sound civil. He wasn't in the mood to talk to anyone right now.

"What can I do for you, Helen?" he asked.

"I'm sorry to bother you. I was taking out the trash behind the diner and overheard Ricky Post and Morgan Reeding talking. I wouldn't have given it a thought, but it's not every day you see a Trinity ranch hand having a casual conversation with the son of the owner of Excelsior Ranch."

"True," he said slowly, but straightened. "Is everything okay?"

"I don't think so, Sheriff." Helen began telling him about the conversation she'd just overheard. "Now I swear by every word of that," she finished.

Trent was already up, pacing the length of his office.

"I'll swear on a Bible," she went on.

"I believe you." If only he knew who was bringing in this trouble. It made his job damn hard when his target was the most prominent man in the county and Trent didn't have a clue what direction the first shot would be coming from.

"There's one more thing." Helen sighed. "If I'm out of line I'll apologize, but I don't think I am. Natasha King overheard this conversation, too."

Trent wasn't able to hold back a spew of profanity as he gripped his phone hard enough to break it. "Where is she now?"

"I'm not sure," Helen said quietly. "She was about to come inside the diner, I think. I didn't notice her until I finished eavesdropping and hurried inside to call you. I guess she was alongside the building, because she took off running across the street toward Pearl's. But Trent, Ricky Post and Morgan Reeding saw her, too. I overheard Morgan tell Ricky not to worry about it, and that he'd take care of it. When Natasha pulled out from behind Pearl's, which was just as I was calling you, Morgan followed her in one of the work trucks."

"Which way was she headed?"

"Toward Trinity Ranch."

"Thank you, Helen."

"You're welcome, and Trent?"

"Yes?"

"I've heard the gossip all morning on my shift. Don't play hard-ass with her. I've known you all my life and I know how you are. Natasha will forgive you about her papa. I liked her. Just don't be your usual bullheaded aggressive self."

"Uh, thanks."

"Now of course, if I'm wrong, I am available this Saturday night," she added sweetly.

Trent was already grabbing his coat. "Thanks for calling, Helen."

"That's what I thought," she said again, and hung up.

Something told him Natasha wouldn't call and fill him in, not this time, not when he'd done the one thing she would view as unforgivable. He'd done his job, though, and with no regrets. It hadn't surprised him a bit when Ethel Burrows had sauntered in this morning, her lawyer in tow, and escorted George King out of there.

Trent had learned what he'd needed to know the night before. George had no desire to go to prison for a crime he didn't commit. The man might be a shitty father, but there was good inside him. Trent hadn't been surprised. Natasha wouldn't have persisted as much as she had to prove her father's innocence if he were a jackass.

George was on the run, but as Trent had started to suspect, King wasn't running from him as much as from the people who'd set him up, made him their scapegoat, and threatened to expose him to Burrows as his wife's lover if he said a word. The man faced murder charges, or the end of a shotgun pointed up his nose. That was about enough to make any man run.

It had been almost one in the morning when George finally told Trent the entire truth, how Pat O'Reilly had killed Carl, enraged by Carl being loved so much by their father and Pat barely acknowledged as blood. George had the incredible misfortune of witnessing O'Reilly torturing Carl Williams. The younger boy didn't stand a chance against the fury and bitterness that had built up in O'Reilly over the years.

George King had done what any sane man would have done. He stepped in, told O'Reilly to leave the boy alone. But King hadn't suspected the depths of O'Reilly's hatred toward Carl, the illegitimate son who was favored. O'Reilly had gone ballistic, slicing and dicing Williams until the boy collapsed. Then O'Reilly turned his rage on King.

Trent bought most of King's story about the fight that followed. King admitted not being as young as he once was, and although the months on the ranch had helped get him in shape, he was on the defensive from the beginning, and he hadn't been armed. King showed Trent the knife wounds he'd endured during the fight. All of them superficial, bandaged and allowed to heal on their own. King didn't think going to the hospital would have been in his favor considering the circumstances.

He'd explained the direction of the fingerprints, too, showing Trent how once O'Reilly got the better of King, Williams had come to and started moaning. King tried pushing O'Reilly away, but the man had gone insane. King wasn't sure where the hunting knife was that O'Reilly had used but suspected O'Reilly either still had it on him or had ditched it somewhere on the ranch property. The man was all over that land. He could have lost it anywhere.

Trent had recorded King's statement, and it was a tape he hoped he didn't have to listen to again anytime soon. King had explained how, in an epitome of rage, babbling insanities about how the loyal Burrows would win in the end and there would no longer be favoritism bought and sold as if it were an item on a grocery store shelf. O'Reilly had decapitated Williams. King admitted he'd damn near puked. He wasn't sure how he lived through that night, but he'd lost enough blood, was weak from fighting, and didn't have the strength left to stop O'Reilly when the man had dragged King over to Williams' body, tossed him on top of the corpse, then used King as a shield, dragging him across the yard with King's arms and hands wrapped around the corpse. That was how King's fingerprints were on Williams and not O'Reilly's. It amazed both King and Trent how someone so incredibly out of his head could still be so shrewd to avoid being pegged to the murder.

Trent had taken King to his house, put him up in the guest room; then the two men had arrived at the station early enough to be there when Ethel pranced in. Helen had called right after Ethel had left.

Trent hurried to his Suburban, pulled out his light bar, and slapped it on the roof. Then hauling ass out of town, he prayed he would be in time to stop Natasha from storming right into the middle of a vicious feud, one that was about to blow up in quite a few people's faces.

Chapter Nineteen

Natasha pushed the truck around the curves, daring to take them faster than was probably safe for her or the Avalanche. She plotted her plan as she drove, deciding the best she could do was warn Jim Burrows. Natasha had overheard too many times now that he was going to end up dead. And it sounded as if it was going to happen very soon. Even if he didn't believe her, or brushed her off as the little lady who possibly wouldn't have all her facts straight, it might buy him enough time and prevent whoever planned on killing him from doing so.

She'd already decided she wouldn't say anything about Ethel. Jim wouldn't believe her if she did. The man adored his wife. God only knew why. Ethel might lack scruples, but it didn't sound as if she were really guilty of anything other than greed and adultery.

Her phone rang. Natasha glanced at it and sent it to voice mail.

"He knows," she whispered, staring at Trent's number before dropping the phone on the passenger seat. Natasha grabbed the steering wheel with both hands as she took a curve too quickly. Hitting the brakes, she forced her heart to quit pounding.

"Damn, Trent, you're endangering my driving." Why not

blame him for her not slowing down in time for a sharp curve?

One of Trinity Ranch's work trucks came up behind her, and she continued gripping the steering wheel with both hands, shooting wary looks at her rearview mirror. The men she overheard were ranch hands. Were the two men she overheard behind her? If they pulled into the ranch behind her, they would want to know why she was there.

Maybe peeling out of the bed-and-breakfast hadn't been her smartest move. In a town like Weaverville, where tension was already running high, the new city girl in town hightailing out of the local bed-and-breakfast might have drawn attention she didn't need. Why did she always figure out the right way to do detective work after the fact? If she didn't learn how to do things right the first time, it might possibly cost her her life. Her heart began thumping in her chest so hard that she had difficulty breathing. Moving her grip on the steering wheel as her hands grew sweaty and continually checking out her rearview and side mirrors were going to distract her even more from driving on these curves.

Natasha wasn't sure if she should slow and see if the truck would pass her, or speed up to get to the ranch before whoever was in that truck got there. She rounded another corner, then tightened her grip on the wheel when the work truck roared up from behind her. It blew passed her as soon as the road straightened.

She exhaled loudly, then tried catching her breath. Of course whoever was driving that truck would know this road like the back of their hand. Her heart barely had time to return to beating normally when another vehicle came up behind her. This one didn't look like he planned on passing.

"God, calm down. Just calm down." Natasha glared at flashing red lights in her rearview mirror.

Trent turned on his siren and accelerated, coming right up on her ass. She had half a mind to slam on the brakes. Fortunately, the rational side of her brain knew it would be stupid to damage her uncle's truck or Trent's Suburban. Trent pulled up alongside Natasha, the outrage in his face obvious. He thumbed to the side of the road and narrowed in on her.

She slowed, letting out a long list of expletives as she did. Trent pulled out ahead but didn't pass her. Instead he herded her in, slowing his Suburban as she slowed the Avalanche until finally she pulled off on the side of the road and stopped.

Trent leapt out of his truck and took long, angry strides toward her.

He grabbed her door handle, yanked open the truck's door, reached in, and pulled her out of the truck as if she were nothing more than a rag doll.

"Are you out of your mind?" he shouted.

Natasha braced herself, which took several steps to do, then spun around, angrier than she'd ever been in her life.

"Who the hell do you think you are?" she demanded, yanking her arm from his grasp so it burned. Then turning on him with both her hands fisted at her side, she got right in his face. "If you ever manhandle me in public again, I promise I will kick your ass whether anyone is watching or not. Also, abuse your rights as sheriff and pull me off the road, and you very well might regret it." She was so mad she was shaking.

Trent stiffened and for a moment seemed taken aback when she spewed outrage at him, but then his eyes darkened until they were almost black. He narrowed them, pressed his lips together, and looked like one of the most dangerous enemies she'd ever encountered as he stalked toward her.

"I'm the sheriff around here."

His tone created an ugly knot in her stomach.

"That doesn't give you the right."

"Like it or not, I'm going to protect you from walking into a situation where you could easily get killed."

Natasha was shaking her head before he finished. "I won't ask what you know or think you know about my business, but—"

"I also think I want to make your business my business."

"I'm sure you do," Natasha shot back. She was pissed and didn't want distractions, like thinking about what he might have meant by what he just said. "But you are so stubborn, so bullheaded, you can't see that I'm capable of taking care of myself. So let me make it clear as glass for you, right now. I'm a big girl, Sheriff. So back off! I know what I'm doing and no one is going to die today because I couldn't get to them in time to warn them."

His expression shifted. There was a tic in his jaw. Apparently, Trent didn't have a lot of people who challenged him. More than likely he had always dated docile, submissive doormats. Well, if he hadn't figured it out yet, she would never be docile or submissive.

"I mean it, Trent. Back off. Go find some pretty little thing who will jump every time you demand it. I am not the one."

"Yes, you are."

"What?"

"You're the one."

Natasha suddenly couldn't catch her breath. She was light-headed. But if he saw her defenses were down, he'd move in and strike.

"What do you mean?" she asked, taking a step backward when he moved closer.

Trent continued closing in on her. Natasha moved toward the back of her truck and paused when she glimpsed a view of the mountains on the horizon.

"Spending the evening with your father last night was a real eye-opener."

Natasha turned around, immediately prepared to defend her dad. She'd done it all her life and the words were there without giving them thought.

Trent put his finger over her lips. "He's one hell of a guy."

She sensed there was a lot more Trent could say but held back. He was right. Her father was one hell of a guy. He had major faults, too.

"Getting to know him explains a lot about his daughter."

"Oh yeah?"

"Yes." Trent's hands moved to her arms.

Natasha wasn't sure when he'd trapped her between the driver's side and his body. But she was suddenly aware of every virile muscle in Trent's hard-as-steel body pressed against her. Trent let go of one arm, gripped her chin, and tilted her head back so she stared into the molten-lava heat smoldering in his eyes.

"I've never met anyone like you before." His voice was raspy.

If Trent had thought about more than whether her father was guilty or innocent last night, she wanted to hear what he might say. Anything to help her understand why he was driving her crazy with need and just as bad with irritation. He'd chosen one hell of a time to share his feelings with her. If she didn't get out to Trinity Ranch soon, someone might die.

"You say I'm stubborn and bullheaded." He began shaking his head, as a smile lit up his eyes. "You were hauling ass out to Jim Burrows' to inform him his life was in danger. More than likely, somewhere in that willful brain of yours you knew he wouldn't listen to you. But did you call for backup? Did you call me?"

Natasha opened her mouth to defend her actions. She knew exactly where he was going with this. Trent plowed forward before she could say a word.

"No, you didn't. And why didn't you? Because you're pissed off at me."

She started to agree with him.

Trent didn't give her a chance. "You're mad as hell that I push you, that I tell you what to do, that I don't appear to be acknowledging that you're fully capable of defending yourself as well as any one person can."

"I'm glad it's finally sunk in." Natasha focused on his eyes and her insides quickened. "Did someone tell you I was going to Trinity Ranch? Do you think it's smarter to stop me than to go out there?" she asked, narrowing her gaze on his and fighting the swelling deep in her womb at the same time.

God, he was so damn sexy.

"Both," he said easily, his voice softening. His features relaxed, too. "And no."

"What?"

"I'm saving your ass," he growled. "Because I don't want you shot, or worse. I want you to stay around."

"Stay around?"

"Yes, damn it. With me. Here. Stay with me, Natasha."

She blinked. When had his face softened, his hands moved to cup her cheeks, and his beautiful eyes filled with passion so deep it terrified her?

"I know what you're feeling," he whispered.

"What's that?"

"You're scared. I'm pulling at emotions you have refused to use before."

"You think so?" She tried making a face at him but wasn't sure admitting yet that she was no longer mad would be in her favor. Hell, she didn't know what to do. That started getting her angry all over again.

Then he laughed, a deep baritone sound that sent shivers rushing over her skin.

"Sweetheart. You've fought all your life. Fought for attention, fought for your place in the world. Fighting comes easy to you. But loving, that is a very different story. And I want you to try loving me."

All the weight she thought had lifted from her chest suddenly swelled in her throat. Her cheeks burned. No matter how she tried, she couldn't catch her breath. Finally, Natasha shoved against him, her hands instantly tingling when she pressed them against his warm, hard body. Even with his T-shirt covering his broad chest, she still felt every finely tuned curve and bulge from all the muscles in his body.

Trent took a step back and dropped his hands. His expression was impossible to read.

"I don't know why you have to bring this up right now," she said, exasperated. Looking at him messed with her head, but dragging her attention elsewhere, even toward the breathtaking view of the mountains, seemed impossible to do.

"It seemed the perfect time to me." Trent had a terrible habit of moving too fast.

He had her in his arms and captured her mouth with his

before his words sank in. Natasha took only a moment to re-act. And even then, it was shock.

Love?

What the hell? Did Trent want her to consider moving here?

Nothing made sense. Trent kissed her with a savage hunger, leaning her backward, and impaling her mouth as if one day had been the worst of tortures to go without kissing her.

It took her a minute to realize how she clung to him. Her fingers pressed against corded muscle that flexed under her touch. She moved her tongue around his, craving every bit he offered her. Even then, it wasn't enough. Natasha wanted to rip his clothes from his body, press him up against the side of the truck, and leap into his arms, both of them naked, and make love until they didn't have an ounce of strength left in their bodies.

A car drove by and honked twice. Natasha leapt backward, her lips swollen as she bent over, fighting for her breath. She tried figuring out what had happened, other than just being busted in the sheriff's arms, all their limbs twisted around each other, embraced in a kiss that possibly borderlined on illegal.

"I'll hear about that one," Trent muttered.

He was watching her when she slowly straightened. He watched her as if he waited to see if she would attack angrily or beg for more.

"Jim Burrows," she said as the fog lifted from her brain. "We can discuss this later. I need to talk to Jim Burrows." On an afterthought and because kissing Trent appealed to her a lot more than fighting with him, she added, "Come with me."

Trent grabbed her car door before she could close it. "Head back into town," he said.

"But—"

"It's pointless for you to run out to the ranch right now. You were spotted leaving Pearl's like a bat out of hell right after Reeding and Post had their conversation. They were following you because I trailed them. They aren't going to do anything right now. They aren't sure if their conversation was overheard or not, so they'll lay cool for a bit. But I have their names and can take it from here.

"I'm going to call Jim right now, ask him to meet me over at my place. I'll let him know it's serious and I want him alone. That should work. He knows how hard it is to have a conversation without ears listening out at the ranch."

"You want me to talk to him at your house? Do you know what I am going to say to him?"

"Helen from the diner called. She overheard Reeding and Post talking behind the Nugget, too."

"Too?"

He nodded, suddenly appearing all business. "The truck that passed you before I pulled you over was Morgan Reeding, the foreman over at Trinity Ranch. He pulled out of the Nugget parking lot after you accelerated on the highway and followed you. If Helen knew you overheard Reeding and Post talking, they might have spotted you as well."

"Their returning to the ranch isn't proof they knew I was there.

"Could have been," Trent said slowly. "Fortunately, we don't have to find out."

"Call Jim," she pressed. She still worried Burrows was in danger. "This is urgent, Trent. If she told you what they said accurately, then you should know that."

"Turn around. I'll follow you back and call him while I'm driving."

"Are U-turns legal here?"

Something glistened in his eyes. "I'll cuff you later," he growled.

"Only if I can cuff you, too," she said in as sweet of a tone as she could master.

Trent hung up the phone after talking to Ethel. Jim was out on the north end of the ranch, dealing with bulls' breaking down the fences.

"Apparently, Trinity Ranch females are just too irresistible to resist," she'd purred into Trent's ear.

Trent grunted, not really caring if he offended her. Ethel was something else, and seeing how Jim Burrows babied her was enough to make Trent want to puke. He told her to have Jim get ahold of him, then hung up. Natasha parked at his house and he intentionally blocked her in.

"What did he say? Is he on his way?" she asked when Trent got out of his Suburban.

She had her coat tightly wrapped around her and her hands stuffed deep in her pockets. Natasha hadn't seemed to notice the cold when they'd been standing out alongside the highway, which he would feel safe to say was at least five to ten degrees colder than it was right here with his house and surrounding evergreens blocking the wind.

"I didn't reach him," he admitted, holding his phone in his hand as he pushed his door closed with his body. "Apparently, he's got bulls breaking down the fence again."

"Do you think he's safe out there?"

Trent almost laughed. Natasha looked really worried. Heading toward her and the porch steps, he placed his hand on her back and guided her to the house.

"Burrows is a lot safer out on his land than he would be if he were up closer to the ranch house. It's open land out there, impossible to sneak up on a man. Not to mention, Burrows is always armed, hand gun on his side and shot gun in his truck." He added, mostly for Natasha's benefit, "Burrows might be an even better shot than me."

He saw her smile, but Natasha was clever enough to wrap her mind around a potential trap. She'd overheard a hell of a lot of disturbing information, if Helen had told it all to him accurately.

"Why don't you tell me exactly what you heard Reeding and Post say to each other?" He fished out his house key and unlocked the front door.

Natasha looked up at him when he pushed the door open and stood to the side for her to enter. "I thought you said Helen, the waitress, told you what they said."

"She did." He saw the skepticism on Natasha's face and wondered if she trusted anyone in her world. Since he'd spoken from the heart out on the side of the highway, mentioning love, something he was still baffled as hell that he'd managed to spit out, he'd take the initiative in showing her what all it entailed. "And Helen is a pretty observant person. She's given me tips before on crimes by overhearing customers talk."

"Sounds like an incredible resource," Natasha said dryly.

Trent walked around her, sliding out of his coat and tossing it on the chair by his front door. "She is. But it wouldn't hurt to hear you share what you heard. Hopefully both stories will match."

She nodded. "You're right. I'd ask for the same thing," she admitted, slipped out of her coat, and tossed it on top of his before he could take it from her and hang it up. Natasha tugged on her sweater.

Goddamn. She wasn't wearing a bra. Damn good thing he didn't know that out on the highway. Especially since a couple of Post's ranch hands had driven by and honked. Trent had never run his hands under her coat. If he had and discovered she was braless, he would have had a hard time stopping. As it was now, part of him didn't want to talk shop; he wanted to fuck her until the two of them had forgotten about the rest of the world.

Trent did an about-face and headed to his kitchen, needing a clear head. "I need coffee. Want some?"

"Sure." She followed him into the kitchen and made herself at home at the table, picking at the newspaper before telling him what she heard. "I'd planned on getting a bite to eat at the Nugget earlier, and had my hand on the door, when I heard them talking. I heard a man say he never would have thought Ethel was smart enough to pull off such a heist right under her husband's nose."

"They were talking about the things she stole out of Nellie's grave."

Natasha looked up at him, shocked. "How do you know that?"

"Your father knew a lot more than he told you." Trent scooped fresh coffee into the coffee maker, just the smell of it helping to clear his head.

"And you just happened to know that when you decided

to haul him in like a common criminal?" The sarcasm in her voice wasn't missed.

Trent had expected getting his ass chewed for bringing in George, although he didn't regret it for a moment. "Tell me what you heard at the Nugget," he pushed, veering her back to what she overheard at the diner.

Natasha made a humphing sound and Trent was glad he had his back to her. After pouring the water in the coffeemaker, he watched it percolate for a minute as Natasha told him what she'd overheard. The grin she'd put on his face over her feisty nature faded as he listened.

"Wait a minute." He turned around and Natasha looked up from where she'd been slowly turning the pages of the paper.

"I found it rather interesting that they knew my dad was being released and no one bothered to tell me about it."

She stuck her lower lip out and Trent almost forgot what he was going to say. He rubbed his forehead, forcing his head to stay clear and not imagine those hot, pouty lips wrapped around his cock. The sooner he fucked her silly, the better he would be at his job; he was sure of it. Natasha was a dangerous distraction.

"That's because I hadn't released him at that point, nor was anyone in town even aware he was there until less than an hour before Helen at the diner called me." Trent turned back to the coffee, willing it to brew faster. There was something here, something in what Natasha had just said.

"Are you suggesting someone watched you bring him in last night?" Natasha asked. But then she snapped her finger and pointed it at him. "I know. The entire town pegs my father as a murderer, but the moment you haul him in everyone knows you'll let him go because they know he didn't do it."

"Not everyone. We knew he didn't do it."

" 'We?' "

"Yes. We," he repeated, and walked up to bop her on the nose.

Natasha slapped at his hand, but Trent grabbed her wrist, pulled her hand to his mouth, and kissed the back of it. Natasha's eyes grew brighter as she watched him, her mouth puckering into a small, tight circle.

It took more than a little strength to keep all the blood in his body from draining straight into his cock. "And apparently at least a few others knew he wasn't the murderer, and knew I'd release him once Ethel lawyered him up."

Trent liked holding her hand to his mouth. It forced her to sit up straight, arch her back, and tilt backward just enough to make her sweater stretch over her full, round breasts.

"Do you think those two I overheard already knew who the killer was?"

"Your father knew."

"My dad told me he killed Carl," she said under her breath.

Trent wondered when George had told Natasha that. Obviously, it wasn't information she'd seen fit to share with him before now. If she asked, he would share the details her father had told him, but if not, they weren't details Trent cared to dwell on any more than necessary and he certainly didn't want the images King had planted in his brain also in Natasha's.

"If O'Reilly bragged about killing Carl, then others know." Trent needed more than one man telling him. Although he believed George and had already put in for a search warrant to comb through the ranch hands' bunks for that hunting knife. He'd searched the grounds after the murder but not anyone's living quarters. At the time, he hadn't thought of the Burrowses or their ranch hands as suspects. He hadn't had any suspects.

Trent had decided to lay low for part of the day and see what O'Reilly might try doing. However, if others knew or were in on it somehow, what might be in it for them? Had someone motivated O'Reilly to kill Williams? The rage and extreme methods used did almost seem beyond O'Reilly's simpleminded MO.

"So we need to go out to that ranch and start talking to people."

Trent let go of her hand reluctantly. The smell of brewing

coffee called to him. He would go out to the ranch with the search warrant. Trent had a few good men, locals he knew he could trust, and had called them already to put some feelers out. Two of them worked out at the ranch. They would text him the moment they heard or saw anything strange or if O'Reilly disappeared. It wasn't foolproof. Trinity Ranch was over a thousand acres, and men could work out there all day and not see every ranch hand until they met for the evening meal. Trent had to play his cards right, though. There were two crimes happening here, and if all went well he'd be making more than one arrest very soon.

He poured two cups of coffee, then brought one over to Natasha as she finished telling him about the conversation she'd overheard.

"I remember they said there was fifty thousand in cash and we counted forty thousand." She accepted the mug and blew on it, looking up at him.

"Interesting bit of trivia Jim Burrows mentioned to me before you two ladies joined us in his den," Trent said, and sipped the steaming coffee. He embraced the burn, willed the fumes to go straight to his brain and keep his head clear. "He told me he'd always wondered, if Nellie's grave were ever found, and there was actually cash buried with her, that if the individual bills had been printed long enough ago, they very well could be worth more than their face value."

"Like a fifty might be worth sixty dollars?"

"Something like that. I think it depends on the year they were printed. But if any of the bills happened to be predepression era, then yes, they would definitely be worth more."

"So how do you know?"

"Research." He shrugged.

Natasha studied him for a moment and he swore he saw her brain wrapping around what he'd just told her, digesting it, and kicking out the obvious hypothesis.

"Did you give Ethel back the cash?"

"Turned over forty thousand dollars, just as her lawyer had worked up in his paperwork."

"Did it happen to be the same forty thousand dollars we

found in the cabin and in the safe-deposit box?" Already she was smiling.

"Old bills pretty much look the same."

Natasha put her cup on the table and jumped out of her seat. "You knew she planned on running away with that cash."

"It wasn't exactly my idea. Sweetheart, I hate to tell you this, but I don't have forty grand I can use to swap with old bills that might, or might not, be worth more. Although the fact that they were buried with someone's ancestor, during a time of so much heated dispute between two ranches, kind of makes that cash worth more right there."

"Jim Burrows asked you to swap out the money."

She stood too close. Trent let that be the reason. He took a gulp of his coffee, staring at her over the rim, and watched her watch him. She was still figuring it all out. He hadn't decided yet if he'd tell her how much he loved watching her brainstorm, especially when her entire face suddenly glowed when it all connected in her mind.

"Jim Burrows knew his wife planned on running off with my dad," she said, looking at Trent to see if she was right.

Trent put his coffee cup on the table with hers and moved in, sitting down and trapping her with her legs straddled on either side of his.

"A good man knows all the secrets of his woman," he murmured, then pulled her on his lap and kissed her before she could accuse him of thinking women were property.

Natasha groaned or possibly tried talking into his mouth. Trent really didn't care. He pressed past her lips, tasting the warm coffee on her as he began devouring her. This time he had no intention of stopping or holding back the desire he'd had building inside of him since the last time he'd made love to her.

Even when she'd pissed him off yesterday, going on about him being too bossy and aggressive and suggesting he couldn't handle the same from her, Trent knew he wouldn't stay angry with her. It dawned on him, and maybe her father suggesting as much might have had something to do with it, that Natasha had always dated *safe* men. That is, men she

could control, who would do as she said. Which of course had
never satisfied her. They had been safe ground for her. Natasha would never fall for a man like that.

George King had said straight up that he'd seen how his
daughter looked at Trent. Trent did push her, and he planned
to continue doing so. She would get pissed. They would
probably have some doozies of fights. But she wouldn't fall
in love with a man who didn't challenge her.

"This is coming off," he whispered against her cheek,
and began lifting her sweater over her breasts.

He felt her full, soft skin and a brush of her hard nipples
when Natasha pulled her head back a few inches to focus on
his face.

"Take your own clothes off," she said, the orneriness in
her expression beyond adorable.

"I think you should."

"Country boy thinks a woman should do all the work."
But already she was yanking at his T-shirt, unbuttoning his
pants, and doing her best to get him undressed without moving off him.

"Not all of it." He made decent work of pulling her sweater
off her but then stood and moved faster than he had in ages to
get out of his boots and shed his jeans.

Natasha did the same, and when he looked up from his
task and saw her standing in his kitchen naked there was no
controlling the unbearable pressure that wrapped around his
dick and balls.

"You're so incredibly beautiful," he whispered, his voice
raw with emotions he wasn't sure she was ready to hear.

Trent had already decided she would start hearing how
he believed he was falling in love with her. It would take her
some getting used to, and there were the demographics to
figure out. None of that bothered him, though.

"Come here." He wrapped his hands around her narrow
waist and lifted her, then again he sat in the chair.

"Find time to put another condom in your wallet?"

He'd even managed to pull his wallet out and place it on

the table before his jeans hit the floor. Natasha moved over him, straddling his legs, her breasts in his face and the heat from her pussy damn near suffocating him from the cock up.

It impressed him that he was able to slide the package out of his wallet, rip it open with his teeth, and pull the latex free from its wrapper. When Natasha took it from him, kept her gaze locked with his, and pressed it against his cock, then slowly began sheathing him, he was pretty sure his eyes rolled back in his head.

"My woman has skills," he groaned.

"Your woman?"

He blinked, fought to focus on her. "Yeah, I think so. My woman."

"You'll never own me," she purred, her fingers gliding up and down the length of his shaft.

"Don't want to own you," he said, and let his head fall back, stopping only when he hit the wall behind him. "Just want you with me always."

"Always?"

"Always."

Natasha pressed her cool palms against his cheeks and he lifted his head, watching her. She moved closer, nipping at his lower lip, and sank down on him, filling herself with his dick.

"Always," she whispered, and moaned.

Chapter Twenty

Natasha stepped out of the shower and dried off, then climbed into clean clothes and pulled her hair loose from the makeshift bun she'd put it in when she'd hopped into rinse off.

"I could go for another cup of coffee, sound good?" she called out, staring at herself through the steamed-over mirror and contemplating putting more makeup on. In spite of taking her time that morning to carefully apply her makeup, thinking at the time if she ran into Trent she would give him an eyeful of what he would not be getting, none of it was left on her face now.

She'd known in the back of her head, buried under her seething outrage at Trent for taking her dad into custody, she wouldn't stay mad at him. Natasha admitted when she'd left the bed-and-breakfast she had really hoped to see him. And now all these words he was throwing at her.

And what was she doing? The normal practice was to run for the hills the first time any man started saying the *l* word.

"Maybe it's because you're already in the hills," she said to her steamed-over reflection, then grinned. Damn. She really felt good. "Do you have a game plan all figured out?" she called out, heading back toward the kitchen.

Trent wasn't there. "Trent?" she called out, turning and retracing her steps, checking his living room, his bedroom, and even the other rooms in his house. It was a large ranch house, obviously too big for one bachelor. It was the house his father had bought when he'd married Trent's mother and apparently had hoped for a larger family. Instead two men had lived here, one raising the other, both of them men on their own. "Trent?" she called, yelling this time. "Where the hell are you?"

The house was suddenly way too quiet.

Natasha marched into the living room, noticed his coat wasn't underneath hers, and yanked open the front door. Trent's Suburban was no longer parked out front.

Natasha wanted to scream.

"You son of a bitch," she hissed. "Where did you go?"

Hurrying into the kitchen and to her purse and cell phone, Natasha downed the rest of the coffee and grabbed her things. If he thought he would make her stay here while he went and solved this case on his own, he would damn well learn otherwise real soon. That's when she spotted the note on the table.

I know you're pissed.

"Damn straight I am," she growled at the piece of loose-leaf paper that appeared to have been torn from a spiral notebook. She picked it up, tearing the many loose paper pieces off the edge and letting them fall to the table as she kept reading.

My forensics team in Redding just called and confirmed the stains on the clothes you found in the cabin were blood, Carl Williams' blood. Pat O'Reilly's fingerprints and body sweat were also all over the clothes. You found the one piece of evidence that secured my warrant. Thank you, sweetheart.

" 'Thank you'?" she muttered, her anger simmering over inside her until she began shaking. "Thank you?" she said louder. The notebook paper crinkled as her fingers clenched into fists.

Putting it on the table, she smoothed it out and read the rest of the note.

> *You're going to try and follow me. So I've tempo-*
> *rarily disabled your Avalanche. You can kick my ass*
> *later, Natasha, but at least you'll be alive to do it.*
> *There is a conspiracy going on over at Trinity Ranch*
> *and you're not going to race into the middle of it over*
> *the excitement of making a bust.*
>
> *I understand your adrenaline. Trust me, I do. I*
> *know how good it feels when the pieces come together*
> *and you figure it all out. Honestly, I wouldn't have it*
> *all pieced together so neatly if it weren't for you.*
>
> *If I'd had time I would have talked this out with*
> *you. I would have explained why there are times when*
> *you simply can't be part of things. I know when you*
> *calm down you'll understand.*
> *Your man,*
> *Trent*

Natasha held up the piece of paper and stared at the final two words before his signature. He'd started to write something else, then changed the letters. It looked as if he'd turned the *l* into a *y*. The *o* wasn't touched. But he'd gone over the *u* as well. Had he started to write *Love,* then changed his mind? Instead he wrote: *Your man.*

"Any man of mine wouldn't treat me like this." She glared at the note, balled it up in her fist, and threw it down on the table. Then ignoring what he'd said in the letter, she grabbed her things and hurried out the front door, although she didn't lock it just in case.

The Avalanche wouldn't start.

"You jerk!" she yelled, and slammed her hands down on the truck.

Natasha didn't feel the cold when she stood outside her truck, staring in the direction of Trinity Ranch. Did Trent seriously think he could make love to her, say all those words that had twisted her brain around into a confused state of mush, then simply leave her to go play sheriff? What did he think she would do, stay here and bake cookies and have them warm on a plate when he returned?

Natasha snorted and kicked the ground hard enough with her boot her big toe stung. Embracing the pain, she pulled out her cell and called him. It rang as she marched up the porch steps but then went to voice mail.

"Damn you." She had half a mind to leave a threatening message, informing him no man treated her this way. Hadn't he forgotten to chain her to his bed? "Damn you," she cursed again.

The pain quickly outweighed the anger. Trent had told her he loved her. He said things that made it sound as if he truly knew her. His words had worked magic, made her believe she might have actually found the one. But then to do this!

"It's just as well," she murmured, and a wave of eerie calm sank into her gut. "Thank you, Sheriff Trent Oakley, for showing me your true colors."

He was a good man, she decided, relishing how clear her mind suddenly was. He had all the qualities needed to make a wonderful lover. Natasha didn't doubt for a moment he would be loyal, make any woman proud to stand by his side, and he would honor and adore his woman until death parted them.

There was one catch with Mr. Perfect, she realized, once again standing in his kitchen and deciding she would drink the rest of his coffee. Trent had said it himself.

His woman.

She'd actually started to believe those words sounded magical when she'd rinsed off in the shower. Her heart had embraced the thought of being wanted, cherished, loved, and adored. She'd overlooked one minor catch.

Possessed.

Trent wanted to own her. Making her his woman apparently also meant he believed he had final say over her actions.

"It's equal all the way or nothing, sweetheart," she said, staring at the crumpled-up note.

Natasha sipped her coffee, slowly pacing his kitchen. There had to be a plan B. There was always a plan B. Remaining here until he returned and put the truck back together was not an option.

She paused at the counter, stared out the window at the backyard, then slowly began to laugh. Plan B was staring her in the face.

"Well, Sheriff Oakley," she said, putting her coffee mug in the sink, then picking it back up, rinsing it out, finding his cup on the table, doing the same, then on an afterthought grabbing his note and brushing the pieces of paper she'd torn into her hand. She threw them away, glanced around, and restacked the newspaper she'd spread around his kitchen table earlier.

Was that really all there was to Weaverville's newspaper?

Natasha grabbed her things, slid her coat on, hurried outside to the Avalanche, grabbed her gun out of the glove box, made sure it was loaded, then double-checked the safety before sliding it into her coat pocket. Then running back inside, she locked the front door, then rushed back through the house to the back door and let herself out.

"If you're going to be my man," she said as she made her way to the barn, "you're going to need quite a bit of training."

She was almost skipping with excitement when she saddled up Midnight, then mounted him. "Come on, boy; put some muscle into it. We've got bad guys to catch."

It probably wouldn't have taken as long to get to Trinity Ranch if she and Midnight had cut through meadows. Natasha wasn't sure who owned the land and she didn't want to get lost. They followed the highway, managing to stay within view of it, until she spotted the entrance to Trinity Ranch. Her heart pounded eagerly in her chest as she slowed Midnight, brought him to a stop, then leaned forward, rubbing his neck as she formed a game plan.

"Miss King, you've decided to join the party."

Natasha spun around on Midnight, twisting her torso and making the horse uneasy when she slid in the saddle at the sound of a woman's voice.

"I was seriously getting bored waiting for the fireworks to end so I could saunter in and claim my prize." Rebecca Burrows walked toward Natasha, a hunting rifle nestled at her shoulder and the long barrel pointed straight at Natasha. "Get off the horse. I have no desire to kill it. I will if I have to, though, so no tricks."

"You're going to kill your father." Natasha couldn't get her brain to shift gears fast enough. She'd been all hell-bent on leaving Midnight here where he'd be safe, hurrying across the highway, and sneaking onto the property until she found Trent. She'd gotten so excited imagining the look on his face when he learned he couldn't tie her to any bed, she obviously hadn't paid close enough attention to her surroundings. But now, as she saw Rebecca, her intentions were clear.

"My what?" Rebecca laughed. "Jim Burrows is no father. He's a slut!" she screamed. "And he cared more about his precious bastard son than my brothers. He chased them off, you know. By the time they were grown none of them gave a rat's ass about this ranch. Jim wanted it that way from the beginning. He wanted to give it all to that stupid bastard of his."

She'd moved closer until she was close enough to poke Midnight in the rear with the end of her rifle. He whinnied in protest, jumping to the side and staring at her with large, wild-looking eyes. Obviously, Midnight didn't like the looks of that shotgun any more than Natasha did.

"Get off the damned horse before I kill it out from underneath you," Rebecca ordered, her voice filled with maniacal coolness.

"Okay, okay," Natasha said, raising her hands in surrender before grabbing the reins. It had crossed her mind to order Midnight to haul ass. They would be across the highway in seconds and able to warn someone that Rebecca was hiding over here, armed and dangerous. Natasha didn't doubt for a moment that Rebecca would shoot Midnight. Natasha wouldn't risk the horse's life. "I'm getting down. Just keep that rifle away from him. He doesn't like it and you won't accomplish anything if he tramples you to death."

"I'm not dying today." Rebecca shook her head as she

spoke. There was enough humidity in the air to turn her hair into a headful of curls. They bounced as she adamantly denounced the idea of failing. "And I'm sure not going to prison. One good thing about bastards, they are so damn willing to fight, and kill, to gain even a small portion of what they think they deserve."

"You used Pat O'Reilly to do your dirty work." Natasha slid off Midnight, patting his side and hoping he wouldn't react to her panic.

"I didn't even know he was my half brother," Rebecca sneered. "Not until—" She broke off, not finishing her sentence.

Natasha released the reins. Trent had told her Midnight knew how to get home. Even if he happened to wander a bit before heading in that direction, someone might spot him. That would be an excellent red flag to draw attention to her predicament. Although the thought of Trent rescuing her left a foul taste in her mouth. Somehow she needed to talk her way through this on her own.

"Not until?" she prompted, needing to keep Rebecca talking.

Rebecca raised the rifle higher, and the long, narrow barrel stared Natasha straight in the eye. It was a one-eyed monster and one she had a hard time staring back at. She looked down, searching the ground around her, but then it hit her.

"You and Pat were going out," she whispered.

Rebecca tightened her grip on the rifle.

"Okay, it's cool. Like you said, you didn't know. He didn't know. And you're right: it is all your father's fault."

"Quit calling him that!" Rebecca screamed.

Natasha swore for a split second she saw her life flash before her eyes. It whirled past her in an array of colors, then exploded with a bright white light as all the scenes bombarded into one another. For a moment it knocked her equilibrium off.

"He destroyed our family. He destroyed Mom. That man is not family to me!" Rebecca snapped, the pain and betrayal filling her and turning her eyes a cold, steely shade. "Now move!" she demanded, gesturing with the rifle. "Oh, and just so you know." Her tone turned into a disgustingly, sweet sound, like a spoiled child, a very insane, crazed child. "That man you keep calling my father insisted me and my brothers and sister learn to shoot at a very early age." Her laughter was chilling. "Thanks to his insistence that we know how to hunt, and defend ourselves, I'm one hell of a damn good shot."

Natasha jumped when Rebecca prodded her with the gun. "Move," Rebecca demanded. "We're going to go pay dear papa a visit."

The two very large barns and the ranch house seemed oddly quiet when Rebecca urged Natasha forward at gunpoint. She walked behind Natasha, so Natasha couldn't see Rebecca's face, but the young woman kept mumbling under her breath, either talking to herself or arguing with herself. Natasha wasn't sure. Instead of trying to hear every word Rebecca said, Natasha darted her gaze across the property, searching for a sign of anyone. She didn't see a soul.

Odd, there weren't any vehicles around, either. Not Trent's Suburban, not a work truck, nothing. Had Trent driven to the far end of the ranch? If that was where everything was going down, it would explain why there weren't any ranch hands by the house. They probably all had hurried to witness the action once word traveled it was happening. Natasha wasn't sure how that word would get out, but she had faith in the power of gossip, even among men.

"Go inside." Rebecca had taken Natasha to a side door, more than likely the door she had always gone in and out of while growing up out here.

Natasha reached for the handle and turned it. It wasn't locked. She opened the door, pushing it hard enough to make it bang against a coatrack nailed to the wall adjacent to the door.

"Don't wake the dead," Rebecca snapped, whispering. She'd lowered her gun so it pointed to the floor and used her other hand to grab Natasha's arm and shove her forward.

Rebecca wouldn't know how well Natasha could fight. She glimpsed the younger woman through her side vision, with her curls windblown around her face. Natasha could kick that gun out of Rebecca's hand. It was cocked, though, and would easily fire if Natasha did.

"What are we doing in here?" Natasha also whispered. "Your—" She stopped, changed her wording. "Jim wouldn't be here. I think I heard he's fixing fences."

"He'll come home," Rebecca said sweetly, and pushed Natasha again.

They moved through the large, incredibly well-furnished home with all of its lavish possessions on display in every room. Natasha remembered Ethel telling her it took a year to make the house her own. She wondered how different it looked from the home Rebecca grew up in. Daring another side-glance, Natasha imagined the pain of seeing her home with another's woman touch imprinted all over it.

"This place is so gaudy." Natasha tried for the sympathy angle.

Rebecca snorted. "I don't give a damn about this house." The rage was too deep for her to see anything other than the end of her tunnel.

Natasha doubted Rebecca saw it through realistic eyes, though. There was no way this would end pretty.

A TV sounded from somewhere in the house, the ramblings of some overly dramatic soap opera adding to the uneasy setting. They moved into the kitchen and Natasha heard someone humming. This time she didn't bother with a discreet glance. Natasha turned and looked at Rebecca.

"What are you going to do?" Natasha asked, still whispering.

Rebecca grinned and by the look on her face she might have thought Natasha had asked her if she wanted to watch a good movie or play a board game. She looked absolutely delighted and incredibly calm.

"Do as I say and don't try and be a hero and I promise you'll walk out of this alive." Rebecca leaned into Natasha, and the faint smell of roses drifted around her. She'd taken care to make herself look nice and even dabbed on perfume for this event. "Cooperate fully and you might walk out of here a richer woman than you were before."

"Really?" Natasha asked.

Rebecca didn't seem to hear the sarcasm. "I promise," she said, nodding. Then without notice, she yelled, "Hey, whore! Get your ugly ass out here this fucking minute!" Rebecca's voice echoed off the walls.

Later Natasha would shake her head in disbelief. But Ethel came running out of one of several doors at the far end of the dining room/family room extension off the kitchen.

"Get out of my house, you little tramp!" Ethel screamed, and pointed a long, daggerlike pink-painted nail at Rebecca, seemingly unimpressed by the rifle aimed at her.

If Natasha screamed, she wouldn't ever admit it to a soul, but the explosion the rifle made when it was fired inside the house was deafening. Natasha did cover her ears and duck. When she straightened, Ethel was rolling on the ground, screaming loud enough Jim Burrows would probably hear her no matter where he was on his land.

"Oh my God!" Natasha yelled, feeling the strain in her throat.

The smell of the gun firing stunk but not as badly as the incredibly pungent odor that quickly filled the room. Natasha gagged when she raced over to Ethel.

"Put your hand on it. Stop the bleeding!" Natasha yelled over the shrill screaming.

"Leave her alone." Rebecca walked up next to Natasha and smiled as she stared down at Ethel. "Feel the pain, bitch. Roll in it. Wallow in it. Know what it feels like to hurt over every inch of your body."

Ethel responded by wailing, her screams slowly turning into hysterical tears.

"You're insane." Natasha didn't take time to think about what Rebecca might do next but ran around the long island in the kitchen and yanked a towel from the refrigerator handle. She hurried back to Ethel and slid to the floor next to her, fighting nausea from the stench of the blood and the open wound spewing blood from her leg.

Natasha pressed the towel on the wound and watched it quickly turn red. Looking away, she grabbed Ethel's hand, fought with her for only a moment when the woman tried pulling away to cover her face, which was where her other hand was. Makeup streamed from her eyes, which were squeezed shut. Natasha managed to press Ethel's hand over the wound.

"Keep your hand there. Don't move it," she instructed. "Do you hear me, Ethel?"

The woman kept crying loudly, her mouth opened wide, giving indication she might break into another screaming fit at any moment.

"I shot her upper thigh. It's a flesh wound." It was hard to hear Rebecca. "She will be fine. But I bet it does hurt like hell," she finished, and giggled. "Now, do you have your phone on you?"

"Yes," Natasha said, turning and looking up at Rachel. Natasha also had her gun on her and would use it if she had to but thought an upper kick to the side of the head would be a lot more satisfying.

"Stand up and get away from her. Do you really want your fingerprints all over her body?" Rebecca was still smiling. "Now, call Jim Burrows and inform him you've just shot his wife."

"What?" Natasha stood slowly. This was turning uglier and uglier by the minute. Rebecca was beyond gone in the head. She would do anything, kill, maim, or torture, to see through her sick, morbid plot. "I will not," she said flatly, facing Rebecca.

"You can't outsmart me," Rebecca told her smoothly. "No one has figured me out yet. The phone call to your office asking about your father." She rolled her eyes. "You have no room to talk when it comes to the dear daddy department," she sneered, but then her features relaxed and she began smiling again. "Not even the sheriff discovered I was the one who put the buck in the road. I just didn't need interference that night, not when I was making sure all our bases were covered and that slut over there hadn't changed the house too drastically."

"You really are clever."

"Yes, I am. And now you will call Jim." She raised her gun.

Natasha leapt, forcing her full weight on Rebecca and sending the two of them flying backward. Carpet burns scorched Natasha's arms. She grabbed the rifle, determined to get it away from Rebecca. It went off again and Natasha jumped backward, doing a crazed crab walk backward as her hair fell into her face.

Something smacked her on the top of the head, and she leapt to her feet, a moment later realizing that it was spackling from the ceiling where the bullet had lodged.

"Do you think I don't already know that you can fight?" Rebecca sneered, moving from her knees to her feet and picking up the rifle, which had fallen next to her. "Get out your fucking phone, now!" she screamed.

Natasha glanced past Rebecca for a second when she saw something, or better yet someone, run past the long, narrow windows that lined the far wall. The thin, see-through curtains that hung to the floor, covering the windows, made it difficult to tell who was out there. Natasha looked down quickly, hoping Rebecca wouldn't notice her moment's distraction. She hoped help was surrounding them as they spoke.

"Fine. Fine," she said, and hated how badly she shook when she reached into her coat pocket and felt her gun. She could pull it out, fire, and take Rebecca down. It would be self-defense. No one would accuse her of anything else. One look at Ethel, who had actually kept her hand pressed against the wound, and Natasha stuffed her other hand into her other pocket. She pulled out the cell phone. "What's the number?"

Her fingers shook almost too much to manage the phone. Rebecca rattled off a phone number and Natasha touched the buttons, backspacing when she actually pushed one hard enough for the phone to register it. Then when she'd tapped the keyboard enough times to make a show of entering the number, she tapped the last number she'd dialed, Trent's phone.

It started ringing as she brought it to her ear.

"Tell him you shot his whore," Rebecca ordered.

Trent answered on the first ring. "What's going on in there?" he barked, although he kept his voice low.

Natasha cleared her voice, determined to sound cool and collected. The situation was out of control, but Natasha wasn't hurt or a prisoner, at least not yet.

"Hello, Jim," she said calmly. "I've just shot your wife."

"Whore," Rebecca corrected, watching Natasha with bright, wide-open eyes.

"Whore," Natasha repeated.

"You didn't shoot her," Trent stated.

"No." Natasha looked at Rebecca. "No, she's not dead."

"Yet," Rebecca said.

"Yet," Natasha repeated.

"Tell him to come to the house and he better be alone or she will be dead along with his unborn bastard." Rebecca raised her rifle with the skill she'd professed earlier to having, moving it into position with one fluid movement. "Tell him that now," she snarled.

"I heard her," Trent said. "We're coming in now."

"Come to the house alone," Natasha said anyway, without taking her attention from Rebecca.

"Hang up."

Natasha hung up the phone.

"Now give it to me." Rebecca reached for Natasha's phone.

"What?" Natasha hesitated. "Why do you want my phone?"

Rebecca pressed the barrel of the gun against Natasha's forehead and yanked the phone out of her hand. Once again Natasha's life flew by before her eyes. Images racing too fast to comprehend spun around her in head, evolving and disappearing from the incredible pressure building where the barrel pinched into her flesh.

Rebecca glanced down at Natasha's cell phone and her smile faded.

"Why, you—," she snarled, her voice reaching screeching tones in less than a second. Rebecca's smile vanished and a snarl so evil, so incredibly filled with hatred, twisted her expression into a cruel frown. "Who the fuck do you think you are?" she screamed, slamming Natasha's phone to the floor.

Natasha didn't want to see her life flash before her eyes again. And she sure as hell wasn't ready to witness the last scene. Slapping the rifle away from her head with her forearm, she yelled when she bulldozed into Rebecca.

"I fucking think I'm tired of your head games, bitch!" Natasha screamed, and grabbed Rebecca's firing arm, twisted it, and sent the rifle skidding across the carpet to the kitchen floor, where it clunked and spun once.

Natasha didn't let go but lifted Rebecca, heaving her into the air, then slamming her to the floor. She reveled in the one moment all air flew from the little bitch's lungs with a loud grunt. Rebecca looked up at Natasha, shocked and confused as if she didn't comprehend what had just happened.

For a moment Natasha swore the gun had fired again. A whirlwind of commotion spun around her. There were men everywhere. But what didn't make sense was that instead of Trent's arms wrapping around her and pulling her away from Rebecca, Natasha's cousin Jake yanked her backward.

Trent slid down next to Rebecca, flipped her to her stomach, and grabbed her wrist, pulling it behind her back as he slapped handcuffs on her. Then he pulled her to her feet, not too nicely, and gave her a quick shake when she began screaming and trying to fight him.

Uncle Greg rushed into the house as well, moving expertly around Trent and sliding to his knees next to Ethel. Greg was feeling her pulse and letting his serious gaze travel over her body, assessing the situation, when Natasha's cousin Marc walked around Trent as well. Marc had his phone out and pressed it to his ear. Natasha wasn't sure if he was talking to anyone or not. But when he squatted on the opposite side of Ethel he looked over at Natasha and winked.

"Good moves there, Cuz," he said.

* * *

Trent had parked his Suburban behind the Avalanche as an identical Avalanche pulled up alongside it. He got out of his truck as the King family unloaded next to him. Every man in Natasha's family was a good couple inches taller than he was, not that he cared. When Greg King had called him he apparently had connections good enough to know the bust was going down. King had offered to assist and Trent agreed.

Greg King and his sons, Marc and Jake, were professionals. They never mentioned Natasha. They asked all the right questions and listened seriously when Trent informed them how it would go down. They didn't argue or inform him that he'd better be taking good care of their niece and cousin. But Trent saw that demand in all of their eyes now.

Natasha slid out of the backseat, arm in arm with Aunt Haley. The two women were talking to each other, huddled close against the wind as they hurried to Trent's house. He followed, key in hand, and unlocked it so Natasha and her family could enter.

It had been a long night. After he'd cuffed Pat O'Reilly and let the Redding police take him in their squad car, the paramedics had taken Ethel Burrows in the ambulance. Jim Burrows had hovered close by. His love for his new wife had been legitimate. The man was a shrewd businessman though, and although family meant the world to him, he knew a bad deal when he saw one. He'd left with the ambulance, but Trent wouldn't be surprised if Jim filed for divorce once Ethel was safe in a hospital bed.

Jim's tormented expression when Rebecca had been hauled off was more of a heartbreaker. It would destroy the man knowing how much his older daughter despised him. She had planned on killing Jim and had screamed it to enough witnesses to make premeditated, attempted murder charges stick easily. Jim Burrows would need a while to recover from all of this. Trent planned on checking in on him here in a few days.

In the meantime, Trent had a houseful of family whom he barely knew and all of them were watching him with scrutinizing stares. Haley King repeatedly looked at him with a stare that said, *I know you're sleeping with my niece.* He wouldn't deny it. Haley's hard, intense attention, when she sent it his way, also made it clear he hadn't met with her approval. Trent wasn't sure what would make her approve of him.

"There's Midnight," Natasha announced loudly and dragged Aunt Haley through the house to the back door.

"Midnight?" Marc asked, following but standing inside the kitchen.

"My father's horse," Trent grumbled, inching around the large man and hurrying outside after the women. Now he knew how Natasha had got to the ranch. He had panicked at first that leaving her at his house had been the worst mistake of his life. He thought Rebecca had shown up, knowing Trent would be arresting Pat O'Reilly, and dragged Natasha from his house at gunpoint. He should have known better.

The three King men followed Trent into his backyard and watched Natasha leave Aunt Haley's side and run up to Midnight. Trent shook his head when the horse actually seemed glad to see her.

"Who would have thought there was so much country in our girl?" Marc said, laughing.

Natasha shoved her long black hair over her shoulder as she turned and made a face at him. "Don't knock it if you haven't tried it." She then locked gazes with Trent and her expression sobered.

He was overly aware of four sets of eyes watching him. Turning to the King men, he nodded toward his house.

"There is beer in the refrigerator. Please, make yourself at home. If you don't mind, I'm going to talk to Natasha alone for a few minutes."

"About what?" Jake stepped forward.

Greg King put his hand on his son's shoulder. "Sounds fine, Son. It's too damned cold out here for any sane man anyway," Greg offered, grinning and using, it appeared, just a bit of force to turn his younger son around and give him a good shove toward the house.

Haley came up around Trent, laughing as she moved

among her men. "You're right. Natasha will freeze before winter even gets here."

"She'll stay warm," Trent said, unable to not be part of their conversation.

Jake turned around, an animalistic growl exploding from him as he appeared ready to lunge at Trent. Greg and Marc moved just as fast. Trent braced himself. He wasn't doing anything wrong, and it wasn't as if Natasha were a child. When the men finally went inside, he turned, and headed to his barn.

Natasha had eased the saddle off Midnight when she spotted Trent. But she glanced past him when he took the saddle from her.

"You were really out of line messing with the truck," she mumbled.

Trent had his back to her as he put the saddle up, but didn't need to see her face to know there was pain there. He imagined she'd been beyond pissed when she read his note. They'd just endured enough trauma to drain all adrenaline and anger out of both of them. Maybe that was why he was inclined to agree with her.

"I knew it would get ugly," he said honestly, that being his only defense. He returned to Midnight's side, then rubbed the side of his head when the horse nuzzled into him. "Even with all the backup in the world, I needed my eyes on everyone out there. I wouldn't have been able to protect you."

Natasha sighed, obviously not having a clue how difficult it had been for him to admit that. "I can protect myself," she said, although her tone sounded almost as flat as his. She began brushing Midnight, and her tangled hair fell in disarray down her front and back. "And I can protect you as well, if needed."

When she shot Trent a look he noticed how her pretty eyes glistened. God, she wasn't close to tears, was she?

"Where is everyone?" she asked, and her voice cracked.

"Inside." He felt like an ass. As much as he wanted her to understand how imperative it was to him that she always remain safe, he also needed her to know that he knew how good she was, at so many things. "I wasn't trying to discredit your abilities."

"Oh yeah?" she accused, dropping her hand and staring at him. "You sabotaged my truck. But worse yet, you were too chickenshit to come tell me you were leaving."

He stared at her. This wasn't the type of woman he should be falling in love with. Trent might not be the best catch in the state, but he had a few things to offer a lady. He had a home, good land, a decent-paying job, and respect in his community. He always imagined the woman for him would always be there for him, anxious to see him come home at night, eager to make the house her own and rearrange all of his furniture. She would adore him, love him, and sit up late at night waiting, worrying, on the occasions when Trent had to chase down a criminal. Trent wouldn't be able to come home to Natasha. She would want to share his day with him. She would always be by his side, caring about what he did. They would end up being best friends.

Trent had always thought his perfect woman would need him. Natasha didn't need him. In fact, she might very well be able to protect him under a variety of circumstances, just as she kept telling him.

"Trent, my family is going to get rooms at Pearl's and in the morning we're heading back to L.A."

He blinked, the dream in his head collapsing, then vanishing altogether. "I was wrong."

Natasha dropped her hand with Midnight's brush in it to her side. Her lips parted, which was probably real close to her jaw dropping in stunned amazement.

"Would you mind repeating that?" she asked, frowning as if she wasn't quite sure she believed he'd just said that.

"Actually, yes, I would." God, he wanted to touch her, pull her into his arms, beg her to stay. "I've always had this image in my head of what the woman for me would be like. I didn't imagine her right," he confessed.

Natasha put her hands on her hips, her coat bunching up

around her, and glared at him. "You were not only wrong. I'm starting to think you're a lost cause." She was trying to sound mad, but her voice cracked and she looked away from him.

Damn it, there were feelings here, strong feelings. Trent couldn't let her get away and he didn't want her crying.

"I know you can take care of yourself." He did touch her then and gave silent thanks when she didn't flinch or slap his hand away from her. "I entered Burrows' home at the same exact minute you sent Rebecca Burrows flying over your shoulder. Woman, you're impressive as hell."

"Yet I need protection."

"No!" he snapped. Emotions spiked inside him and he turned away, needing a distraction, so heading for Midnight's food. "You don't need a damn thing," Trent shot at her, over his shoulder. "You've got it all. You're perfect in every way, sweetheart. I've never met a woman like you, and I mean that," he added, fighting not to yell or to break down and beg. More feelings than he could handle attacked from all sides so that his hands shook. He gripped the edge of the stall in front of him and watched his breath cloud up in front of his face as he searched for the right words. "I'm not sure there is anything you can't do. And yes, that scares me. What the hell do I have to offer you?"

There was silence between them. Her small hand touched the back of his shoulder and Trent spun around, not having heard her approach. But she had. That had to be good. He needed her to stay, wanted her to stay, and even knew, somewhere in the back of his brain, what he needed to say to keep her with him. But the words were so foreign to him, he didn't know how to say them.

"I think you offered me love." Her voice was so soft he almost didn't hear her.

Trent tried taking her hand, but she pulled it out of his and dropped it to her side. She didn't back away, though. "There is really only one thing I need from you."

"What?" He sounded anxious, like a dog willing to dance or do any trick for the treat being offered him. Oddly enough, Trent didn't feel humiliated or manipulated. His insides rejoiced, a flutter of excitement daring to build in his chest. "Tell me, Natasha. What can I give you?"

"Well, there is that love part," she said hastily, and dropped her attention to her hands clasped in front of her.

Trent barely had to move to touch her. He took her chin, gently easing her head up, then tilted it so her eyes focused on his. "I think you already have that, sweetheart."

When she blinked he saw the moisture pooling in her eyes. She moved her hands quickly, rubbing her eyes, then looked rather put out when she focused on him again. She was tough as nails, raised in a world where strength was required, not only physically but also emotionally. It didn't surprise him a bit her family watched him warily. Natasha meant the world to them and for obvious reasons.

"Equality."

"What?"

"Equality," she repeated. "If we're going to give this a shot, then we do it as equals. You have no more right to restrain me than I do you." She raised her finger and poked him in the chest. "And believe me, mister, if you try again, I promise I'll do the same to you."

He believed she would. Life with Natasha would be a challenge, and one he couldn't wait to embrace.

"All right, darling. I accept your terms."

The corner of her mouth twitched, but he didn't wait for the full-fledged smile. Trent wrapped his arms around her, lifting her off her feet, and devoured her mouth.

A loud whooping and instant cheers damn near made his heart explode.

"I thought I was going to freeze my ass off waiting for you two to figure it out," Marc announced loudly as he bounded into the barn.

"I don't know, Natasha," Jake said, stalking in alongside his brother. "Seems you were going to freeze to death waiting for him to agree to treat you right."

"Shut up, both of you." Natasha turned, had her back to Trent, and looked ready to take both of her cousins on at the same time.

Greg and Haley King were right behind their sons and Haley rushed around the men to hug her niece. "Ignore all of them," Haley said, loud enough for everyone to hear her. "I say he's one hell of a catch."

"Just let me know if he turns out not to be," Jake said, giving Trent a warning look.

Natasha punched Jake in his chest and he feigned pain as he backed up and hugged himself, wailing to his parents to make Natasha quit abusing him. All of them broke into laughter and Natasha turned, looking up at Trent.

"Don't worry, my dear," she said, moving into his arms. "I'll protect you from these brutes."

"She will, too," Greg said, obviously having overheard his niece. He moved alongside Trent and slapped him on the back. "Our little girl cares deeply for those who mean the most to her. She will protect and care for them with her own sweat and blood."

Although Greg smiled and looked relaxed and happy, Trent got his meaning and nodded. The older man nodded back, then took Natasha from Trent and gave her a bear hug.

Trent was more than overwhelmed. He'd just been invited into a very close-knit, protective family and was very aware of the honor they bestowed on him. He wondered, if this was their reaction to him and Natasha agreeing to a committed relationship, how they would react if he proposed marriage. Suddenly he felt weak in the knees. When he looked around him all three King men were watching him, grinning. If they'd read his thoughts they seemed to understand and told him so with knowing looks.

He returned their attentive stares and hoped they saw what was inside him. He would be all Natasha needed and wanted from him. Equality wasn't such an unreasonable request. As he watched her, jabbing at her cousins, laughing with her aunt, and hugging her uncle, Trent's love for her grew. And with that came an overwhelming desire to do whatever it took to keep her smiling and laughing always. All she'd asked was they treat each other the same. He was one lucky guy.

"I'm starving," Marc announced. "And freezing."

Everyone immediately agreed with him.

"I haven't had a chance to tell you," Natasha said, returning to Trent's arms. "Dad called on the ride back over here. He wants to take you and me to dinner. His way of saying 'thank you.'"

Trent had no doubts how the town would react to seeing him eating dinner with Natasha's family. He decided it might be the easiest way to let his town know he'd taken his name off the available bachelors list.

"I'll finish feeding Midnight," he offered. "Take everyone inside before their thin L.A. blood does them in."

This time, Natasha rode with him, her hand in his, as her family followed them into Weaverville. When her phone rang she was still glowing as she pulled it out and answered it.

"Hi, Dad," she said cheerfully. "We should be there in a few minutes."

As the town came into view Trent slowed and glanced over at Natasha when the first city lights flashed over her expression.

"What's wrong?" he whispered.

"No. It's okay, Dad. I understand. Love you, too." When she hung up her phone she rested it on her lap.

Trent stared at the woman, his woman, who'd lived her entire life loving a father who simply didn't have the capability to give her everything she gave him in return. At that moment Trent made a silent vow never to do the same.

Natasha looked at him. "Looks like there will be one less of us at supper. Dad is already putting California behind him. He said he forgot about our supper invitation and wanted to call before he hit the evening traffic in Seattle."

"Natasha, I'm—"

"No." She held her hand up. "It really is okay," she said, and sounded like she meant it. "Believe it or not, I think Dad is growing up a bit."

Trent signaled, then pulled into the diner's parking lot. "How so?" he asked, and parked as quickly as he could so he could pull Natasha into his arms.

"He called," she said, then opened her car door and hopped out of the Suburban without waiting for Trent to come around. "Before he might have left a message with someone else."

Dinner was everything Trent expected. Everyone eating in the diner found a reason sooner or later to stop by their table and learn who the people were who were eating with their sheriff. They each walked away with knowing smiles on their faces.

"I hope I'm not interrupting."

Trent was surprised when Jim Burrows stood next to him, the man's loud, commanding voice as strong as a rock, just as it had always been.

"Of course not." Trent stood and shook the man's hand, then made quick interruptions. "I admit I didn't expect to see you in town for a while."

"Got the family in order," was all he said.

Trent seriously doubted Jim had bounced back as quickly as he appeared but gave the man his pride. "Join us, please," Trent insisted, and signaled for the busboy to grab a chair.

"I'd like that. There's something I want to talk to you about, and all of you might as well hear this." Jim had everyone's attention when he sat, his chair at the end of the table, with Jake and Marc on either side of him.

Trent figured the way Jim would see it, he sat at the head of the table. Once a cattle rancher tycoon, always one. The older gentleman was even dressed up, as if he'd planned on meeting them and on speaking to all of them. For all Trent knew, Jim might very well have planned it.

"I took all the cash that was found on my land to some folks I happen to know in Redding," he began. "It turns out over half the bills have a face value well over their initial worth."

"Really?" Trent shook his head. "That's great, Jim." It was the least the man deserved.

"The old wives' tale of Nellie Burrows was that she was buried in cash, literally, meaning when her mama put her to rest she filled that coffin up with all the money she swore no one in her family would ever see. We found the coffin yesterday. I hadn't had a chance to tell you that, and I shipped it out to be gone over with a fine-tooth comb as well. Turns out all those old wives had their story straight. There was a sizeable amount of dust in the coffin, which turned out to be the cash that wasn't properly preserved and turned to dust over the years. They did find several more compartments my beloved wife overlooked in the coffin and they were also filled with cash." Jim paused, accepted the beer the waitress had brought to him with a smile and a wink, then drank.

Trent leaned back and slid his hand under the table, resting it on Natasha's leg. Her face glowed when she grinned at him. Jim didn't wait long in building his suspense. Possibly he guessed some of his audience didn't care as much about money as they did about being alone later.

"Trent, my boy, you're one hell of a good sheriff, just like your daddy was. And this little lady you've found," Jim added, and lifted his bottle of beer in a silent toast to Natasha, "I'm glad you saw fit to take my advice and not let her get away."

Natasha looked at Trent. He gave her leg a squeeze and didn't take his attention off Jim. "It was a no-brainer, Jim," Trent said easily. "It's really the only thing a man can do when he finds perfection."

"Hear! Hear!" Jim agreed, and the King men willingly lifted their drinks and toasted Natasha, the lot of them only getting louder when Natasha protested and warned them to quit embarrassing her.

"I'm going to give you a gift, Sheriff."

Everyone at the table grew quiet.

"I can tell your woman loves you unconditionally, but a lady does love to make a home her own. God knows with you and your father having hung around in that house alone all these years, she's got her work cut out for her." Jim simply pressed on when Trent started to protest, having a good idea where Jim was going with this. "I know what your salary is and you sure don't have a gold digger by your side, but any young couple finds a better go of it when life is easy." Jim finished off his beer and stood, making his way to the other end of the table and to Trent. "You're a good man and even better sheriff." He looked at Natasha. "Go easy on him, little lady," he said. "Most of us are completely clueless when we first shack up. Forgive him when he gets too bossy. Hug him when he makes a mess. And most of all, remember your gender is a hell of a lot stronger than ours. You'll get him trained in no time flat. I see the love and determination in your eyes." With that he handed Natasha an envelope and headed out of the diner.

Natasha's family leaned in, encouraging her to open it. She offered it to Trent, but he shook his head. "Go ahead."

Trent watched Natasha and barely heard her exclaim with excitement over how much the check was for. He was content to simply stare at her, pride and love filling him up inside to where he barely had room for his food. He remembered how Jim had acted differently around his wife. She was a bad seed, but Jim had loved her and might still. The man was powerful, an aggressive businessman, shrewd as hell, and had made an enemy or two along the way. But when it came to his women, his love for them was unconditional. His first wife couldn't handle illegitimate children. His second wasn't satisfied with all Jim gave her. Yet he had adored each one. He'd been crushed watching his daughter being arrested. He'd stood tall and silent alongside Ethel. Jim wasn't a perfect man and had made some serious mistakes in his lifetime, but through all of that, he had been blessed with knowing true love. Trent would never make the mistakes Jim had made but heard the man's words and saw that inside this imperfect, successful business-man were words of wisdom Trent took to heart.

Natasha leaned into him, showing him the check. "What are we going to do with fifty thousand dollars?" she whispered into his ear.

Trent didn't hesitate with his answer. "Whatever you say we're going to do with it."

Natasha studied him a minute, then smiled. She leaned in to kiss him and Trent wanted to sweep her out of there instantly. "I love you," he whispered, and believed he truly understood the meaning of those three little words for the first time in his life.

Read on for an excerpt from Lorie O'Clare's next book

SLOW HEAT

Coming soon from St. Martin's Paperbacks

Maggie O'Malley glanced up from her books when she heard the cook talking to someone out in the kitchen. Max was back there alone and would be for another hour until the club opened. He worked better alone and did an incredible job of setting up all the meal preparation if he didn't have to share the work load with anyone else.

She cursed under her breath when Max continued talking to whoever was out in the kitchen with him. Uncle Larry might be an idiot, but she'd sworn more than once that he'd given her this office, right off the kitchen, on purpose. Uncle Larry knew Maggie would jump in and put his kitchen in order once she heard the chaos that occurred there daily once she started working there. And she had. The kitchen was run like a smooth-sailing ship today. It would stay that way, too, damn it!

Heading around her desk, the mixture of Irish and Italian blood inside her brought Maggie's temper to a quick boil. She would never be like her mother but a glance at the small statue of the Mother Mary holding baby Jesus, a gift from her parents after landing this job, gave her pause.

"Saints preserve me," she grumbled, crossed herself, then blew out an exasperated breath as she headed out of her office. Max knew he wasn't allowed to have friends in the kitchen while he was working.

"Max," she said, using his name as a warning when she stared at the tall, dark-haired man facing Max from across the large, cutting-board counter.

"He showed up at the back door with some questions." Max stuck his chin out stubbornly and turned to stir something that smelled strongly of garlic and oregano. Max was making his famous spaghetti sauce, one of Uncle Larry's favorite food items.

"Who are you?" Maggie crossed her arms, possibly more as a shield than out of frustration. The man she stared at was incredibly sexy. There was something in his eyes that bothered her though. They were a soft brown shade and his lashes and eyebrows were a thick black. The lashes didn't quite hide the way his eyes appeared doused with danger. "What questions do you have?"

"I'm looking for Larry," the guy said, his deep baritone crisp and a bit too confident.

"Larry isn't back here. This is the kitchen. Larry would be up front. Are you lost?" She watched something spark in his brown eyes. "And you didn't say your name."

"You're right." He didn't look like a vagrant wanting free food, or in need of a job. He looked healthy, very healthy and dangerous. "Are you a cook also?" he asked, and walked around Max's prep counter, then moved between the stocking shelves.

"I work here and you don't." No matter how big, or how muscular this man appeared, Maggie had had her fair share of dealing with bullies. She wasn't easily daunted or intimidated. Coming from a large family, Maggie had learned at an early age to stand her ground, or she'd never get what she wanted. "Tell me your name, why you're here, and what you want—or leave."

She met him at the end of the short aisle where cooking supplies were stocked on shelves. He didn't appear interested in anything on the shelves but reached the end of the aisle and turned, then stopped when she blocked him.

The top of Maggie's head probably wouldn't have touched this man's nose. He was tall. And muscular, damn! When she stared at him straight on, she got an eyeful of roped muscle pressing against his t-shirt. Where his shirt sleeves ended, corded biceps began. He had a tan, and she noticed a couple small puckers, old scars remaining from some previous trauma in his life. She imagined him fighting like a mercenary late at night on some loading dock against bad guys.

"If you want to go out front, you can leave the way you came and walk around the building." She again crossed her arms, but this time felt the solid beat of her heart grow stronger against her chest. "The back door is that way." She nodded in the direction of the door, proud of herself for not trembling as adrenaline started pumping through her.

He glanced at her for only a moment before looking over her shoulder. Maggie couldn't physically stop him and wasn't sure touching him would be to her advantage. The way he brushed against her when he walked past her suggested he wanted her doing just that.

"Is there a place we can talk?" he asked and took determined steps toward her office.

"Stop, now!" she ordered, hurrying after him and grabbing the door, then damn near skidding in front of him before facing him again.

The amusement in his eyes pissed her off. Who the hell was this guy?

"Anything you want me to do?" Max asked from behind the man. His voice was a lot deeper and meaner than he usually sounded.

"I don't know yet, Max," she said, focusing on the man facing her. She caught him glancing down her body before meeting her gaze. No way would she look away, but she was very grateful for Max being close, just in case. "Who do you think you are prancing in here as if you had a right?"

The man stepped closer, moving into her space, and lowered his head so when he spoke, his breath tickled her skin. "Because criminals don't have rights. The police are going to be here any minute."

Oh God! This man really was dangerous. The law was looking for him and he had to choose her place to hide. Maggie had to think fast. She hadn't made the deposit yet. No way in hell would he take her and Max hostage. Not if she could outthink him.

"Why are they coming here?" she asked, trying to match his cool, soft tone.

"They're about to make an arrest." Now he looked amused, as if her question were ludicrous.

Maybe it was. Hell, she didn't have a clue how to talk to a criminal.

"Oh, really?" she asked, wondering how genuine this man was. "And you sauntered into the back door of my kitchen just to tell me that?"

"Your kitchen? I thought Larry Santinos ran this place."

"He does." She didn't need to explain herself to him, and apparently the look on her face made that clear.

The buzzer next to her desk went off, letting her know someone had just come in the front door. She turned, glanced at it, and shifted her attention to the small box next to her phone. A second later it beeped, letting her know Larry was here.

"Who do they want to arrest?" she asked, trying for a different tactic.

"Is that telling you Larry is here?" the man asked, nodding at the devices on her desk.

"That's enough." She pointed behind him. "Turn around and march out that door. Now."

"I will in a minute."

When he reached for his back pocket, Max moved faster than Maggie had ever seen the man move. For a giant black man, his looks could intimidate. But in the year and a half that he'd been their cook, all Maggie had seen was an oversized teddy bear with a heart of gold. At the moment, though, he looked terrifying enough that Maggie took a step backward. Max grabbed the man before he could get his hand to his back pocket.

Max stood over six feet tall and this man was as tall as

Max. Where Max was very large, Maggie imagined this man would be all steel and packed muscle. Instead of struggling, the stranger stepped to the side, turning to face Max and holding his hands up in surrender. Max looked mean as hell. The stranger didn't look scared. That same annoying, amused look was still on his face.

"Easy now," the man said, holding his hands out in front of him when he slipped out of Max's grasp.

Maggie noticed he was now also in her office.

"I was just taking out my ID to show the lady here who I am," the man said. "Is she your boss? You're a good man to keep an eye on her."

Max grabbed the man. His expression never changed, and again, he moved so fast a cry escaped Maggie's lips before she could hold it back. Pressing her fingers to her lips, she stepped backward until she leaned against her desk. Did she have time to call 911?

Max flipped the man around and her office wall shook when he shoved him against it. The man's face was turned to the side, his cheek against her wall, terribly close to the crucifix hanging there. The amused look was gone. He blinked once, twice, and exhaled. Maggie swore she could see his brain working through the expressions that changed on his face. He was trying to decide if he should try throwing Max off him or not.

Thick, dark brown hair tapered around his face but didn't hide his intense features. This man was doing a really good job of controlling his reaction to Max's sudden attack. And Max, with his back to her, didn't look like the soft and cuddly teddy bear she'd always pictured him up until this moment. His large body looked hard as steel, just like the stranger he held. His thick, dark arms were like small tree trunks. And although defined muscle didn't bulge against his black skin, he held the man where he was and didn't appear to be struggling to do so.

"Take it out where I can see it," Max said, his voice a guttural growl.

"I will, man," the guy said, his voice still calm. "Best to

let go of me so we don't fight over a piece of ID. I have a feeling your boss wouldn't like her office destroyed if you and I go at it."

"No, I wouldn't." Maggie wished she could say she hadn't seen grown men fight before. But with brothers both older and younger, she'd witnessed them scrap as children and more than once go at each other as adults. Italian and Irish blood were a bad mix, but it was who they were. Nonetheless, her heart pounded in her chest with two huge men standing just inside her office door and adrenaline pumping through the air thick enough to slice with a knife. "Pull out your ID," she managed, speaking softly so she wouldn't start screaming.

Suddenly she understood why her mother always spoke softly, almost whispering. She was trying to maintain control while raising five children and not instantly losing her temper. Maggie was on the verge of screaming at both of them.

Max adjusted his hold on the man, not willing yet to release him, but allowed the man to pull his wallet from his back pocket. The man flipped it open and held it out, his cheek still pressed against the wall. He strained to watch her when Maggie stepped closer.

She glanced at it but stepped back when the stranger applied a bit of strength and turned against Max, forcing him to take a step back as well. Did this stranger really possess the strength to push Max off of him?

The man turned slightly, looking at Max. "Just a wallet, my friend." His tone changed just a bit when he added, "It's never smart to carry a gun in your back pocket."

"Hand your ID to me," Maggie instructed, deciding it would be smarter to keep her distance from both of them just in case one of them made a quick move. Another thing she'd learned at a young age. Two boys, or men, fighting worked on blind rage. Get too close and get hurt.

Max dropped his arms, taking his hands off the man and stepped back until he filled her doorway. He was still so unlike her usual teddy-bear cook. Maggie was grateful for him being there. She gave him a quick glance, hoping her look showed as much. There wasn't time to express her gratitude right now, though. She shot her attention back to the man when he turned, faced her, tugged on his t-shirt to straighten it, and gave her an eyeful of richly defined curves and bulges.

Maggie swallowed even though her mouth was too dry and forced composure through her body. Shifting her attention from that virile body to his hand didn't help much. She glanced at the laminated card he held out to her but couldn't read it from that distance. Her legs didn't wobble when she stepped forward and took it, then stared at the picture of the man standing in front of her, then his credentials. Her stomach did a small flip-flop.

"Micah Jones," she read. "Bounty hunter."